cpsmith

Wallflowers

Double Trouble

Published by CP Smith

First Edition: July 2017

Editor Julia Goda
Formatting: CP Smith
Cover design: Dark Waters Covers
Cover Photograph Depositphoto @inarik
Information address: cpsmith74135@gmail.com

ISBN-13: 978-1548930882
ISBN-10: 1548930881

Titles by CP Smith

a reason to breathe

a reason to kill

a reason to live

Restoring Hope

Property Of

FRAMED

Wallflowers: *Three of a Kind*

Wallflowers: *Double Trouble*

Acknowledgments

To my family. *All* of this is for you. Thank you for putting up with me!

Julia Goda and Mayra Statham. I love you both, to the moon and back. You ladies keep me sane!

Deb Hawblitzel Schultz, I love you like a sister. Thank you for always having my back.

Nichole Hart, Gi Paar, Jane S Wells, Angela Shue, Kelly Marshall-White, Sallie Brown Davis, Michelle Reed, Joanne Thompson, Karen Hrdlicka, and Allison Michaels. Thank you for taking time out of your busy day to find my errors. It means a lot to me that you care as much as I do about these characters I bring to life.

Julia Goda, you're the best damn editor out there. Thank you!

Tracie Douglas-Rabas, thank you for always understanding my vision. Your covers make me happy!

And to my original Dream Team. I love you more than you know! 'Thank you' isn't a big enough word.

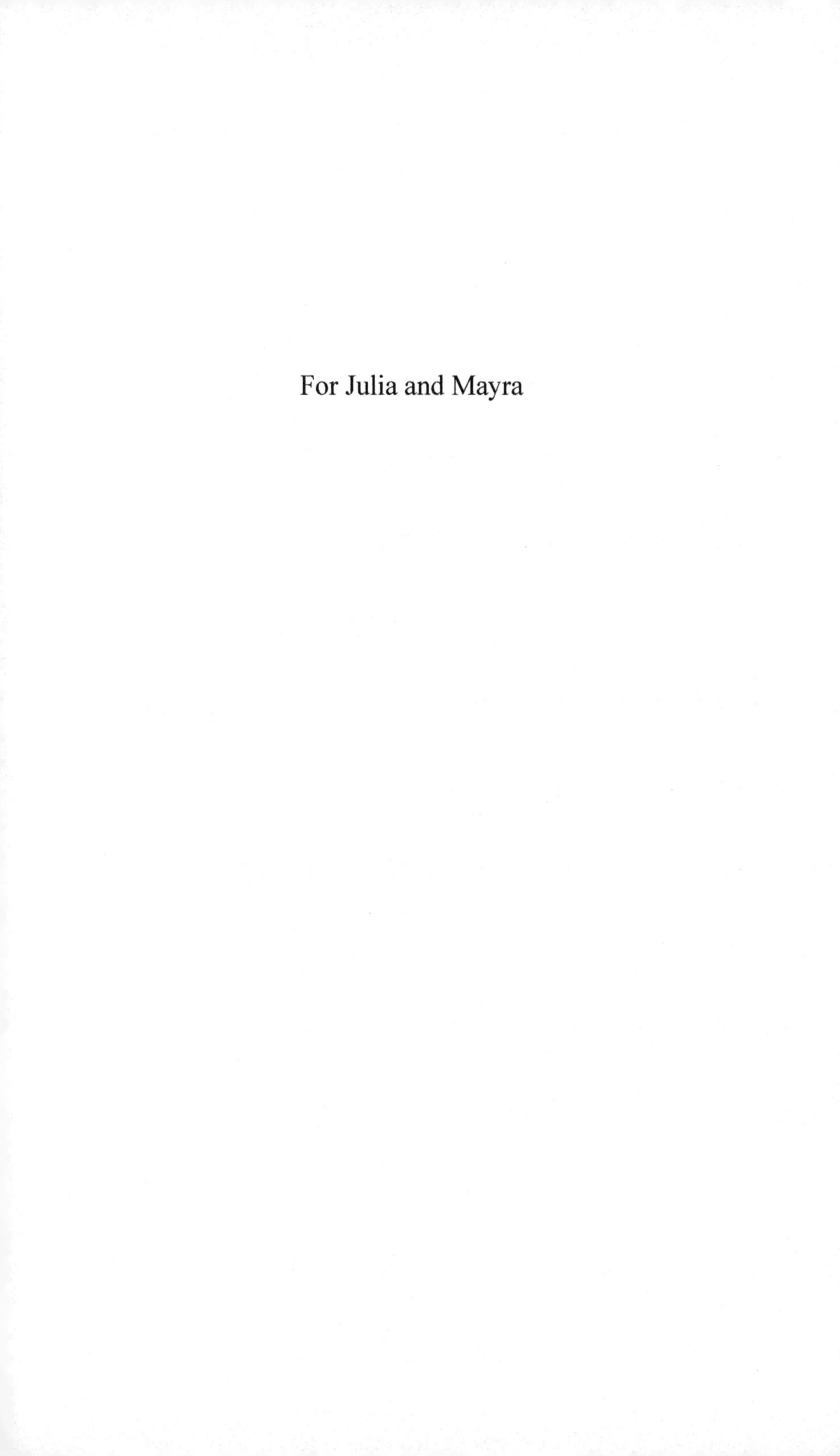

For Julia and Mayra

Prologue

NOT HAPPENIN'

Three days earlier . . .

RACING THROUGH TRAFFIC AT A high rate of speed, dodging cars as his siren blared, Bo Strawn tried to rein in his temper as he headed for Tybee Island in pursuit of Gayla Brown, a psychopath who'd kidnapped his friend's woman. What hold he had on his temper, after three nights with little to no sleep, was slipping. His lack of control was due in part to two infuriating Wallflowers. Or, more to the point, the one behind the wheel who wouldn't pull the fuck over.

He was five minutes behind Devin Hawthorne when he should have been in the lead because he couldn't get Calla's friends to pull over. Since he was losing valuable time arguing with the two irrational women, he'd asked for Poppy's phone number and called them back from his cell as he headed for his truck. But no matter what he said, the stubborn woman behind the wheel wouldn't listen.

"Swear to Christ, Sienna. I will lock you up and throw away

the key if you don't stand down. NOW!" Bo roared into the phone.

Law and order were paramount to Bo, so when Poppy Gentry scoffed in his ear, then relayed his message to Sienna Miller, whose only reply was a sexy chuckle, he gritted his teeth and slammed his hand against the steering wheel.

Don't lose control.

Drawing a deep breath in through his nose, he counted to ten before trying *again* to talk some sense into two of the most infuriating women he'd ever encountered. No. Scratch that. Two of the *three* most infuriating women he'd ever encountered. Their cohort and ringleader, Calla Armstrong, who was currently in the hands of a madwoman, was equally infuriating. None of them listened to reason. *None of them* followed the rules he held sacred.

"Poppy!" he barked into the phone. "You'll only get yourselves killed. Leave this to Devin and me, and pull over."

"Is he still yappin' his jaw?" Sienna shouted. "Tell him to save his breath. Wallflowers *do not* leave a woman behind."

His eye twitched, and his hand followed suit. He didn't know if he wanted to strangle Sienna or put her over his knee until she listened to reason.

"I'm done playin' this game," Bo growled low. "Pull over now or face the consequences."

"We aren't pullin' over, so you can save your breath. Besides, Gayla stopped," Poppy whispered. "They pulled in front of a cottage facing the ocean. We'll get out and see what she's up to when they go inside."

"For fuck's sake, stay in your—" The report of a gun being fired stopped Bo mid-sentence, and his heart dropped. "Talk to me. What's happening?" he shouted.

No response.

"Poppy, did you hear me? Stay where you are. Devin will be there any minute."

He was still met with dead air.

Bo's blood ran cold, and he jammed the pedal to the floor.

Now all three Wallflowers were at the mercy of a madwoman. A woman who had stalked Devin with the intent to kill him for ruining her life. The same woman who had killed a man to keep her identity a secret.

Eight minutes later, he came to a screeching halt next to a police cruiser and Devin's hog. Barreling out of his truck, Bo took off toward the beach with his heart in his throat. As he stepped off a berm into the soft white sand, his heart stopped then started again. Fifty feet in front of him, Sienna stood next to a prone Gayla Brown, whose arms were cuffed behind her back, and Sienna's hands were waving wildly as she spoke to an officer.

Scanning the beach for Devin and Calla, he saw Poppy standing at the water's edge shouting at the horizon. He searched the waves until he saw Devin swimming toward a leg of the pier. He squinted and made out the figure of a person hanging on, their arms wrapped tightly around the leg.

Jesus, it's Calla.

He began to breathe again.

Safe. All three were safe.

Bo heard a commotion over his shoulder and looked back. The press had shown up along with the paramedics. He'd need to deal with the vultures before things got out of hand, but the adrenaline pounding through his veins had turned from fear to anger at how close these women had come to being corpses in his morgue. He needed a target for his anger to calm down before he dealt with them.

His eyes shot to Sienna, and they narrowed. Two seconds

later, he was zeroed in on her location, moving quickly toward her while his hands opened and closed for control.

Sienna looked up as he approached and actually smiled at him. Her blatant disregard for her safety and the casual way she ignored his anger caused his left eye to twitch again.

She smiled wider.

His hands shook with the need to strangle her.

"We took her out," Sienna cried out as he approached. "She wasn't watchin' her back, so we snuck up and . . . What's wrong with your eye?"

"Reckless. Irresponsible. You could have gotten yourself killed," he thundered.

Men had cowered in the face of his anger, but not this woman. No, she had the nerve to place her hands on her hips and narrow her eyes.

"Bite me, lawman. I told you already; a Wallflower *never* leaves a woman behind. So you can take your righteous indignation and shove it where the sun don't shine."

The officer standing next to her snorted at the insult.

Bo shot him a lethal look, and the rookie cleared his throat then took several steps back and turned around.

"You could have been shot," he bit out, turning his attention back to the matter at hand.

"Maybe, but Cali needed our help. What would you have done in the same situation? Sit in your car and do nothin' while your friend took a bullet?"

Her dark brown eyes lit with fire as he glared at her. He could read the conviction in their depths, and his anger ebbed by a degree. The fierce defense of her actions left him without a solid argument. She was right, and he knew it, but the thought of Sienna in danger was unacceptable to him.

He'd, unfortunately and to his extreme disapproval, been

highly attracted to her from the first time he'd laid eyes on her. An attraction he'd tried to ignore without success. He wanted her, that much he knew, but he also knew she was completely wrong for a man like him. He needed a woman who could be reasoned with, who listened when he needed her to, one who followed the law without question. But Sienna broke the rules when it suited her, never listened to reason, and had no respect for authority. It was a dangerous combination in his line of work and a trait he didn't need in his woman. Not after growing up without a mother who put her own needs over those of her family.

Crowding in closer to Sienna until her head tipped back and she met his eyes, Bo tried to use his size to intimidate her into listening to him once and for all. She might be all wrong for him, but that didn't negate the fact he wanted her safe, and he would use any means necessary to ensure that.

"Pull that shit again, and I'll put you over my knee," he hissed.

The quick intake of her breath directed his attention to her mouth. And just like that, he went from angry to hard.

Her full, pink lips called out to him, begged to be taken. Taken by him so he could kiss some much-needed sense into her.

Before he knew what he was doing, Bo leaned in closer for a taste of what he knew would be heaven and hell. Heaven because he'd spent more than a few moments thinking about doing just that, and hell because he knew it could never work between them and the taste of her lips would always haunt him.

Her eyes widened as he moved in to take her mouth. Bo could see flecks of gold dancing in their depths as the light reflected their color. *Christ, a man could get lost in her eyes, could drown in those dark pools and never want to come up for air.*

Lost to the world around him, Bo inched closer to Sienna, determined to know what heaven tasted like. But when her hands came up and clutched his shoulders, and her mouth opened slowly in preparation to be kissed, whispering, "Bo?" on a sultry broken breath, it stopped him dead in his tracks.

Jesus, what am I doing?

Diverting his descent at the last second, Bo whispered in her ear. "You're right, I would have done exactly what you did. But the difference is, I'm trained to do it, and you're not. If you ever disobey a direct order like that again, I promise you I'll lock you up and throw away the key."

She swallowed hard, nodding in quick, jerking motions, but didn't answer him.

Bo should have stepped back from temptation immediately, but Sienna's warm body was pressed close to his, and the soft curves burned a trail of heat through his own, igniting a white-hot desire.

At that moment, he was helpless to move.

Lingering a half-second longer than he should have, Bo got a lungful of sweet almonds for his troubles. Sienna's unique scent was like a drug to his system. He wanted to pull it further into his lungs until he was addicted, but years of disciplined control were on autopilot, and he stepped back.

When she locked confused eyes with his, eyes that were hooded with lust, he turned toward the pier without a backward glance before he claimed the woman for his own. A woman who'd undoubtedly make his head explode before he turned thirty.

"Not happenin'," he hissed as he set his sights on Poppy, Devin, and Calla. But the fuck of it was, he had a bad feeling he was lying to himself.

One

YOU CAN'T START CHAPTER ONE OF YOUR LIFE IF YOU KEEP RE-READING THE PROLOGUE

ALFRED, LORD TENNYSON ONCE WROTE in the poem *In Memoriam A.H.H* "'*Tis better to have loved and lost than never to have loved at all.*" Standing on the second floor of Jacobs' Ladder, stunned to be face-to-face with a man I once thought I loved, I decided that the line of the poem should be rewritten to say, "'Tis better to *never* have loved and lost than to live with the regret of your stupidity."

Since meeting Cali and Poppy, and banding together as Wallflowers, the topic of letting go of past hurts had been in the forefront of my mind. I'd traveled down memory lane this past week, examining my feelings so I could move forward, and what I discovered is, regret for prior behavior clouds the mind until you're drowning in false memories. That what had once been a clear picture of the events becomes distorted, eroding over time until those memories are a twisted figment of the truth.

And the truth about my past was now glaringly obvious as I stood less than three feet away from Chase Winters, the man I'd stupidly thought I'd loved for the past five years.

Looking at him now, it's no wonder I'd fooled myself into believing I was in love with him. With dark hair and light blue eyes, Chase had reminded me of one of the white knights I read about in romance novels. The kind who swept the heroine off her feet, saving her from whatever perceived threat she was under. And just like those fictional heroines, I needed rescuing.

Growing up, my life had been less than perfect. My mother had been a straight-A student and a former Miss Georgia State. My father, a former quarterback who got his master's degree in engineering. They were a golden couple who married and had two golden children. Their life continued to be golden until baby number three came along two years later. I was the odd child out. The one who didn't make sense in their golden life.

You see, my parents had breezed through school, and I preferred my daydreams to studying the Civil War. My sister was homecoming queen, and I stayed home on Friday nights with my face buried in a book. My brother was a chip off the old block and high school quarterback, and I was, well, invisible for the most part to both my parents.

I also didn't look like my sister or my mother.

Or my father or brother, for that matter.

They all had dark hair. I had hair the color of wheat; a fact my father didn't miss and repeatedly joked about until I turned fifteen. Then one day, he stopped joking and moved out.

My mother, it turned out, had cheated on him. That's why I didn't look or act like the rest of them. I was, according to my mother, the bastard child of a testosterone-filled gym manager. Overnight, I went from being invisible to forgettable for both my parents, and the cause of their separation to my siblings.

It was the pain from those years of neglect that put me on a collision course with Chase Winters. After years of finding solace from my parents' divorce between the pages of a book, I began to see myself as a damsel in need of rescuing. I would escape into my head as a shield to block out the pain, praying for a knight of my own to carry me away from the heartache.

That's where Chase came in.

I met Chase my first year in college. My brother and I had just arrived back in Athens, after a long weekend home, when Chase walked up to my brother's car.

I was infatuated immediately with his good looks and slow smile; positive he was the man for me. So I proceeded to tie myself into knots for the next two years to no avail, convinced he was the one who would finally rescue me from a lifetime of being invisible.

But I was invisible to him as well.

When he graduated and moved to Atlanta without so much as a backward glance, I tried to move on from my foolish dream, but I'd been infatuated with him for so long, it wasn't easy. Three years after he graduated, on one of the few times I stopped in to visit my mother, an announcement of his engagement came in the mail.

It hit me harder than I expected.

Even though I'd seen him from time to time with his girlfriend, some foolish part of me had hoped he'd wake up one day and finally see me, and forget about her. But the wedding announcement shattered those dreams into teeny tiny pieces. In a moment of emotional insanity, I'd grabbed a bottle of Jack from my mother's liquor cabinet and proceeded to drown my sorrows for all the time I'd lost waiting for a man who didn't care.

Unfortunately for me, and my rotten timing, Chase was in town visiting friends. He chose that exact day to hang out with my brother, who'd yet to move out of my mother's house.

I was muddle-brained and sulking when he showed up, and I proceeded to stalk his movements throughout the house like a trained assassin, convinced if I told him how I felt, it would change everything.

When he excused himself to use the bathroom, I saw my opportunity and barged in on him, throwing myself into his arms, confessing my love like the idiot I was. Fortunately for everyone involved, my brother heard the commotion and stopped me before I made a bigger fool of myself. He told me to pull my head out of my ass, then shoved me into a cold shower—which shocked some much-needed sense into my alcohol-filled brain—then sent me home in a cab with orders to, "Chill the hell out or don't come back."

When I awoke the next morning, I was sicker than a dog—not to mention humiliated, angry, and full of regret for being so foolish—and that's the moment, when the harsh reality of what I'd done kicked in, that I swore off men completely until I got my head screwed on straight. I knew then I needed to rescue myself from my past, not the other way around. And I'd done that, I realized, as the source of my greatest humiliation stood in front of me.

Chase hadn't changed much in the years since I'd seen him, but that didn't surprise me. He was good-looking in that boy-next-door sort of way that aged slowly over time, retaining a youthful appearance well into their fifties. What did surprise me, though, was the spark that had always sent my heart racing when he walked into a room was suddenly absent. I felt nothing looking at him. There was no flutter in my stomach, no shallow breaths, no sweaty palms or stuttered words. Nothing. The only thing I felt when I looked at Chase now was embarrassment for my behavior toward him—and a painful, vivid truth. The truth was, I'd never been in love with him in the first place. No, I'd been in love with the idea of being rescued by the white knight. In love with the idea of someone sweeping me off my feet and carrying me away from my family. In love with the idea of love.

I was such an idiot.

Until that moment, my greatest regret had been throwing myself at Chase when he was engaged. But now, face-to-face with the *once* object of my affection, my greatest regret was for a whole other reason. It was for the time I'd lost fixated on him when I should have been focused on having fun. My yesterdays were behind me and I'd spent them irresponsibly. I should have forgotten about my parents and charted my own course for my life. Instead, I'd watched from the sidelines, licking my wounds, waiting for the day my storybook knight would look my way and see me. Save me.

If I'd spent less time fixated on my parents' shortcomings, I might have tasted the variety of man-boys at my fingertips rather than focusing on one, and would have learned the difference between infatuation and soul-deep attraction, saving myself years of heartache.

Real attraction, one that melts your bones and leaves you unable to speak, leaves you tossing in your bed with a burning need that can only be tamed by one man, is completely different than a crush.

Looking at Chase, I knew the difference now. I'd experienced that stomach dropping, mind-numbing attraction recently, and the difference was glaringly obvious.

Sneaking a peek at Bo Strawn as Chase went on about how great it was to see me again, I bit my lip to keep from groaning. I'd had a visceral reaction to Bo when he'd yelled at the Wallflowers for butting into Devin's case, but I'd written it off as nerves. I knew better now. Bo was like no other man I'd met. He was arrogant, bold, in-your-face-dominant, and had a body that made my mouth run dry. He gave the impression of a man who was coiled with power. Power he kept in check. The attraction I felt each time I looked at him was off the charts, and I knew if my twenty-year-old self had seen Bo standing next to Chase, there would have been no contest. Bo would have won hands down.

Where Chase was lean, Bo was broad and muscled. Where Chase was spit-shined and coiffed in his linen pants and sparkling white shirt, Bo was rugged in Wranglers, boots, and a faded T-shirt. Where Chase's hair was styled, not a strand out of place, Bo's hair was longer, wilder, sexier. The two men couldn't be more different. In the best possible ways.

I was attracted to Bo in a way I'd never been to Chase. That much was clear after he threatened to put me over his knee and the thought made my legs go weak with want. And when I'd thought he was going to kiss me, I'd grabbed hold of his arms in welcome anticipation, further solidifying how attracted I was. We were standing on a beach full of police officers and reporters, and they'd all disappeared from view when Bo had leaned in close. I'd wanted him, no ifs, ands, or buts about it. Wanted him to claim my mouth with half of Tybee Island watching. But he hadn't kissed me. He'd only been leaning in to whisper in my ear.

Like Chase, he'd left me standing alone on the beach without so much as a backward glance, verifying what I'd already suspected. The attraction was one-sided. I was invisible to him just like I'd been invisible to Chase.

That hadn't stopped my growing attraction, though. In the last three days, I'd dreamt about his hot breath on my neck, his hard lines pressed against my body, and his firm hand on my ass, which only fueled more fantasies. Fantasies that included being tied to a bed as his body moved over mine or using my mouth on him as he controlled the rhythm. Fantasies that a Wallflower with no experience shouldn't be having, and I called myself all kinds of an idiot. Because once again, I wanted a man who couldn't have cared less about me.

In light of this revelation, I concluded that I had to be fundamentally screwed up by my parents to only fall for men who didn't want me. Though, in Bo's case, he didn't just dislike me. No, he *hated* me for repeatedly ignoring his orders when Cali was kidnapped, and I had *no* doubt if he knew I fantasized nightly about him, he would laugh in my face.

Since I was clearly a masochist in disguise, I stole another glance at Bo out of the corner of my eye and caught him looking up at us. If his expression was anything to go by, I'd say he still wanted to throttle me within an inch of my life. Yet, even in the face of his obvious dislike, all I could think about was how handsome his face looked when his brow drew into a hard line across his face. Or that his set jaw, ticking with anger, was sexy as hell.

See? I'm fundamentally screwed in the head.

Who knowingly wants a man who can't stand the sight of them?

"Sienna?" Chase questioned.

"Hmm?" I answered, distracted.

Bo's gray eyes had turned into slits as he scowled up at us. Their color reminded me of quicksilver, but they morphed into a raging storm cloud when he was pissed. Unfortunately, I'd seen storm-cloud gray more often than the shimmering silver.

Chase reached out and touched my arm, and I jumped, looking up at him. I regarded him for the first time through the eyes of an adult who had learned her lesson and saw nothing but my brother's friend.

It was such a relief to finally be free of my infatuation, that the tension I'd been holding on to since he walked up evaporated, and my face softened with the realization that I was truly free of him. Free to move forward and not look back.

"Like I said, I'm in town for a few days, and I'd love to catch up," Chase went on. "So what do you think? Do you wanna have dinner with me tonight?"

What?

I mean, WHAT?

Am I in The Twilight Zone?

No way was I going to dinner with this guy. For one, I threw myself at him like an idiot when he was engaged. And two, I threw myself at him like an idiot, *and* it was humiliating!

"Umm," I answered, then looked at Poppy and lied through my teeth. "Sorry, but Poppy and I have plans."

"Right," she answered, not missing a beat, taking my back like any good Wallflower would.

"Then we can catch up tomorrow," he tried again, and I panicked.

"I, ah . . . I have to go out of town on important publishin' business. I'm, um, leavin' in the mornin'."

That wasn't exactly a lie. Alexandra was out of town for a whole week, so Poppy and I had scheduled our vacations to coincide with her trip months ago. Neither of us had to report back to work for eight days. We'd planned to go to Atlanta for a week of shopping and nightlife, but with all the excitement surrounding Cali's kidnapping, we hadn't left.

He looked between Poppy and me and then smiled knowingly.

That's right, Chaser, I'm making excuses. Just accept it and move along.

"Sorry to hear that. When I saw you sittin' here, I'd hoped we could get together and catch up. You know, for old time's sake."

A tinge of guilt hit me, since he was obviously trying to mend fences that I'd torn down, and I *almost* gave in. Then wI remembered how humiliated I'd been, and I bit my lip. I'd lost enough time because of this man, and just as my sweet grandmother always said, "Nothin' good comes from visitin' past hurts."

"You know how it is. No rest for the weary. Gotta keep pourin' out those romance novels for the masses," I rattled on like a loon.

Please leave before I humiliate myself again!

He smiled and nodded, then pulled out his wallet. "I tell you what. Take my card, that way you can call me if your plans change," he said, pulling a business card from his wallet. Then he hesitantly leaned in, to my surprise and confusion, and brushed a soft kiss across my cheek, mumbling, "Good seein' you again. Hope you call so we can catch up," before turning to head down the stairs.

"Tell me that didn't just happen?" I whispered to Poppy as I watched Chase leave with two men who were waiting for him by the front door.

"Oh, it happened," Poppy chuckled next to me. "And considerin' you threw yourself at him the last time you saw him, it shows he's a nice guy."

I started to say, "He must have had one too many drinks during lunch because that's the only explanation for this Twilight Zone moment," but Bo Strawn stood from his stool and started to make his way toward the door, glancing up at me with a scowl before he left. He looked pissed like always, and I was tempted to stick out my tongue again to cover my attraction, but my heart flipped instead and plunged into my stomach like a lead ball. He would never see me as anything but an annoyance.

Time to nip this attraction in the bud before I lose any more time to unavailable men.

"It doesn't make sense," I answered. "Why would he want to

have dinner with me after what happened?"

Poppy looked back at the door and shrugged.

"I think we've already established that Wallflowers don't understand men very well, so I'd only be guessin'."

I looked at Chase's card for a moment, then tossed it on the table—done with the man—and grabbed my purse from my chair.

"You know what else Wallflowers don't know much about until it hits them smack between the eyes?"

"You mean *besides* men, clothes, and identifyin' crazed killers you work with day in and day out?"

I nodded firmly. The crazed killer one definitely got past us.

"Yes. Besides those glaringly obvious ones."

"Okay, I'll bite. What else are Wallflowers uniquely unqualified to understand?"

"The difference between infatuation and soul-deep, unadulterated attraction," I replied with authority.

Poppy's eyes shot to the bar below, then back to mine. "How do you know the difference?" she asked curiously.

"Simple," I answered. "One makes your heart go pitter-patter."

"And the other?" she questioned on the heel of my answer.

"Your heart doesn't go pitter-patter. It stampedes like a wild mustang, *never* to be tamed."

Her eyes grew wider at my explanation, and in a hushed voice she asked, "Is that what you felt talking with Chase?"

I smiled again. "Not. Even. Close. I'm *free*, Poppy. I *don't* love him. I never did. I was in love with the idea of love, and it scrambled my brain. I didn't understand that until today."

Poppy's eye began to twinkle with delight. "You know what that means, don't you?"

"That I'm free?"

"Oh, no. It means you're next. Cali found Devin; now it's your turn."

"Ah, we're *both* next," I explained as I leaned over and grabbed my laptop from the table and shoved it into my bag. "And since I lied about goin' out of town with Alexandra, it's time we decided what we're doin' next week. Why don't we go out tonight and practice flirtin' while we decide if we're headed to Atlanta or not."

Poppy slipped her arm into mine, and we headed for the stairs. "I'll be your wingwoman, but I don't think I'm ready to try yet."

I started to argue with her, but Cali emerged from the back with Devin as we hit the first floor. Her hair was tousled, and the glassy look in her eyes said Devin had done more than talk like Cali had said. And from the condition of her clothes, I say he used his hands to get his point across.

"Are you leavin'?" Cali called out.

"We have to get ready for a Wallflowers' night out," Poppy answered.

"You're goin' out?" she asked with a fair amount of enthusiasm.

"Yep. Sienna had a breakthrough, and we're gonna celebrate while we plan our vacation."

Cali looked back at Devin and gave him a pouty lip. He narrowed his eyes for a moment, then pointed at her and growled, "No speed datin'."

She rolled her eyes. "Yes, sir," she replied, saluting him.

His lip twitched, then he grabbed her neck and crushed his mouth over hers. When she melted into him and opened her mouth, Nate threw a towel at them both and grumbled, "My patrons are tryin' to eat. Take that shit back to my office."

Poppy snorted at Nate's reply, then moved behind the bar. She grabbed plastic to-go cups and began filling them with cold drafts of beer. Nate turned to look at her with more than a little bit of surprise and raised a brow. She countered with her own and said, “What? We need refreshments for our night out.”

Nate dropped his head back and bit out, “Christ,” then grabbed Poppy by the arm and led her out from behind the bar. “If the Health Department catches you behind my bar, I’ll get fined,” he grumbled, but I noted he went back to the draft and finished filling our cups, placing them on the bar for us.

We each grabbed one and raised them in salute to Nate before leaving.

Cali blew Devin a kiss before we turned and headed for the door, snorting at the man when he sighed heavily. “Try not to get kidnapped. I’d like one quiet weekend to get settled into my office before you drag me into another mess.”

“He has a selective memory,” Poppy chuckled. “You didn’t drag him into anything.”

“He says if I’d stayed inside like I promised, I wouldn’t have been kidnapped by Gayla,” she explained.

“Of course, he does,” I scoffed. “He clearly forgot who brought Gayla to your doorstep in the first place.”

“Right? So, what was your breakthrough?” Cali asked as we hit the sidewalk on River Street.

I looked at her and grinned. “You missed it while you were tangling tongues with Devin.”

“Missed what?”

“My past settin’ me free.”

Bo pushed through the crowded sidewalk, his attention zeroed in on the back of a man he didn’t know but instinctively hated. He told himself to get in his truck, to let it be and leave, but he'd ignored his better judgment and kept following the man and his friends as they wandered River Street in historic Savannah, Georgia. There was something about the guy that bugged him, something that put his protective instincts on high alert. *Something* other than the fact Sienna seemed affected by him, and he was determined to find out.

Her reaction to the man, who his friends called Chase, unsettled him for reasons he wanted to ignore. But the memory of her expression, as it softened in response to whatever Chase had said, rattled him in a territorial way. He didn't want to want her, but that didn't negate the fact that he did, and seeing her brown eyes turn from shocked to relaxed, then wistful as the man spoke burned a hole in his gut and had him reacting irrationally.

His jaw ticked at the memory, and he kept moving, staying a safe enough distance behind them so he could observe the man without being detected. He'd hoped they would make their way to a vehicle so he could grab a tag number; he preferred investigating someone in the anonymity of his office as opposed to tailing at close range. He had no choice, though. If the guy was bad news, he needed to know in order to protect Sienna. At least that's what he told himself as he stopped to watch the three men cast their eyes on a woman as she strutted past, whistling while gesturing vulgarly behind her back.

Definitely an asshole who needs to steer clear of Sienna.

The fact that her intoxicating scent followed him into his dreams each night or that her soulful eyes called out to him in the early morning hours as he wrapped his hand around his cock to ease the ache she'd caused had nothing to do with his suspicion. No, it was the smug look on the man's face as he descended the stairs that had him on alert. He reeked of player. The type of man an innocent Wallflower should steer clear of.

Bo inched closer to Chase and his friends, the need to expose him as an asshole directing his actions. When the group stopped at a souvenir store and went inside, Bo started to follow, but he paused when he caught sight of his reflection in a mirror. The image reflected back at him was wired, on edge, and it stopped him in his tracks.

What the fuck am I doing?

"Losin' your fuckin' mind," he answered.

Staring at his mirrored image, he recognized the expression. He'd seen it before on his own father's face. Knew then it was time to throw in the towel before he got sucked in deeper, but Chase moved into his line of sight before he could leave, so he watched him a moment longer.

That's when he noticed the wedding ring.

He saw blinding red then, and all thoughts of abandoning his pursuit for the truth flew out the window. He'd seen the lust in the man's eyes when he'd looked at Sienna, and knowing he had a wife sitting at home ignited his anger further.

Moving to the side, Bo leaned against the doorjamb and waited. He'd finish what he started. He'd find out who this guy was and warn him off Sienna, then he could forget about the Wallflower once and for all.

While Bo waited, Chase bought a woman's T-shirt, explaining to the cashier it was for his wife, and Bo's teeth ground together. As the group exited the shop, one of his friends finally asked the question that Bo needed answered: who was this guy to Sienna?

"So the blonde at the bar? You never explained about her."

"Nothin' to explain. She's a hot piece of ass who was hung up on me in college. She threw herself at me when she found out I was gettin' married, so I figured I'd throw her a bone. I played the nice guy angle, and she fell for it hook, line, and sinker."

"So you're hookin' up with her later?"

Chase shrugged arrogantly. "The way she wanted me," he

chuckled, "I figure she'll call any minute, then I'll wine and dine her until the alcohol sets the fuckin' mood."

An overabundance of testosterone can send rational men into fits of rage. Bo had more testosterone than the average male, and he kept a close check on his temper because of it. Then there were times like these when rational thought fell by the wayside and his natural instincts kicked in.

In one fluid motion, Bo pushed off the doorjamb, grabbed Chase by his pristine white shirt, and shoved him into the wall, bearing his teeth as he growled, "Stay the fuck away from Sienna."

The crowd around them stopped and stared, and the once loud sidewalk hushed as they waited to see what would happen. Bo didn't care. His focus was on the asshole in front of him.

"You want to fuck around on your wife, that's your business. It's an asshole move that doesn't surprise me in the least, but you're not draggin' Sienna down with you. Stay the fuck away from her."

"Get off me, man," Chase barked, pushing against Bo's chest.

"I see you're not listenin' to me," Bo bit back. "The correct response is, 'I'll forget Sienna existed.'"

"And I'll repeat, get the fuck off of me," Chase bit back, trying to wrench Bo's arm from his neck. When that didn't work, he tried to shove Bo in the chest to move him back. It was like trying to move an angry mountain. Chase tried once more as Bo held him easily in place. When Bo didn't budge, Chase finally threw his hands in the air and surrendered like Bo knew he would. Cowards backed down easily, while men stood their ground and fought for what was right. Chase was no man. "Fine. I'll forget she existed. She's not worth this much trouble anyway."

A gasping, "Oh. My. God," caught Bo's attention, and he

turned his head. Sienna was to his left with Calla and Poppy, her mouth opened in surprise, her eyes glued to the man pinned to the wall. "Chase?" she asked, the tone of her voice pained.

Bo stepped back and dropped his arm, keeping his attention on Sienna as he addressed Chase. "Tell her how you planned to get her drunk, then take advantage of her."

"Jesus Christ," Chase sighed, straightening his shirt. "I'm a fuckin' married man, not a rapist. I was just tryin' to make her feel better after what happened."

"I don't need to feel better, you ass," Sienna snapped. "I'm fine!"

"Yeah? That's not what your brother said. Seems you haven't been able to move on since I got married. I was tryin' to be nice, explain it was time for you to get on with your life, and this is the thanks I get?" Chase spit out, jerking his head toward Bo.

The crowd around them chuckled, and Sienna spun on her heel, her face growing scarlet in response. Then she spun back on Bo and leveled him with a look that would bring most men to their knees.

"Why are you doin' this?" she whispered, panic written clearly across her face. "Is this payback?"

Bo blinked, then cocked his head in confusion. "Payback?"

"Of course, it is," she murmured, scanning the crowd, looking like a fox trapped in a hole with no way to escape. "I get it. You hate me for not listenin' and humiliatin' you in front of that officer," she continued, "but I think you've more than paid me back, and then some."

"You think I planned this?" Bo growled, stepping in closer so the gathering crowd couldn't overhear. "I don't play games."

"Maybe you do, maybe you don't. I really don't care at this point. You've made it clear how you feel, so do me a favor, just stay the hell away from me!"

For five days, this woman had been inside his head, creeping in when he least expected it, an unwelcome visitor in his nightly dreams. He knew when he met her she spelled trouble for him, that she would make his head explode, and he was right.

Leaning down until he was nose-to-nose with her, Bo growled low, "Sweetheart, it would be my fuckin' pleasure to never lay eyes on you again. In fact, it's all I've been able to think about for the past five days."

Calla and Poppy gasped at his reply, but Sienna jerked infinitesimally, like she'd been struck by an imaginary fist, and her eyes welled with tears as she stared back at him. Seeing her pained expression, Bo regretted his words immediately, but he ignored the guilt and pushed past her, heading for his truck.

This was what he'd wanted since he laid eyes on her, to be free of the attraction. To be free of a woman who reminded him of his mother. A mother who left him for her own selfish purpose and destroyed his father in the process.

As a teen, he'd watched his father drink himself to death because he couldn't get over the loss of Bo's mother. A woman who was headstrong, who bucked the rules like Sienna did, who left his father high and dry for some asshole who got her hooked on drugs. Bo had lived through the aftermath her bad decisions had caused, and wanted no part of it in his life again. He wanted stability, order, a life where the only surprises were in the cases he investigated, not in his personal life. And a woman like Sienna would turn that on end. At least that's what he told himself every time he looked at her.

Pushing through the crowd, he made it five steps and then stopped, unable to walk away after the damage he'd caused. Growling, "Fuck," he dropped his head back then took a deep breath to calm down before he apologized. When he turned to make his peace with the woman, Sienna had already disappeared into the crowd. He searched the street, but couldn't find her or the other Wallflowers. Turning back to the souvenir shop in case she'd ducked inside, Bo found Chase in the same spot wiping beer from his face.

Sienna must have gotten in the final word and used a beer as an exclamation point.

Needing an outlet for his frustration, Bo decided Chase was as good a target as any, so he grabbed him by the collar again and threw a right hook into his jaw. When he hit the ground, Bo leaned over him, got right in his face, and hissed, "You go near her again, and I'll bury you. You hear me? Stay the fuck away from Sienna."

Chase grabbed his jaw, throwing his other hand up to block any additional punches that might come his way, asking what Bo himself wanted to know. "Jesus, man. What the fuck? Who is Sienna to you?"

Bo's answer . . . "My worst nightmare. A woman I can't have."

Sweetheart, it would be my fuckin' pleasure to never lay eyes on you again. In fact, it's all I've been able to think about for the past five days.

Bo's voice. Those words. They kept repeating in a loop.

Since the moment he'd laid eyes on me, he hadn't wanted a thing to do with me. I was that unappealing to him, and that knowledge stung.

I looked over my shoulder at Cali and Poppy. They were huddled together in deep conversation. Conversation that no doubt was centered on Bo, Chase, and myself.

After the scene on the sidewalk, I'd wanted to be alone to lick my wounds, but the girls wouldn't allow me to. They'd followed me to my car and jumped in when I unlocked the doors, but kept quiet, both watching me carefully. Needing space, I'd pulled into the first bar I came across for a much-needed drink, hoping the alcohol would block out the last thirty minutes. Or more to the point, block out the past ten years.

I didn't want to discuss Bo with them. It would require admitting I'd fantasized about him. Admitting that Bo never wanting to lay eyes on me hurt more than it should. As for Chase? I didn't want to discuss him either. I'd lost enough time on him.

Lesson learned. He's a big ole jackass who doesn't deserve a minute more of my time.

Racking pool balls together, I centered them on the pool table like I'd seen on TV.

"Are we playin' or what?"

Cali popped her head up and nodded.

"Stripes or solids?" I asked.

"Do you know how to play pool?"

"No. You?"

She shrugged. "I've played once. I think it's easier if you turn the stick around and use the larger end."

I looked down at the pool cue. "That's brilliant. You can't miss usin' the wider end."

"If we divide the balls into threes, all of us can play. You take numbers one through five. I'll take numbers six through ten, and Poppy can play eleven through fifteen."

Poppy jumped up from her barstool carrying a shot and grabbed a cue. "We'll play for shots. Every time you miss, you have to take a drink."

"Poppy, none of us have played. We'll need a cab to take us home after one game," I stated.

"Exactly," Cali said, carrying a shot glass and grabbing a cue of her own. "What better way to forget about asshole men?"

"I'm over it," I lied, lining up the cue ball. "I'd already discovered I wasn't in love with Chase before he showed his true colors, so there's nothin' to get over."

"And Bo?" Poppy asked.

Ignoring her question, I leaned over and pulled the cue stick back and whacked the cue ball hard enough to send all the balls crashing in every direction. None of them dropped into a pocket, though.

A shot glass landed in front of me. It was filled with green liquid, and I followed the line of the arm up to meet Cali's stern face. "And Bo?" she repeated for Poppy.

I shrugged. "Definitely an asshole. What's there to say?"

Cali looked at Poppy then back at me. "We thought we saw a look."

"A look?"

"Yeah, a look. When he said it was all he'd been thinkin' about for the past five days, there was a look on your face that said it hurt more than it should."

I pfft'd. "You're seein' things."

She crossed her arms and raised a brow. "You forget what I just went through with Devin. You can't lie to me and get away with it."

"You're comparin' what you and Devin have with Bo and me?"

"No. I'm comparin' your reaction to one I've had recently. I'm not a ninny, Sienna. You reacted to his declaration like you'd been slapped in the face. Now spill, what's runnin' through that mind of yours?"

I looked at Poppy and sighed. In that moment, I understood Cali's reactions that last week. And just like her, I would have killed for a Wallflower divorce rather than confess.

"Bo's who you meant when you talked about the difference between infatuation and soul-deep, unadulterated attraction, isn't he?" Poppy asked.

Damn, but these women are perceptive.

Now what?

Wallflowers don't lie to each other. That's what.

I grabbed the shot to stall them and threw it back.

I should have learned from the toast we made the other night that it was a bad idea to just toss a drink back. This one burned worse.

"What," I gasped, "was that?"

"Absinthe" Poppy beamed.

It took about two seconds for the liquor to make its way to my cerebral cortex, relaxing me immediately. "Doesn't this cause hallucinations?" I asked, feeling better by the second.

Poppy put another shot in front of me and said, "Let's find out."

I looked at the emerald-green color of the liquid. If it took away my memories of the past five years, I was game.

Grabbing the shot glass, I threw it back and noted the second shot was easier to handle, then closed my eyes. A warmth coiled around my limbs, relaxing me, and even though I felt light-headed instantly, I also felt clear-headed, like I could answer the question to the meaning of life.

"Well?" Cali asked. "You're supposed to filter it with water and sugar, but my granddaddy prefers it neat. He sips it, though."

I ran my hands through my hair and smiled. It felt like a thousand fingers were massaging my scalp. "This stuff is great," I said then moved to a barstool and sat down, closing my eyes so I could enjoy the high. "Can I have more?"

"Will you answer our questions about Bo?"

"He makes my heart race, my legs weak, and my breath leave

my lungs."

Huh? That was easier than I thought.

"He does?" Cali gasped.

"I want him to tie me to a bed and do naughty things to me."

Silence.

I opened my eyes to find two sets staring back at me with varying degrees of shock.

"That's right," I giggled. "I want him to—"

Poppy threw her hand over my mouth. "Big biker guys in here. No more talk about bein' tied up, capiche?"

I nodded, and she stepped back. "Gotcha. I don't want any ole man to tie me up. Just Bo."

"Are you sure he hates you?" Cali asked. "He did go after Chase. Maybe that *means* somethin'."

I tried to stand but sank back on the stool. They should really bottle this stuff for daily consumption. There'd be no need for antidepressants.

"I'm sure," I answered, smiling back at them.

"I think we gave her too much," Poppy said.

Cali pulled out her phone and began typing. "It says here that Absinthe should be sipped. It's the third strongest liquor produced and was illegal in the US until 2007 because of its effects."

"What effects? I feel great. I feel like I could fly," I laughed, throwing my arms wide like a bird.

"We need food. Greasy food," Cali stated. "I'll pay the tab then get the car. You bring her out back."

"What? No. You'll kill this feelin'."

I felt like I could take on the world and win. In fact, Bo who? Who needs a man when there's magical green fairy liquid to take away all your problems?

"Up," Cali said, grabbing my arm. "It's gonna take two of us to get her out."

Poppy moved to the other side, and they started walking me toward the back door.

"Can we stop on the way home for more magical green fairy potion?"

"Suuuure," Cali answered, so I kissed her on the cheek. She was the bestest Wallflower ever.

"I need to use the facilities before we leave," I announced, pulling away from Poppy and Cali. "Are the bathrooms down this hall?"

There were three doors in the darkened hallway, so I reached for the first doorknob and turned it. It was a supply closet.

"I think the bathrooms are the other way," Cali said as I opened the second door.

This wasn't a bathroom either. It was an office. And there were two scary biker dudes having a conversation. Cali and Poppy appeared over my shoulder, and one of the biker dudes stood and glared at us. I mumbled, "Whoops, my bad," and shut the door before they could bellow to get out of their meeting.

"This way," Poppy chuckled, grabbing my arm to lead me to the ladies' room, where I relieved myself and splashed cold water onto my face.

Looking at my reflection, I turned my head from side to side. For a moment, I wondered if I looked like my father. I'd never met the man. I wasn't even sure he knew I was his daughter. We never discussed him. It was the family secret that we all ignored. All I knew about the man was that he worked in a gym, and it was a short-lived affair that my mother regrets. Regrets most likely because she ended up with me.

"You know, I wouldn't want me either," I told my reflection.

"What are you talkin' about?" Poppy asked as she washed her hands.

"My eyes are plain old brown, and my lips are too large. I wish I had dark hair like my brother and sister."

"What's she goin' on about?" Cali said.

"Somethin' about her lips bein' too large and wanting dark hair."

"Women pay good money to have lips like yours," Cali said.

"Then why does every man I like find me repulsive?"

"Sounds like the fairy potion is wearin' off," Poppy mumbled.

"Time for a fill-up," Cali said and grabbed my arm.

They hauled me back to the bar and ordered another shot of Absinthe. I threw it back like my life depended on it, and waited for the calming effects to lull me back into not caring about anything but world peace.

"Better?" Poppy asked.

Tiny pricks of delight swirled through my brain, and I smiled. "I'm so buying stock in this stuff."

"Let's hit the road," Cali said. "We can pick up greasy burgers and take them back to the courtyard."

"Barkeep, I need my tab," I shouted.

The man turned, grabbed the tab hanging from the back wall, and looked at me. "You Calla Armstrong?"

I snatched the slip of paper from the man and scribbled Cali's name at the bottom. "I am," I replied, "But I prefer bein' called Cali."

Cali snorted and grabbed my arm. "Come on, *Cali,*" she chuckled.

I slid off the barstool and kept on going. The sweet effects of the Absinthe had settled in my legs, turning them into JELL-O in heels. Poppy and Cali grabbed me under the arms, giggling as they led me back down the long narrow hallway toward the back alley.

My phone began to ring in my pocket, so I halted and pulled

it out. The screen said *David Calling.*

"It's my brother," I explained, swiping 'Answer.' David never called me unless it was important.

"David?"

"You threw beer all over Chase?"

I bugged my eyes out at the girls.

"He wanted to get me drunk and have his way with me. It seemed like an appropriate response," I giggled.

Silence ensued.

"David?"

"That's not the way he told it. Who's the guy who punched him?"

"Bo punched him?"

Poppy and Cali gasped.

"Just stay away from my friends. I'm tired of cleanin' up after your messes," he growled, then the line went dead.

A lump caught in my throat. David tolerated being around me, but I knew he blamed me for our father leaving.

"Shit," Poppy exclaimed and turned back toward the bar. "I think she needs another round."

I pulled my arms free and headed back the way we'd come. "I'm fine. I'm used to it," I lied.

The girls followed me out the exit as I stumbled toward my car. Unable to drive, I climbed in and sprawled across the back seat. I loved my car. I loved my car's back seat. I loved the ceiling of my car. It was very gray. Like a storm cloud. Like Bo's eyes.

"Bo has great eyes," I called out as the car rocked forward then stopped sharply. "And lips that would feel amazin' working their way down my body."

Neither replied.

"Are you guys still here?"

I sat up and looked at both women. They were staring straight ahead with their hands in the air.

"What are you doin'?" I asked. Leaning forward to look out the front window, I caught sight of what held their attention. "Do we know him?"

Standing in front of my car was a grumpy-looking guy pointing a gun.

"I thought Devin told you not to get kidnapped again?" I reminded Cali.

"It must be a robbery," Poppy whispered. "Sit back and do as he says."

Grumpy Gus—who was sporting an MC cut and wearing sunglasses and a bandana to disguise his identity—moved toward the driver's side, so I rolled down my window to negotiate with the man. "We don't have any money."

"Out of the car," Grumpy Gus growled, and I could have sworn he was looking at me.

"Don't you mean her?" I asked for clarification, pointing at Cali. I don't know why he'd want me. Cali was the one with a bazillion dollars.

"Out," he bit out again.

And ruin this lovely high? I don't think so.

"NO!"

The man jerked his head to the side in confusion. "No?"

"That's right. I don't feel like comin' with you. You'll ruin my magical green fairy high, and after the day I've had, you *don't* want to ruin my high."

"Jesus," Poppy grumbled. "Man with gun, Sienna. Try not to piss him off before Devin's sixth sense kicks in, and he comes to the rescue."

"Does he have a sixth sense?" I asked Cali.

"I'm thinkin' he does," she replied, then whispered, "hold on, I'll make a break for it when I get my chance."

"No more talkin'," the man shouted, pointing his gun at me. "Out of the car."

"Why?" I asked, because it was a logical question.

"Because I said so."

"That's not good enough," I retorted. "I do not go home with strange men."

The man looked confused, and, I'll admit, a wee bit pissed off by my answer.

Maybe this is his first robbery?

Tired of waiting for me to comply, the man lowered his gun and approached my door. Cali, who clearly thought she was Jeff Gordon, punched the accelerator as he approached, the tires screeching for all they were worth as we shot out of the alley. When she hit the main road, she took a quick right then another, and for some reason doubled back the way we came behind the bar.

"What are you doing?" Poppy shouted.

"He ran to his truck. He thinks I'll keep going. If we double back, he won't expect that and we'll lose him."

"Devin's rubbing off on you," I sighed, falling back against the seat, my magical green buzz temporarily deflated due to an overabundance of adrenaline. "He'll never let you go out with us again when he finds out we were almost robbed."

Cali creeped around the back of the building just in time to see the taillights of his truck as it peeled out of the parking lot at a high rate of speed. We turned in our seats and looked out the back window, holding our breath until we saw the truck speed down the street in the direction he thought we went.

"Genius," I said. "You can keep Devin."

"Devin didn't teach me that," she answered.

"Book?" Poppy asked.

She nodded. "Linda Howard, I think."

"Blair Mallory?"

She shrugged. "Not sure, but Blair would have thought of it if she didn't."

"You know Bo reminds me a lot of Wyatt in *To Die For*," Poppy added. "Maybe we should call him and report the incident?" Her eyes lit up at the thought of Bo coming to the rescue, and my stomach dropped, the buzz I'd been riding lessening more in the face of seeing Bo Strawn again.

"NO!" Cali and I both cried out.

Poppy looked between us with wide eyes.

"Sienna's right," Cali rushed out. "Devin would lock me up and throw away the key. It was just a random guy hopin' to cash in on three women out alone. Let's just keep this between the three of us."

I nodded emphatically in agreement. "What she said. The last thing I need is Bo Strawn yellin' at me again. I'd need a *whole* bottle of magical green fairy potion to survive that."

"You sure?" Poppy asked. "He could impound your car as evidence, forcing you to deal with the rude detective like in *To Die For.*"

"You're missin' an element to that plot," I pointed out.

"What's that?"

"A dead body."

"Oh. Right," she mumbled, her nose scrunching at the thought. "But what if he's *your* Wyatt like Devin is Cali's Devil?"

"Bo Strawn is more likely my Voldemort," I snorted, "*not* my knight in shining armor. Besides, if I had to pick a fictional character to sweep me off my feet, I'd choose Iain Maitland from *The Secret* by Julie Garwood."

"Nice," Cali sighed. "Nothin' like a Highland warrior to get your juices flowin'."

Poppy cocked her head in introspection. "Bo's a little like

Iain as well."

"He can't be both Wyatt and Iain."

"Uh, yeah, he can. He's got the whole broodin' cop thing down like Wyatt, but protective instincts like Iain. Why else did he confront Chase?"

"To humiliate me," I threw out. "He was gettin' back at me for not pullin' over."

Cali groaned. "You don't really believe that, do you? Devin respects Bo. He wouldn't be friends with him if he was anything but a stand-up guy."

She had a point. A point I couldn't argue at that moment due to my muddled brain.

"Then why did he go after Chase?"

"I know," Poppy interjected, "why don't we call him and tell him you were almost kidnapped at gunpoint and find out?"

"NO!" Cali and I shouted again.

"Just a thought," Poppy grumbled.

"Let it go, Poppy. Bo and me, it's never gonna happen."

The adrenaline that had surged during our adventure leaked from my body and the green fairy potion took over again. I wanted to lie down in a cool field somewhere and stare at billowy clouds as I pondered my life.

I settled for the back seat of my car.

"We should get goin'," I yawned. "I doubt he'll find us now."

Turning so I could lie down, I glanced out the back window and gasped. Before I could cry out, "Go. Go. Go," the sound of metal meeting metal exploded around me as Grumpy Gus crashed into the back of my car.

Two

LET'S GET THE HELL OUT OF DODGE

SIENNA'S PAINED EXPRESSION HAUNTED BO like a ghost wandering Bonaventure Cemetery at midnight. He needed to find her, to explain he'd spoken out of anger and frustration. That he'd lashed out at her for reasons he couldn't explain.

After searching up and down River Street, he'd stopped by the Armstrong sisters' resale shop, Frock You, to see if she'd headed there with the other Wallflowers. Calla's aunts had informed him they'd seen all three women leave in Sienna's car.

Now what?

"I should let it be," he grumbled as he headed to his truck, well aware he wouldn't. Not after the way her dark pools had brightened with tears. Since he'd met Sienna, she'd been argumentative, stubborn, and steadfast in her convictions. Never sad. He didn't like that he was the one to put that look on her face.

Folding his six-foot-four-inch frame into his truck, Bo made the decision to head to his office, where he could access Sienna's personal information. He'd find out where she lived and head there to apologize. Then maybe the weight in his chest would ease. The last time he remembered feeling this way, he was a boy whose mother had just abandoned him, and it wasn't lost on him that a woman who reminded him of her was now the object of his self-inflicted torture.

Traveling south on Bay Street, Bo was about to turn west toward his station when a silver car passed in the opposite direction at a high rate of speed. Grumbling under his breath, he switched on his siren then waited until traffic cleared before executing a U-turn.

Weaving in and out of traffic, he caught sight of the car turning onto the River Street entrance he'd exited minutes before, bouncing off the curb as it sped down the ramp.

Just what he needed. Drunk tourists.

Punching his accelerator, Bo followed them down the ramp that led to the back alley and parking for the historic buildings on the river's edge. As he made the turn, searching for the silver car, movement caught his eye. It was Sienna and her friends. They were rushing through the gate that backed to Calla's building. He also saw the silver four-door parked at an angle next to the fence. It was empty, and the rear end was damaged.

Suspicion reared its head, so he parked behind the car to keep it from leaving, then peeled out of his truck, his eyes glued to the spot the Wallflowers had rushed through a few moments before.

Ripping open the gate, Bo found the three women huddled together in the back garden of Calla's building. He'd been there twice in the last week, and it still amazed him how her aunts had created an oasis from the world in the back alley of the two-hundred-year-old building. Flowers of every color bordered the fence, while a Pergola and water feature drew your attention to the center. Wisteria vines covered the structure, their scent blocking out the fumes of passing cars as they wound their way down to street level. In Bo's estimation, it was a thousand square feet of pure fucking paradise.

Calla saw him first as she fumbled with her phone, and elbowed Poppy. Poppy looked up, saw him, and then nudged the object of his frustration with her shoulder, pointing in his direction. Sienna turned her head and froze. He expected her reaction to be aloof after his harsh comments. It was anything but.

Before he could ask, "What the fuck is goin' on?" Sienna started moving toward him. Her long blond hair shimmered in the afternoon sun like spun gold, partially hiding her face. But not enough that he couldn't still see tears running down her cheeks.

That's when he went on full alert.

"Talk to me," he bit out as Sienna approached, but she didn't say a word. Instead, she kept moving until her head banged into his chest and she'd grabbed a handful of his shirt. The heat from her body bled through his clothes, and he folded his arms around her without a second thought, tightening his hold as her body began to tremble. It was as natural to him to comfort this woman as it was to breathe, and he stored that information away to think about later. Right now, he had a puzzle to solve.

"Hey?" he mumbled low, leaning down so he could whisper in her ear. "Talk to me."

"You need to arrest me," she sobbed.

His brows pulled together in confusion, and he looked to Calla and Poppy for clarification. Their heads were bowed, their eyes averted. Not a good sign.

"Why do I need to arrest you, honey?"

She hiccupped, buried her face deeper into his chest, then cried out, "Because I killed a man."

Bo stiffened at her answer but didn't let go of her. "You wanna say that again?"

Pulling her face out of his chest, Sienna wiped her tears away with the backs of her hands, then tried again. "I killed a man," she answered on a broken breath. "A robber."

"You killed a robber?" he questioned.

"With a Yeti."

He blinked.

"With a what?"

"With a Yeti. A metal cup."

The sweet smell of liquor filled the space between them as she tried to explain her weapon of choice, and he sighed.

She'd been drinking and was confused.

"You've been drinkin'," he stated.

"I know. Does that mean I'll get more jail time, since I'm under the influence?"

"You didn't kill anyone," he explained. "You're imaginin' it."

She shook her head. "Yeah, I did. I threw a Yeti out the window after he chased us down the street, and it hit his windshield. He crashed his truck because he couldn't see. He's dead. I just know it."

Bo looked over her shoulder and saw the other Wallflowers nodding in agreement. Something had happened, that much was certain. The question was, what?

Releasing Sienna, he grabbed her hand, pulled her toward Calla and Poppy, then pointed at lawn chairs, ordering them all to, "Sit."

All three obeyed immediately, and he thanked God for small miracles.

"You," he bit out, pointing at Calla. "Explain."

"After the scene on the, uh, sidewalk," Calla's eyes darted to Sienna then down to the ground. "Well, we stopped at a bar for drinks."

"So you were assaulted inside the bar?"

She shook her head. "When we left in Sienna's car, a man stepped out in front of us with a gun."

"Is that when he chased you?"

"No."

"No?"

"No, we got away first then doubled back behind the buildin' to hide until he was gone."

"That was brilliant by the way," Sienna interjected. "Too bad it didn't work."

"Totally brilliant," Poppy added. "I never would have thought—"

Bo's jaw began to twitch from holding his temper in. "For Christ's sake," he barked, interrupting, pinching the bridge of his nose for patience, "finish the story."

"Right. Sorry. Well, we were waitin' to make sure he was gone before leavin', but he found us."

"And that's when Sienna threw the Yeti?"

"No, he slammed into the back of Sienna's car first, so I took off. That's when he gave chase. Then Sienna rolled down her window like she said and threw a thirty-two-ounce Yeti full of Coke at him. It shattered his window, and he crashed into a light pole. We didn't stop when he crashed, considerin' he had a gun, and came straight here. I was about to call Devin when you found us."

Bo could feel his blood pressure rising, so he counted to ten before he spoke. "Let me get this straight," he asked through clenched teeth as an image of Sienna hanging out the window of a speeding car made his blood run cold. "You were confronted by an armed robber, and instead of handin' over your cash, you tried to evade him. Then he found you while you were hidin' in your *car,* instead of inside the bar where it was *safe*, and you proceeded to try and outrun him. *Then*, while drivin' erratically, puttin' the public in danger, Sienna risked her life by hangin' out the window to throw a metal cup at an *armed* man? Is that what you're tellin' me?"

All three Wallflowers grimaced.

"It really didn't seem that stupid at the time," Poppy tried to argue, and Bo saw red.

These women had no fear. Not a lick of sense.

"Oh, boy, his eye is twitchin'," Sienna mumbled. "That means he's about to blow."

"Enough," Bo growled—shooting Sienna a look that dared her to say another word—then pulled out his phone. "Devin should have his head examined for gettin' himself tied up with a woman like the three of you."

"What's that supposed to mean?" Calla gasped.

"It means none of you have the sense that God gave you. You'll all end up dead if you don't learn self-preservation, for Christ's sake," Bo shouted. "Now, give me the location of the wreck before I lock all of you up for leavin' the scene of an accident."

"Liberty and Habersham," she squeaked out, bugging her eyes out at her friends.

At least one of them had sense enough not to push him.

"No one leaves this location," he ordered, leveling each woman with a hard stare, then he started moving toward the back gate. "I'll be back once I know what the fuck is goin' on."

"Should I call Devin?" Calla called out.

Bo looked back at her and shook his head. "I'll do it. If you spout off the shit you just told me, he'll lose his mind. I don't need Hawthorne goin' cowboy on this guy if he lived through the accident."

She nodded, then Bo's eyes landed on Sienna before leaving.

She still looked shaken by their encounter, and his protective instincts kicked in for the second time that day. She may not be his woman, but the need to keep her safe hummed through his body like a battle cry. He needed to find this guy quickly. No armed robber he'd ever arrested would keep searching for a target unless they wanted something else, or worse. In his estimation, all of the Wallflowers were in danger until he found the man who dared to raise a gun on them.

On Sienna.

Devin rode up on his hog as the fire department put out the last of the flames. Bo watched him carefully as he approached. The set line of Devin's jaw told him all he needed to know. If the man hadn't already perished in the fire, Devin would have been on the war path.

"Lay it out for me again," Devin bit out as he turned his eyes on the smoldering wreckage. "I need to know if this is related to Calla's grandfather."

Bo jerked his head for Devin to follow so they weren't overheard by the forming crowd. Once they were a good distance away, Bo laid it out like he asked.

"According to Calla, this guy tried to rob them at gunpoint. They got away, and a chase ensued. Sienna threw a Yeti at the truck while he was in pursuit, and it shattered his window. He hit that pole," he explained, nodding toward the wooden light pole that had split at the base and was currently lying across the hood of the truck, "and it burst into flames."

"Witnesses?" Devin asked, scanning the street.

"None. No one saw Sienna throw the Yeti. No one saw the crash. The explosion's what alerted nearby residents."

"*You* know," Devin stated, holding his eyes.

Bo took a deep breath and looked at the smoldering wreckage. "Yeah, I know. And I'm keepin' it that way."

Devin's brows shot to his hairline. "You're not reportin' what you know?"

Bo's teeth ground together. He was by the book. Followed the letter of the law. Always. Until today. "It serves no purpose. Calla and her friends were the victims, not this guy."

Devin grinned slowly. "You know the first time's the hardest."

"The first time?" Bo questioned.

"The first time you look the other way instead of reportin' what you know. It'll get easier."

Bo's teeth continued to grind. "I don't plan on makin' a habit of—" Lieutenant Turner, with the Savannah Fire Department, waved at Bo, interrupting him. "They've got somethin'."

Pushing through the crowd, Bo and Devin made their way over to Turner and Jose Dejesus, the beat cop who'd responded to the accident.

"Truck's empty," Turner announced without prelude.

Bo swung around and scanned the crowd. "He's still on the loose. We need to find this guy. Have you run the VIN?"

"Just did," Turner responded. "It was reported as stolen a week ago."

"Dust for prints," Devin ordered.

"For a stolen vehicle?" Dejesus asked, but Bo ignored him. He swung back and looked at the truck. The driver's side door was closed, but the passenger side door was open. He'd assumed SFD had opened it, but he was now convinced it was how the perp escaped the wreck. "Passenger side door. Dust the door handle. It's how he got out."

"Why the full-court press for a stolen vehicle?" Dejesus questioned.

Bo stepped in closer to make sure he got his point across. He wasn't taking any chances this guy got away and went after Sienna or the other Wallflowers. "Because," he growled, "this truck matches the description of one of my cold cases, so tell Vargas to find me a print and that I needed it yesterday."

Dejesus swallowed hard and nodded, then turned and headed back to the crime scene investigators who were waiting to clear the area.

Devin watched the cop retreat with his tail between his legs, then turned to Bo, smiling as he pulled out his phone to call Calla. "Like I said, it gets easier each time."

Bo turned slowly and scowled at his friend, hissing, "Bite me, 'Dashing Detective,'" referring to the YouTube video of them both taking down Fang Yoo, a huge Asian woman.

Devin's smile pulled wider across his face, and then he threw his head back and laughed.

"All right. Someone needs to tell me what's goin' on," Bernice Armstrong, Cali's colorful yet lovable aunt demanded. "Bo Strawn was here lookin' for you not an hour ago, and now you all look like jackrabbits in a den of wolves."

I turned my head and looked at Bernice. She was dressed in acid-washed jeans, popular with her generation in the 1980s, and a Pink Floyd T-shirt. She had stitches near her hairline—courtesy of the butt of a gun Gayla Brown had used when she kidnapped Cali—that stood out in sharp contrast to her peaches-and-cream complexion.

Cali referred to her aunts as from the Madonna generation, and she wasn't wrong. Any day now I expected them to stroll out wearing rubber bracelets, Madonna's trademark hair bow, and a belt that said 'Boy Toy.'

"Nothin' we can't handle," Cali answered.

"I didn't ask if you could handle it or not. You're an Armstrong, sugar, that goes without sayin'. What I asked is, what the heck is goin' on?"

"Hold on a minute," Poppy jumped in. "You said Bo Strawn was here an hour ago lookin' for us?"

"That's what I said."

Poppy looked at me and smiled. "Did he say why he was lookin' for us?"

I threw my head back and banged it against the chair. "Let it go, Poppy. You heard what he said on the sidewalk, not to mention, the bit about how a man would have to be a glutton for punishment to tangle himself with the likes of us. He's a jerk, and I want nothin' to do with him," I lied.

"Maybe he's bein' a jerk 'cause he's fightin' his feelin's for you. *Maybe* he's all bluster and deep down he doesn't mean it. And just *maybe* he enjoys a little punishment," she suggested, wiggling her eyebrows, referring to my slip about wanting to be tied up by Bo.

I groaned. Me and my big mouth. I just *had* to open my big mouth about Bo.

"When pigs fly," Bernice chuckled. "That's a man's man if I ever saw one. He hands out punishment, not the other way around."

I banged my head against the back of the chair again to erase the image of Bo handing out *punishment* of any kind. It didn't work. My ass tingled as if it had been struck by a very large, warm hand.

"What's wrong with her?" Bernice asked.

"I need a vacation," I whined.

"She needs a man," Cali chuckled.

I raised my head. "Men are the least of my worries right now."

"This is true," Poppy answered. "You'd look horrible in prison orange. It'll make you look sallow."

"Sallow? Really, Poppy?"

"Just tryin' to lighten the mood," she smiled.

"She's not goin' to prison. It was self-defense," Cali added.

"Now we're gettin' somewhere," Bernice said, pulling up a chair. "Tell Bernie all about it. What did you do that Bo Strawn is lookin' for you?"

I looked at Cali. "Why does she seem giddy at the prospect of my incarceration?"

Cali shrugged, flicking her hands out in 'who knows' gesture. "I stopped tryin' to figure out my aunts years ago."

"Enough stallin'," Bernice sighed. "I knew when I saw you three sittin' out back that trouble was a brewin'. When the three of you get together, you're like a magnet for it. So, spill. What did you do?"

Oh, what the hell. She'd find out soon enough when Bo came back and slapped the cuffs on me.

"I killed a man with a Yeti."

Bernice opened her mouth, then closed it. "Say again? I think I need a hearin' aid 'cause I could have sworn you said you killed a man with Bigfoot."

"A man tried to rob us at gunpoint. While pursuin' us, Sienna threw a *Yeti tumbler* out the window, and it smashed in his windshield, causin' the man to crash. She thinks he's dead, therefore she killed him and must face the consequences," Poppy enlightened.

Bernice stood without a word and turned, heading for the back door of Frock You.

"Where are you goin'?" Cali called out.

Bernice turned back and looked at us. "A story like that

requires refreshments. Midnight Mojitos comin' right up."

"Your aunts are nuts," I chuckled.

"You have *no* idea."

Cali's phone began to ring. I sat up and looked at it as if it held my fate in its tiny electronic hands. "It's Devin," she gasped, swiping 'Answer.'

My heart began to race, and I forgot to breathe as I watched Cali for any signs that prison might be in my immediate future.

"Then he got away?" she cried out. "He didn't die in the crash?"

Her eyes shot to mine as she listened to whatever Devin said. When she relaxed and smiled at me, I took my first breath.

Thank you, thank you, God.

"Okay, I'll tell the girls," she finally said, then her face grew softer, and she ended the call with a whispered, "Love you, too."

"Well?" I asked.

"Devin says no one saw the crash or us. The truck exploded and burnt to a crisp, but he wasn't inside. You're in the clear. We all are!"

I sunk back in relief. "What a way to start a vacation. First, you get kidnapped, then this."

"Yep," Poppy said. "A trip to Atlanta will seem pale in comparison."

"Then do somethin' you'd never do in a million years," Cali stated. "What did you dream about when you were a little girl? Climbin' a mountain or maybe tourin' France?"

Poppy cocked her head, then chuckled. "I dreamt about slayin' Orcs."

"As in *Lord of the Rings*?" Cali questioned.

She nodded.

I snorted. "I think we slayed one today."

"True," she chuckled. "So what was your dream as a girl?"

"That's easy. Before I discovered romance novels, I was obsessed with the adventures of Laura Ingalls Wilder. I wanted to be Laura."

Poppy perked up. "I read those books. But the romance between Laura and Almanzo held my attention the most."

"So you wanted to live in the wild frontier?" Cali asked.

I thought about that for a moment. "I suppose. The long skirts and bonnets fascinated me. And the strappin' men who were real men instead of these snivelin' idiots who live at home with their mothers till they're thirty definitely held my appeal. They were manly, like Laura said."

"Sounds like someone else we know. A certain lawman with attitude?" Poppy threw out.

I looked at her and rolled my eyes. "You're like a dog with a bone."

"I can't help it. Sienna, he's perfect for you, and you're bein' stubborn if you don't pursue it."

I looked at Cali. "Help me out here? You heard him, why can't she get it through her thick skull that the man isn't interested in me?"

"No talkin'," Bernice shouted as she exited the building carrying a tray full of glasses and a pitcher of mojitos. "I don't want to miss anything, so hold all discussion."

Once she'd deposited the tray on the table, she took her seat and began to pour, saying, "Continue," as she handed me a glass.

"I'm in the clear," I told her, shrugging. "Grumpy Gus didn't die."

She paused her pouring, looking crestfallen. "I wasn't gone that long. How'd you manage that?"

"Devin called and said he got out of the truck alive. That's all we know."

"Now we're tryin' to decide how to spend our vacation,"

Poppy said.

Bernice looked between Poppy and me. "You sure you should travel? The way things are goin', you could end up kidnapped and on a slow boat to China, or wherever it is they take sex slaves these days."

"Wait a minute," Cali called out, "I have it. Bernie, do your friends still have that dude ranch?"

"Dude ranch?" I questioned.

"Yeah, you said you were obsessed with *Little House on the Prairie,* which made me think cowboy, which made me think horses, which made me think hunky cowboys herdin' cattle, and then it hit me that Bernice has these friends who own a dude ranch. It's actually a workin' ranch, but they rent out cabins and have all sorts of fun stuff. Horseback ridin'. A pack trip with a covered wagon, complete with trail cook and cattle wranglin'."

"You'd love Boris and Natasha Winkle," Bernice interjected.

"Your friends' names are Boris and Natasha?" I asked. "Like in *The Rocky and Bullwinkle Show?"*

"Yep. And they're a hoot, too. I can call in a favor if they're full. But they normally have plenty of room seein' as it's a workin' ranch and most don't see feedin' chickens and milkin' cows as a vacation."

I looked at Poppy and shrugged. "It's definitely different."

She mulled it over for a moment, then nodded. "I haven't been on a horse in years, but I'm game if you are. Maybe we could learn to lasso; it might come in handy the way our luck is runnin'."

"Then we're decided?" I asked.

Poppy beamed. "Let's get the hell out of Dodge and wrangle some cattle."

"No bigger than you both are it's more likely the cattle will wrangle you," Bernice chuckled, pulling out her cell phone. "I'll call Natasha and set you up."

Excitement bubbled in my chest. Horseback riding, campfires, and maybe a few manly cowboys might take my mind off the past few hours, *and* Bo Strawn if I was lucky.

The back gate ripped open, startling me, and I turned to watch Bo storm through followed by Devin. One look told me no amount of manly cowboys would temper my attraction any time soon. He was, in my opinion, almost the ideal man. Tall, strong, protective, and sinfully gorgeous. It was his jerk status at the moment that kept him from being perfect.

His gray eyes landed on mine for a moment as he approached. He looked ready to kill, which upped his hotness factor a thousand percent, and I wanted to bang my head against a wall until I got over this stupid attraction.

I looked away before he could read my thoughts. There was so much intelligence working behind those eyes, I felt sure if I looked at him too long, he'd see right through me, would know what I was thinking.

"We need a description of this guy," Bo stated as he walked up.

Devin moved to Cali and hauled her into his arms, hugging her before curling her into his side. "We'll talk about your Jeff Gordon impersonation later."

Cali beamed at Devin. "I could give Jeff a run for his money."

Devin looked incredulous. "Jesus. I thought fearless was cute until today."

"You love me," she whispered back, and his face softened.

"I must if I put up with your antics," he mumbled softly then brushed a kiss across her lips.

I turned away from them. I wanted that type of connection with someone.

Bo sat down across from me and pulled out a notepad, breaking me from my thoughts. Then he looked up at me. Our eyes caught and held long enough for my heart to pick up its pace. Then he scanned my face, taking my measure. "You better?" he asked softly. So softly it almost seemed as if he cared.

Remember he's a jerk.

I nodded my response.

He scanned my body for some reason, and I swear it felt like he was undressing me, so when his eyes made their way back to mine, I raised a brow.

"Were you hurt durin' the altercation?" His voice had grown deeper as he spoke. The resonances curled around me, increasing my heart rate with each word like a slow seduction, so I cleared my throat and shook my head. There was no way I could have answered in that moment. He would have heard how aroused I was.

Bo scowled at my non-answer.

"Cat got your tongue?"

I shook my head.

"So you can talk."

I nodded.

He narrowed his eyes, so I narrowed mine back. "All right, describe this guy for me."

I looked at Cali and Poppy and caught them looking between the two us, grinning like loons.

"Um, medium to tall height, brown hair. He was wearin' sunglasses and a bandana, so I couldn't see his face."

"He was wearin' black jeans, a black hoodie, and a leather vest," Poppy added. "Who wears black in Savannah after February first?"

"Did you see him in the bar?"

"He may have been inside, but I don't remember seein' him," Cali remarked.

"Name of the bar?"

Oh. Dear. Lord.

I cleared my throat and said on a quick exhale, "The Tap Room."

Bo stopped writing and looked up. "You went to a biker bar?"

I looked at the girls and bugged out my eyes. "We were in the mood for a game of pool."

"We'll be havin' a discussion about biker bars as well," Devin grumbled.

I snorted at Devin, and Bo's attention shot to mine. "Do you frequent biker bars regularly?" he growled.

The judgment in his voice piqued my temper. I'd only been in that bar because of him. "Only when it's made clear that I'm a thorn in someone's side, and they rue the day they ever met me."

Bo jerked slightly, then took a long, slow, deep breath. He looked, for lack of a better word, like he felt guilty. "About that," he muttered.

I raised my hand to stop him. "Don't. The truth comes out when people are mad, so don't get all 'I didn't mean it.' You did. I'm way over it," I lied, "so move on to your next question."

His jaw tightened, so I looked away. It wasn't my job to ease his conscience. If he was regretting what he said, he could stew on it for a while.

Bo stood abruptly and closed his notepad, shoving it into his back pocket. I ignored him and assumed an air of 'not giving a shit,' because the more I thought about it, the more I believed it was his fault we were held at gunpoint to begin with. If he'd been a nice guy instead of a jerk, I wouldn't have stopped at the damn bar.

"I'll let you know when we find him," Bo bit out and turned to leave.

"You do that," I mumbled under my breath.

I kept my eyes off his retreating backside as he and Devin left. It was past time to get him out of my system, and watching his muscled body as he marched across the courtyard wouldn't help. Bo filled out his Wranglers like they'd been custom made for him alone.

"If you two weren't goin' out of town tomorrow, I'd give it two days max before you and that man are rippin' each other's clothes off," Bernice chuckled.

"What?"

"Butterbean, you're as clueless as Calla Lily was. That man wants you; he's just fightin' it."

Cali and Poppy both nodded.

"The sexual tension was off the charts," Poppy added.

"You're all nuts. Certifiable. The only thing that man wants from me is for me to live in a different zip code."

"That's the ticket," Bernice replied. "Make him come after you. A gentleman should always do the pursuin'."

God, help me. She thinks she's Dear Abby.

"The only way Bo Strawn would pursue me is if handcuffs were involved."

"He's got a kinky side, does he?" Bernice asked.

I opened my mouth and then closed it. Then I banged my head on the chair again.

Nope. Didn't help.

Why me?

"Poppy, let's hit the road and pack. I need a distraction from my life."

Bernice jumped up from her chair. "I'll print off the directions before you go."

"What's the name of this place?" I asked.

Bernice cocked her head and smiled. "Why, Bullwinkle Ranch, of course."

Perfect. My life was a comedy show, why not graduate to cartoons?

Bo placed his gun on his kitchen counter, then headed for a beer. It was after midnight, and he was still waiting to hear back on the smudged print they'd pulled off the passenger side door of the burnt-out truck. They'd found no other evidence to point them in the right direction. If the print didn't ping back to his perp, he'd have no leads and a ton of unanswered questions.

Pulling an ice-cold beer from the refrigerator, he popped off the top and took a long draw. Then he looked around his quiet apartment, and his mind wandered. Despite being surrounded by his carefully structured life, he couldn't keep his thoughts off the one aspect of it that didn't fit.

His attraction to Sienna Miller.

She'd gotten under his skin. Buried herself there, and he couldn't get her out. And now with the threat to her and the other Wallflowers, he was tweaked, felt off-balance. He wanted to lash out at something.

Bo thought back to that afternoon. He'd hurt Sienna, that was apparent. Her interaction with him had been guarded when he'd returned with Devin, and he hated it. Hated that he'd been the one who caused her to turn cautious with him. If he could take it back, he would have done so.

Closing his eyes against the memory, Bo's thoughts wandered to the moment she'd buried her face in his chest, as if she thought he was the only man who could help her. He tried to ignore the way she'd felt pressed close, but it was no use. The heat from her body had seared a memory into his.

Rolling his head from side to side to work out the kinks, Bo lifted the bottle to his mouth for another long pull. The sound of a clock ticking in his apartment amplified how quiet his life was when he wasn't on the job. He told himself for the hundredth time it's how he wanted it. How he'd organized it after a childhood full of chaos, but what had once been a necessity to block out the pain, locking it behind bars like an unwanted criminal, now seemed like a self-imposed prison. He looked around his apartment and noted how sterile it was. There were no pictures from his twenty-eight years of life, no clutter to distract him. Only organized boredom. His life was gray.

Clenching and unclenching his fist, Bo looked down at his beer then turned and threw it at his fireplace in a fit of rage. The bottle shattered, splattering beer and glass on the polished hardwood.

He stared at the destruction peppering his carefully planned world, then looked at the clock. Moments passed as the second hand ticked by, a metaphor, he thought, for his life. Looking back at the shards of glass, Bo realized it, too, was a symbol for his childhood, but it was also a sign of things to come if he didn't move forward.

He had a decision to make.

He could live in the past, holding his mother's actions against a woman he craved more than air, or he could pull his head out of his ass and move forward before another man saw what he did. Sienna was the sun in his gray world.

"Fuck it," he growled, heading for the door.

It was time to leave the past where it belonged. Dead and buried.

He made the drive to Sienna's apartment in ten minutes, then parked and peeled out of his truck. He looked up at the darkened windows of her unit and knew she was asleep.

Bo didn't hesitate to take the stairs two at a time to her landing. He was done fighting what he wanted. Done denying what he felt for the woman. He wanted her, and he knew she felt something for him. He'd seen it in her eyes on the beach. It was time to drop the subterfuge that he didn't want to claim Sienna for his own. He'd played by the rules his whole life, and he had nothing to show for it but a lonely existence.

Rules don't keep you warm at night. Rules didn't fill a void that's been empty since he was ten. He wanted Sienna more than he'd wanted anything in his life, except for his mother's love, and when he wanted something, he normally went after it with both barrels blazing and hung on tight. Why he'd let his past stop him from grabbing hold of Sienna with both hands, he'd never know. Chalk it up to stupidity. But he was done being stupid. Tonight, he'd let Sienna know exactly where he stood, and that her days of searching for her white knight were over.

Raising his fist, Bo pounded on her door. He waited thirty seconds for her to wake up, then pounded again. When he heard no movement inside, he looked over the railing into the parking lot and saw her beat-up car. She was home but not answering. He smiled. His woman slept like the dead.

Pulling his lock pick tools from his back pocket, Bo went to work on her deadbolt. It wasn't lost on him that he was pulling the same maneuver Devin had in his attempt to track down his Wallflower.

When the bolt finally gave, Bo turned the knob and entered. He was standing in a hallway, so he moved to the living room on quiet feet. Finding the light switch, he flipped it on and then blinked. He'd walked into an English garden of soft pastels and wicker furniture. The walls were painted a soft pink, like the color of her full lips. The wicker furniture was upholstered in shades of pink and purple floral print that was neither loud nor subtle. There were bookshelves lining two walls, jam-packed with paperback novels that looked as if she'd read them multiple times. But the structure that caught Bo's eye the most was the large queen trusses supporting the open ceilings. Her building was an old Tannery that had been remodeled and converted into apartments years ago. The space, though small, was as appealing as the woman who lived in it.

Moving to the open bedroom door, Bo pushed it wider until the light from the living room filtered in and he could see inside. A king-size wrought iron bed with a snow-white quilt and matching shams took center stage in the room. It looked soft, inviting, like a man could crawl inside and sleep for years while he held his woman tight.

It was also empty.

"You better not be out speed datin'," Bo growled, then pulled out his phone to call Devin.

When he swiped his phone awake, he noted he had a text message waiting for him and tapped it open, hoping it was the station with a match on the print. He wasn't disappointed.

Print came back to a Larry Dwayne Daniels. He's a prospect with the Serpents. Goes by Purge in the club.

Bo was beginning to think Wallflowers was the wrong name for this particular set of women. They were better suited for the name Calamity Janes. *How in the hell did they get on the Serpents' radar?*

Swiping Devin's number after reading the text, he waited impatiently for his friend to pick up. The call went to voicemail. He didn't have time to waste, so he hit redial. In their line of work, Bo knew Devin wouldn't ignore a second call from him at midnight, even if he was with his woman.

"This had better be good," Devin growled.

"Ask Calla where Sienna is," he growled back.

Devin sighed, aggravated, then muffled the phone. He came back a few moments later with laughter in his voice. "You're not gonna believe this shit. Bernice has friends who run a dude ranch. Sienna and Poppy are headed up there for a week of ridin' horses and milkin' cows."

"And huntin' men. The ranch is full of hunky cowboys!" Calla called out loudly.

Bo narrowed his eyes. "You wanna repeat that?"

"You heard me. And Calla. The Wallflowers are spendin' their vacation on a ranch."

"Jesus. They'll end up ridin' off a cliff."

A low rumble of laughter sounded over the phone.

"I told you earlier she needed to be locked up," Bo chuckled.

"You also said you pity the man who takes her on."

"That opinion hasn't changed."

"Are you sayin' you're not the man for the job?" Devin questioned. "I've seen the way you look at her."

"Oh, I'm the man for the job, but I have to find her first," Bo bit out.

"Fuckin' déjà vu," Devin muttered. "I feel your pain."

"Ask Calla the name of the ranch."

Devin covered the phone again, then stated, "Calla said Bullwinkle Ranch. Like the cartoon."

Bo saw a computer sitting on her nightstand, so he walked over and opened the lid.

"You gonna hunt her down?" Devin questioned as the screen came to life. It was password protected. Bo remembered what Calla had said about women using their birthdates for passwords, so he shoved the phone between his ear and shoulder and pulled out the slip of paper he'd written Sienna's information on at the office.

"You still there?" Devin asked.

"Yeah, I'm tryin' to Google the address of the ranch."

"That answers my question at least. What about the print? Did you get a hit?"

"Yeah. Belongs to a biker by the name of Purge. I'll have him picked up in the mornin'. In the meantime, keep an eye on Calla till he's hauled in."

"That's a given," Devin answered. "She's in my sight at all times 'til we figure out what the fuck he was after."

Bo punched in Sienna's birthday and smiled when the screen sputtered then logged in. Then he barked out "Christ," when an image of a scantily dressed woman, handcuffed to a bed, appeared on the screen.

"You got somethin?" Devin asked.

"Yeah," Bo bit back. "A mystery wrapped in an enigma tied up with leather and lace."

"You've lost me," Devin said.

"I gotta go," Bo growled.

"You find what you were lookin' for?"

"Yeah, and then some."

Bo ended the call and scanned the website Sienna had logged into. She'd left the page open to an article titled "Are You A Submissive?"

"Jesus," Bo said, then opened a tab and Googled Bullwinkle Ranch. Then he remembered what Calla had said about Sienna and Poppy huntin' cowboys and grabbed his phone. He left a message for his captain on his voicemail.

"This is Strawn. You know that vacation you've been yellin' at me to take? I'm takin' it now. I'll be back in a week . . ."

Three

GIT ALONG, LITTLE DOGIES

A CROW DARTED ACROSS THE periwinkle horizon, its sharp cry bouncing off the valley, and I looked up, squinting my eyes against the morning sun. Then I took a deep, cleansing breath. The quiet that surrounded Bullwinkle Ranch was like a Band-Aid to my soul. I could kiss Cali for suggesting we come here. The ranch was isolated in a valley that was bordered by rolling hills and mountains. This was God's country. Peaceful. Serene. The only noise that could be heard was the intermittent cry of a cow, chicken, or horse. It was as if time stood still in this little pocket of heaven.

The main house at Bullwinkle Ranch was a sprawling log cabin, complete with a front porch that twenty people could easily sit back and relax on. It faced the mountain range—which rivaled any view in the world—and a small lake on the border. Windmills dotted the property, which brought water to the ranch as well as the livestock, adding to the impression of having stepped back in time. Their mute presence guarded over the ranch like silent sentries.

And everywhere I looked, there were animals . . . and men.

In every shape and size.

Every age.

Young, old, and in-between.

Unfortunately, not one of them held a candle to Bo Strawn, and that was my dilemma. How was I supposed to get over my attraction to the man if everywhere I looked I saw examples of why he was my ideal?

Poppy and I had arrived the night before. After the day we'd had, I decided I didn't want to wait, so she and I headed out early evening and arrived close to midnight.

We'd called ahead, so Boris and Natasha had kept the home fires burning, waiting for us to arrive. They'd stood on the front porch, arm in arm as we pulled up, greeting us with warm smiles, bear hugs, and warm apple cobbler.

For this overworked, overstressed city girl, it was much-needed medicine.

Boris was big, bold, and fatherly, with a high and tight haircut reminiscent of a man who'd spent years in the military and hadn't let go.

Natasha . . . Well, Natasha was a plump woman with silver hair and skin the texture of leather. She clearly had worked the ranch right alongside Boris and didn't believe in sunscreen. She also wore the pants, and Boris loved it, and her. I guessed their age around late sixties, since, according to Boris, they'd been married almost forty years, spending only five days apart in all that time.

I'd wanted to adopt them instantly as my very own grandparents.

"Why does that horse look like he wants to take a bite out of me?" Poppy whispered as I took in the glorious day.

Turning my head, I peered at the impressive animal. I'd

ridden a horse exactly twice, so I knew nothing about them. This particular one was big, black, and staring at us through the split rail fence surrounding the corral. We were feeding the chickens in a coop bordering his enclosure, tossing seed on the ground as the hens darted around our feet.

"He's just curious, I suppose. Maybe he's hoping you have an apple?"

A loud bang caused us both to jump, and we directed our attention to the horse stalls. By eight a.m. the ranch was in full swing, and one of the ranch hands had thrown open a door and was currently hauling a bale of hay inside.

"Is it just me or is the sight of a sweaty man throwin' around hay a turn-on?" Poppy whispered.

I crinkled my nose and snorted. Then I pictured Bo as the man hauling the hay around, his muscles bulging as he easily hoisted the bale into a stall, and my opinion changed. "Definitely," I answered, then frowned.

Will I ever get the man out of my head?

"Hey, you two," Natasha shouted. "Quit your lollygaggin', or you'll miss out when Boris checks the herd."

Poppy turned back and looked at the horse currently watching our every move. "He's all yours," she mumbled, jerking her head in the horse's direction.

"You're bein' silly," I replied, tossing out my final handful of seed. "I'll prove it to you."

Dusting off my hands, I moved to the beast and put out my hand, intending to scratch him between the eyes. The horse jerked his head back before I could pet him, then opened his gaping mouth and bit me.

Snatching my hand back, I glared at the satanic animal. "See if I bring you an apple anytime soon," I snapped.

"Goliath," Natasha shouted, "quit bein' an ass."

"Told ya he wanted to bite us," Poppy snorted.

I glared at her, too.

"Please tell me we won't have to ride him," I asked Natasha.

"Not unless you're an experienced horsewoman. Goliath can be…" She bobbled her head back and forth like a bobblehead doll, looking for the right word.

"An ass," I supplied.

"I was gonna say stubborn, arrogant, and full of himself. Only the most experienced riders can handle him, and he prefers men."

"So he's a typical male, is what you're sayin'," Poppy laughed.

"Exactly," Natasha said. "Are you girls ready for a nice long ride?"

Poppy and I looked at each other. "I'm game if you are," I stated.

"Count me in."

Natasha jerked her head toward a group of horses that were saddled. Boris was climbing on top of a stunning snow-white horse that seemed to bear his weight with ease as we walked up. He settled a cowboy hat on his head, then looked back at us and winked.

"You ladies ready for some fun after milkin' cows and feedin' the hens?"

Natasha pointed to a pretty little speckled mare for me, and a buckskinned mare for Poppy. They were both handsome creatures and a little more my speed. The speckled mare was much smaller than Goliath and not near as intimidating.

"What's her name?" I asked, running my hand down the center of her long head.

"This here is Tiny Dancer," Natasha said. "And the buckskin is called Harriet."

"Harriet?" Poppy chuckled.

"She's named after my dear departed mother," Boris called out. "On account she looks just like her. Those big brown eyes and long snout, it's like lookin' at her, I tell ya."

Natasha leaned in with a smirk and mumbled low so he couldn't hear her, "He's not lyin'. His mother was as sweet as they come, but, *Lord,* was she homely."

I didn't know how to respond to that, so I smiled and grabbed hold of the horn to pull myself up into the saddle. I put my foot in the stirrup, then tried unsuccessfully to get on top of Tiny Dancer. On the third try, a pair of strong hands grabbed me by the waist and pushed me up. I looked down as I tucked my right foot into the stirrup and found one of the ranch hands smiling up at me.

"Thanks," I said, smiling in return.

He tipped the brim of his hat at me, mumbling, "Ma'am," before winking and turning to leave.

"That's another stud to steer clear of," Natasha informed me. "Duke's a good seasonal hand, but he's what your generation calls a player."

"All right. Let's head out," Boris called out.

I looked around and found it was just Boris, Poppy, and me who were on horseback.

"It's just the three of us?"

"Yep. You're our only customers right now."

"Where are we headed?"

"Boris is goin' to check on the herd. We have them up in the high-country grazing. He'll bring them back down in a couple of days. You'll have fun with that. Nothin' like herdin' cattle to get your juices flowin'."

I could think of a few other things that would get my juices flowing more than rounding up cows. A good romance novel being at the top of my list.

With a, "Yee-haw," that had to be for their guests' benefit—though I will admit Tiny Dancer perked right up at the exclamation—we took off in a cloud of dust.

We made it halfway down the trail that led to the foothills before Tiny Dancer broke into a canter. That's when I realized I wasn't a very good horsewoman, nor was Poppy. We bounced and bobbled all over the seat, holding on for dear life to the horn.

"I should have worn a sports bra," I told Poppy, wishing I could let go of the reins to adjust my bra. My boobs were getting a workout. If Tiny Dancer went any faster, they'd knock me out.

"Harriet needs a smooth-ride button," Poppy grumbled. "I'm gonna break a tooth."

Boris shook his head at our commotion and stopped, so I pulled on my reins.

Looking back at us, he studied our form. "Sit your ass deeper in the saddle so you move with the horse. Right, now bear down with your heels in the stirrups so you don't bounce your insides out. Heads up. Now straighten your backs, but not too straight." We complied and then looked at him for more instructions. "Right, that's right. Now loosen your grip on the reins, and whatever else you do, for God's sake, don't fall off."

"Right. Don't fall off," I muttered.

Definitely an order I wanted to follow.

Boris picked up the pace after our instructions, and I was beginning to feel less awkward in the saddle. In fact, I was feeling downright comfortable, like a real cowgirl.

"I think I'm gettin' the hang of this," I called out.

"Good. Good," Boris replied, absentmindedly.

Feeling adventurous, and a little rebellious 'cause *Dad* wasn't paying attention, I kicked Tiny Dancer so she'd trot a little faster, and caught up with Poppy. "Race you," I chuckled, not really meaning it.

Poppy, who was always one for an adventure, raised a brow at me and kicked her horse into a higher gear with the flick of her reins, shouting out, "First one to that pine tree."

I should have known better, but my competitive spirit kicked in like a sibling competing for their parents' attention, and I copied what Poppy had done. That was my first mistake. Tiny Dancer took off like a rocket, and it was then I realized I'd screwed up. Galloping was a whole other level of horsemanship. I made it twenty feet before I started sliding off her side. Rather than hanging on and being dragged to death, I let go. That was my second mistake. I landed hard in the middle of a wild raspberry bush. A raspberry bush with thorns.

"What did I say?" Boris shouted as he pulled up quickly next to me.

"Don't," I grumbled, pulling leaves and berries from my hair, "fall off."

"And did ya listen?"

I wiped blood off my arm and looked up at the man, smiling between clenched jaws. "No, *Dad,* I didn't."

Poppy rode back, clearly having mastered galloping, and looked down at me. "Nice fall. Very graceful."

"Bite me, snowflake."

"Girlie, you shouldn't have worn a white shirt. You've got smashed berries all over the front. You look like you've been shot," she chuckled.

I climbed out of the bush, snagging the front of my shirt on the way out, and looked down at my appearance.

Yep. I looked like I'd been in a shootout with a raspberry bush.

This was not my day, which pissed me off 'cause it had started out so promising.

Tiny Dancer came prancing up, and I swear she had a smirk on her face. "Yeah, I suck at riding. Go easy on me from now on," I grumbled as I pulled myself onto her back. I made it up but hadn't swung my leg over when my hand slipped and tugged the reins down. Tiny Dancer started turning in circles as I grabbed the horn and pulled myself up. She was moving too quickly for me to get my leg over and I ended up draped across her back like a sack of flour while she danced in circles. On the second turn, I caught Poppy with her phone out. "What are you doin'?" I asked while trying to pull my leg up.

"Filming your humiliation, of course."

That was the icing on my shitty week.

"I . . . Want . . . A Wallflower divorce," I cried out as I held on tight.

"Sorry, no can do," Poppy chuckled.

"Are you ladies done horsin' around?" Boris asked as he grabbed hold of Tiny Dancer, stopping my spiral of death.

I pulled myself up, threw my leg over, then pointed at Poppy and bit out, "It's all her fault."

Boris looked between the two of us and shook his head, grumbling, "Thank God I had a son."

Whatever!

After my little mishap, I kept Tiny Dancer on a tight rein. It took us a good hour to make it to the top at the slower pace, but the ride, my fall notwithstanding, was worth it. Looking out onto the valley below, I sighed with contentment. Tall pines rose straight and even, their old needles coloring the ground like a rust-colored carpet. The rolling hills were breathtaking. The different hues of green took on the appearance of a patchwork quilt that touched the clouds.

"Breathtaking," I whispered.

"You can almost see the ranch," Poppy said, pointing toward

a red-colored roof peeking out between the green.

Boris began circling the herd, so I took the opportunity to slide off Tiny Dancer and rest my legs. Poppy followed suit, and we laughed when we took our first steps.

"Now I know what they mean by cowboy legs."

"Yeah, it makes sense why women used to ride side saddle," Poppy added.

"Or rode sitting across a man's lap."

"True that. I'll definitely have a new appreciation for Jamie, Brenna, Judith, and Gillian when I re-read their books. They traveled for days on horseback at a breakneck pace."

I stretched my back and groaned. "I once wished I lived in their century. The way Julie Garwood wrote their stories made you want to step back in time. Then I remembered they didn't have epidurals for childbirth, and I changed my mind." I laughed.

"How many kids do you want?" Poppy asked.

I shrugged. Kids were the last thing on my mind. I'd just be happy to find a good man at this point.

"I'm not sure I want any. If their father left like mine did . . . You know what I mean." She sighed.

Poppy's daddy issues were deep-seated. It would take a patient man to break through the wall she'd put up, that much was clear.

"I get it," I jumped in. "But not all men are like your father,"—*or mine,* I thought—"so keep an open mind like Cali said."

Poppy nodded, then scanned the herd. "Maybe Boris has a brother?"

"He has a son," I reminded her. "But he's probably our parents' age."

The cry of a cow directed our attention up the ridge. We both watched as a heifer called out over the edge, dancing in place as if in distress.

“What’s she looking at?” I asked, then moved behind Tiny Dancer and looked over the edge. Below on a wide outcrop was a calf. “How did you get down there?” I shouted at the baby cow.

Two brown eyes looked up at me, fear radiating from its young face.

“We should get Boris,” Poppy stated, then turned to find him.

I scanned the ridge looking for a way down. There wasn’t one. It was a steep drop except for a few trees that had grown above the ridge line.

“If one of us climbs down there, maybe we could pull her up with a rope?” I mumbled to Tiny Dancer.

She snorted in reply.

“I climbed a tree once,” I argued. The speckled mare jerked her head up and down, and I took that as an agreement I should try.

Only one tree looked like it could hold my weight, so I pulled Tiny Dancer behind me and tied her off, then squatted to my haunches and looked over the edge. “You still with me?” I called out to the calf. She looked up at me with just enough attitude I knew she was thinking, “Where the hell else would I be?”

“Okay, take this one foot at a time,” I whispered.

There was a small ledge about ten feet down, so I sat my ass on the ground, scooted over the edge, and climbed my way to the ledge. Then I reached out until I had a good hold of a branch and said a silent prayer that I didn’t fall and break my neck.

“On three,” I told Tiny Dancer. “One. Two. Three!”

Pushing off with my legs, I was suspended in the air for half a second before my weight shifted. I grabbed hold of the branch with my other hand like an aerial artist, tensing my biceps so I wouldn’t fall. My hands slipped for a moment as gravity tried to pull me down, but I held firm.

Now what?

I looked below, but I was too far from a limb that would hold my weight. I needed to make my way to the trunk of the tree.

I was too afraid to move my hands, so I brought up one of my legs and hoisted it over the limb. Then I followed with the other. I looked back at Tiny Dancer and found her watching me. "Don't worry. I work for the circus on the weekends," I huffed out while trying to hang on.

"Sienna?" Poppy called out as I hooked an arm around the branch and pulled myself over until I could sit up.

"Here," I called out.

Poppy and Boris appeared at the edge of the ridge, their faces saying what neither had. 'What in tarnation is wrong with you?'

"I'll climb down. You guys throw me a rope, and we can pull her up."

They both stared dumbstruck at me for a moment, then Boris moved out of my line of sight.

"And you call me crazy?" Poppy shouted. "Boris has a radio. He's gonna call down and have some ranch hands come up."

Well, hell.

"I didn't know he had a radio," I called out. "I figured we were on our own, and considerin' Boris' size, I knew it would have to be one of us who went down."

Boris appeared at the edge with a radio at his mouth. "Copy that," he answered. "How long ago did he leave?"

Static crackled, then Natasha's voice rang out. "About fifteen minutes after you left. He should be there any minute the way he took off out of here on Goliath."

"Copy that. I'll let you know if I need more help gettin' the calf up and Sienna out of the damn tree."

"I'm not stuck," I argued, reaching up to the branch above me. "I just need to make my way—"

A loud snap echoed as I grabbed hold of the limb and felt the branch beneath me give slightly and then bend.

"Oh, fudge," I mumbled, reaching up with my other hand to take the weight of the branch. "Houston, we have a problem."

Boris dropped the radio, then got to his knees and reached out to me. "Grab my hand," he ordered.

I shook my head. "If I release my hold, I'll put more weight on the branch, and it will break off."

"Sienna, grab his hand," Poppy argued as she dropped to her knees and lay down next to Boris. "We won't let you fall."

I gauged the distance between us and decided it was too far to risk. "I can't reach you without lunging. You won't be able to catch me."

The branch beneath my feet gave again, so I repeated the move I'd made before and looped my legs on the branch above me. Tipping my head back, I looked at Boris and Poppy. "I'll make my way to the trunk now and climb down."

Even with my head upside down, I could see movement on the horizon. There was a man in the distance making his way toward us. He was riding Goliath, who was a huge beast of a horse, yet the rider wasn't dwarfed by his size.

"Your man is here," I told Boris, then began to work my way down the limb toward the trunk.

"He's not my man," Boris said, huffing with exertion as he got to his feet. "He's here for you."

I dropped my head back. "Me?"

"That's what Natasha said."

Peering between them as blood rushed to my head, I cocked it sideways so I could get a better look at the man.

"Is that—" Poppy gasped.

"What's Bo Strawn doin' here?" I cried out, then lost my hold on the branch.

Bo pushed the stallion harder as he flew across the meadow. He wouldn't relax until he saw for himself that Sienna was safe. That her free spirit hadn't landed her at the bottom of a gully. Scanning the herd, a group of three horses came into view, so Bo headed in their direction. Within fifty feet of their location, Bo's heart began to race. Poppy was lying on the ground next to a larger, older man, and both were looking over the edge. He scanned the area for Sienna but didn't see her, and knew instantly what they were looking at.

"Bo! Help!" Poppy shouted as he pulled the stallion to a stop.

Bo bailed off the horse, ran to the edge, looked over the side, afraid of what he'd see, then bit out, "Why am I not surprised?" Sienna was hanging upside down from a tree limb. "Move. Give me some room."

Poppy moved immediately, and Bo took her place.

"What are you doin' here?" Sienna snapped.

"Savin' your ass, it looks like."

"I don't need savin'. The calf does."

Sienna pointed toward the edge of the outcrop, indicating a young calf. Ignoring her, Bo scooted over the side and climbed down onto a narrow ledge. "Crawl toward me," he ordered.

Sienna dropped her head back and looked at him through narrowed eyes. "I'm goin' down, not back up. You can either help me or keep quiet."

"You'll break your fuckin' neck," Bo bit back, then he noticed her shirt was covered in blood. "Jesus, don't move, you're already bleedin'."

Sienna ignored him, which didn't surprise Bo, and started making her way slowly toward the trunk. "It's raspberry juice, not blood."

"Goddamnit, Sienna," Bo shouted, scanning the tree for a way to reach her before she fell. The limb closest to him was bent, and Sienna was on the one above. He could climb lower or jump for the trunk. When she lost her foothold, and struggled to wrap her leg around the limb, Bo took a deep breath and lunged for the trunk. He smashed into the pine and slid a short distance, stopping himself with his armpits on the lower limbs, then began making his way up toward her.

"Show-off," Sienna huffed as she finally found her footing.

Bo kept his mouth shut. If he said anything now, he was liable to shout her out of the tree. He'd tear into her once he got her on the ground.

He reached Sienna just as she made it to the trunk, hooking his arm around her waist as she lowered her legs. When she wrapped her arm around his neck and reached for the trunk, Bo growled, with as much control as he could muster, "Don't say another word until we're on the ground or so help me God . . ."

She opened her mouth to argue, then got a good look at his expression and shut it, rolling her lips between her teeth to keep from popping off.

"Smart move," he snapped. "Now follow me down and step exactly where I step. Understand?"

"You girls are gonna be the death of me," Boris grumbled. "I swear I can feel my blood pressure risin'. First, you fall off a perfectly good horse, and now you're tryin' to break your neck."

Bo had started down, but stopped when he heard Sienna had been unseated by her horse.

"Don't forget about her graceful dance laid out across the horse's back," Poppy laughed. "That was priceless."

Bo's head began to pound.

"Sienna?" Bo said, pinching the bridge of his nose. Visions of her being thrown from a horse and breaking her gorgeous neck battled with his need to roar at her.

Tipping her head over her arm, she looked down at him.

"What?"

"You better be worth the heartburn you're undoubtedly gonna cause me."

"What's that supposed to mean?"

"I'll tell ya when we reach the ground," he sighed.

He knew she would turn his world upside down; he just didn't know she would do it hanging from a tree.

With less than three feet to go, Bo jumped to the ground, then turned and lowered Sienna safely to her feet. He opened his mouth to lecture her about using her head, but stopped when her brown eyes hit him with a questioning look.

"Why are you here? Is Cali ok?"

Sweet almonds invaded his senses, waylaying his anger and replacing it with lust. He'd driven all night to get to Sienna, to apologize for being an ass, but the words wouldn't come.

"Bo? Why are you here?"

Rather than explain his reasons for coming, Bo grabbed her by the neck, jerked her to his body, and slammed his mouth over hers. There was a time to argue, and there was time to take matters into your own hands. Bo wasn't good with words, so he'd let his actions do the talking.

Heat sparked to life the moment their mouths met, and any lasting reservation he may have had about Sienna melted away. Wrapping his hand in Sienna's hair, Bo tilted her head to the side and deepened the kiss until she melted into him and wrapped her arms tightly around his neck. He ignored the shouts from above asking if they'd made it down safely. He didn't want to pause long enough to answer them. He wanted to savor the moment. Drink it into his soul to remember for the rest of his days. Because he knew from the sweet whimpering sound she made, to the way her body arched into his, this was the *last* first kiss either would have. Sienna belonged to him now. And God help any man who tried to take her from him.

Sienna broke from his embrace with a shove to his chest and stumbled back. Her eyes were heavy with lust, so Bo started to reach for her again. She narrowed her eyes at him, rather than respond, then drew back her arm and swung for his head. He dodged the punch with ease and smiled.

His woman was feisty.

"You can't kiss me like that after you were a jerk the day before," Sienna shouted, raising her fist again for a second try. Before she could attempt punch number two, Bo wrapped her up tightly and claimed her mouth again.

Lifting Sienna off her feet, Bo backed her into the tree, leaning his weight into her so she couldn't move. "You've had me in knots since the moment I laid eyes on you," Bo whispered against her mouth. "You got under my skin the minute you opened your mouth."

"That doesn't make any sense," she gasped. "You hated me yesterday."

"I never hated you," Bo returned. "I was just bein' an ass."

"Yes, you—"

He captured her lips a third time, hoping to delay her questions until they could be alone. Sienna melted into him again, so he deepened the kiss. He was determined to show her with his mouth she could trust what he said.

She responded with equal vigor, then seemed to remember herself and pushed him back yet again. "If you care so much, then why did you humiliate me the way you did with Chase?"

"You weren't supposed to see that," Bo sighed.

"If it wasn't to humiliate me, then why did you go after him?"

"Because I wanted to rip his fuckin' head off for kissin' your cheek," Bo growled.

Her eyes grew wider at his admission.

"Yeah, that's right," Bo said. "In my heart you were already mine, and I don't like when another man touches my woman. I don't share, and Chase crossed that line."

"If you felt that way, then why did you push me away?"

"I'd had little sleep after Calla's case, and I hadn't had time to work through my feelin's," he admitted because that much was true. Chase had escalated matters, then their brush with death had brought him full circle until he could see clearly.

"But you said a man would have to be nuts to get involved with a woman like me."

"He would," Bo agreed, then leaned in and brushed a kiss across her lips. "Good thing I'm nuts."

"Helloooo down there! Did you die or what?" Poppy shouted.

Bo looked up and gritted his teeth. He needed more time to make up for the hurt he'd caused her.

"Not yet. But the day isn't over," he shouted.

Sienna rolled her eyes. "I was never in danger."

Bo raised a brow.

"Okay, maybe a little, but you know you would have done the same thing. That calf needed my help."

Shaking his head, Bo pulled back and brought Sienna with him. "I'll deal with the calf. You're gonna stand right here where it's safe."

"Wait," Sienna said, throwing up her hands to stall him.

"What?"

"Did you really come all the way out here for me?"

"I'm here, aren't I?"

"Yes. But why?"

"Why?"

"Don't parrot me. Why are you here?"

"I thought I made that clear."

"You came all the way out here to kiss me and tell me you

don't hate me?" she asked suspiciously. "Why not wait until I got home?"

"Because you two together, unprotected, after the week we've lived through?" Bo shook his head. "Nothin' but double trouble. You'll end up ridin' off a cliff or *climbin'* down a fuckin' tree and break your gorgeous neck."

Her eyes softened. "You think I have a gorgeous neck?"

Pulling her closer, Bo leaned in slowly like he had that day on the beach. At the last moment, before he could brush his lips across hers, he detoured to her ear and whispered, "Every part of you is gorgeous. Your *eyes*, your *hair*, your *great* fuckin' rack, but most especially, *your heart*."

She shivered from his warm breath against her ear. "I'll let the 'great rack' comment go," she whispered, "since you brought up my heart."

"Good. Now let's get the calf and get the hell out of here."

"One more thing," she said, clutching his arms to keep him from moving back.

"Now what?"

"I still don't understand why you were confused. If you say you wanted me from the moment you laid eyes on me, then what held you back?"

"You guys ready? Boris fashioned a harness out of a rope," Poppy shouted.

"I'll tell you, but not now," Bo promised, then pushed away from the tree.

"Toss it down," he instructed, then waited with his back to Sienna to try to discourage more questions.

"Bo?"

"Yeah?"

"Whatever it is, I can handle it."

He closed his eyes. The urge to lie so she wouldn't take

offense was strong, but Bo believed in being truthful, and starting a relationship on a lie would only mean disaster.

"Please tell me," she asked softly.

He dropped his head in defeat. One sweetly spoken plea, and he was ready to tell her anything she wanted. His future didn't bode well if she used that tone on him whenever she wanted something.

"Can you handle the fact you reminded me of my mother?"

"Yes."

Bo took a deep breath and let it out slowly. "She was beautiful," he began, to soften the sting. "Had the voice of an angel, and hair the same color as yours. But she was headstrong, never listened to reason. She always did what she wanted no matter what my dad said . . . just like you."

"Being an independent woman who knows what she wants and how to achieve it is not a negative in my book," she bit out, incensed.

Bo closed his eyes and waited a beat before he answered. He'd spent the whole drive up trying to figure out the best way to explain his mother to her. In the end, it had to be the truth.

"It is when you put your *own* wants and needs over those of a ten-year-old boy and then leave him behind."

"Are you sayin' your mother left you behind?" she whispered.

"I am."

"So, what you're sayin' is, you think I'm the kind of woman who would neglect a ten-year-old boy?" He could hear the hurt in her words and turned back to look at her. Her face had paled, and the pain reflected in her expression almost brought him to his knees. Shaking his head, Bo responded with conviction. "I wouldn't be standin' here right now if I thought you would."

"But you said—"

"I said you reminded me of her. Not that you were like her.

Your loyalty to your friends, the way you rush in without any fear to help those you love? That's not like my mother. Devin was right when he said Calla was fearless. It's a trait all three of you Wallflowers share."

Her bottom lip began to tremble, and it cut like a hot knife through his gut. He started to take a step toward her, but she lowered her head and asked, "Do you have a relationship with your mother now?"

The knot that always seemed to constrict his throat at the mention of his mother threatened to choke him. Swallowing hard to clear his voice, he started to answer her, but Poppy shouted, "Incoming," a few feet further up the ridge. She'd found a spot where she could easily toss the harness while avoiding the trees.

He stared at the harness, then turned back and looked at Sienna. He'd come this far, and he needed to finish it no matter the outcome. Whatever her reaction to the truth was, he wouldn't sleep until he'd made up for the damage he'd caused.

"My mother is dead," he finally said, then prayed to God he'd made the right decision. "She left me behind because her need for drugs was greater than her love for me. She overdosed."

Sienna's eyes grew wider, then brightened with moisture. When a single tear fell, he hissed, "Fuck," and turned to pick up the harness to avoid seeing the pain he'd brought about.

He needed to get the calf up to its mother so he could concentrate on repairing the damage, but before he could turn back to Sienna and attempt an apology, there was a shriek from above. Bo turned toward the ridge line and looked up just as Poppy emerged and screamed, "Bo! Please, help me. Boris collapsed, and he isn't breathing."

Four

MAN OF ACTION

I CLOSED MY EYES AND said a prayer for Boris and Natasha, asking God to save his life and to give Bo the strength he needed to help the man as they sped away in a Bullwinkle Jeep.

Everything happened so fast, my head was still spinning. When Poppy had cried out, Bo had ordered her to tie a rope to the horn of a saddle and pull him up. She'd done as he said, and I watched with trepidation as Bo was lifted into the air, then up the ridge at a rapid pace. What seemed like hours passed before Poppy shouted that a Jeep was on its way to help. When they arrived, I was pulled out of the ravine just like Bo had been, and when I reached the top, I found Bo performing CPR on Boris with a portable defibrillator. I jerked when Boris contracted with the shock and held my breath as the machine's electronic voice advised, "Hands off. Analyzing rhythm." I held on to Poppy as this was repeated twice more until Boris' color turned from a cold gray to a soft pink. When Boris' leg moved, Poppy and I finally took a breath.

It was a surreal scene, set in the high country surrounded by cattle and a stunning vista, but the impact of how close we came to losing Boris was never clearer than when Natasha grabbed his hand, and cried out, “You will not die, you old coot. I forbid it.”

Bo checked his pulse as his chest began to rise and fall on its own. When Boris moaned, Bo nodded to the ranch hands, and they began preparing to load him onto a stretcher made from heavy canvas and wooden supports. I wanted to help, but it was clear that Bo had everything under control. His ability in any given situation was another reason I was attracted to him. He oozed authority and confidence. He was an alpha male with piercing eyes that said he’d lead in any situation, *and* he expected to be followed. In short, he made me feel safe in an otherwise dangerous world.

He was a man of action rather than inaction, and that side of him was hard to resist. So hard to resist that when Bo turned and marched over to me, hauling me up against his body, I said nothing. Instead, I let him cover my mouth with his own and kiss me speechless, leaving my knees weak and my mind muddled.

“I’ll be back after I see Boris to the hospital. We’ll talk then, and I swear to Christ I’ll make this right between us,” he vowed. My heart started to soften toward him at the anguish in his tone, until he started barking out orders. “‘Til then, I don’t want you on anything with four legs. And, for God’s sake, don’t climb any more trees. Head to the ranch house and stay there so you don’t get into trouble.”

If I’d been clear-headed enough, I would have told him what I thought about him bossing me around. Instead, I’d bit my lip and watched silently as he’d walked away, talked to a ranch hand, and then jumped into the Jeep and started barking out more orders as they’d pulled away and disappeared over the hill.

“He’ll be okay,” Poppy whispered beside me.

I nodded in agreement. “Natasha won’t let him die.”

"I take it from that kiss Bo just planted on you that you've worked out your differences?" Poppy said as a slight smile pulled across her mouth.

"I wouldn't say that," I mumbled. "There are obstacles that concern me."

"Sienna, he came all the way out here for you. What's there to think about? He's your Wyatt slash Iain, just like I said."

My heart began to beat wildly at the reminder of what Bo had done. She was right, the sight of him riding Goliath at full speed to find me was like something out of a romance novel. But the fact he came all the way out here to apologize for being a jerk didn't overshadow the reason he pushed me away in the first place. I hadn't had time to process all he said or come to any conclusions about how I felt. There'd been no time—nor had it been the right time—for me to tell Bo that his reasons for keeping me at arm's length concerned me.

Being friends with Poppy, as well as my own turbulent adolescence, had taught me that neglect or abuse caused during childhood were some of the hardest disappointments to overcome. The idea that I would be a constant reminder of his mother if we started seeing each other was a concern. My own mother couldn't look at me without a constant reminder of what she'd done, so I was scared to risk my heart. What if he got up one day, just like my father had, and said the similarities were too much to overcome?

A soft cry from below pulled me from my troubled thoughts. "Poppy! The poor calf," I cried out, rushing to the edge of the ridge.

Two of the ranch hands had stayed behind to tend to the horses, so I turned to them. "Can you get her out?"

Both men looked over the edge, nodded, then got to work rescuing the poor thing.

"I still can't believe she fell all that way and doesn't have a scratch," I said to Poppy.

"She probably fell farther up where the drop is only ten feet," Poppy informed me.

I turned and looked at her, incredulous. "Are you telling me if I'd walked farther up, I could have climbed down on my own?"

Poppy beamed. "Yep."

"Do me a favor," I sighed. "Don't mention that little fact to Bo."

Snorting, Poppy twisted her thumb and forefinger in a 'my lips are sealed' motion.

We watched as they pulled the doe-eyed baby from the ravine, further up where it was less steep, I might add, and we smiled like loons when it raced to its mother and began to drink from one of her tits as if nothing had happened.

"Thank you," I shouted to one of the men. "I'm Sienna, and this is Poppy."

I put out my hand as I walked to the one Bo had spoken with, and he took it, mumbling, "Ma'am. This here is Brantley, and I'm Troy."

Both men looked to be under thirty. They had kind eyes, broad backs, and they were covered in dirt from a hard day's work.

"Are they sending a Jeep back for one of you?"

"No, ma'am. We were instructed to bring you back with the horses."

Poppy turned to me with a grin. "Didn't Bo say you weren't allowed on anything with four legs?"

I rolled my eyes. "He can think what he wants. A kiss or two and an apology doesn't give him the right to demand anything of me."

I started to move toward Tiny Dancer, but Troy stayed me with his hand. "Sorry, ma'am. Detective Strawn threatened me with arrest if we let you back on a horse by yourself. You're supposed to ride back with me."

"What? You must be jokin'!"

Poppy barked out a laugh, and I swung around on her. "This isn't funny."

"Uh, yeah, it is."

"You're supposed to be on my side. Remember the Wallflower creed?"

"What creed?"

"Hoes before arrogant assholes," I bit out, then moved toward Tiny Dancer. "Troy, I won't tell Bo you let me ride alone."

"Ma'am, I'm not about to lose this job because you're stubborn."

I rounded on him and put my hands on my hips. "I'm not stubborn."

"That's not what Detective Strawn said. He also said you'd disobey me unless I hog-tied you. I don't want to hog-tie you, ma'am."

"You wouldn't!" I gasped.

Troy grinned. "There's one way to find out."

I looked at Poppy for backup. She'd ducked her head and was laughing. I was *so* getting a Wallflower divorce when we got back.

"This is ridiculous," I bit out. "Why is he doin' this?"

"He's your man," was Troy's only response.

I narrowed my eyes. "You're all a bunch of Neanderthals. This *is* the twenty-first century if you hadn't noticed. I don't *want* or *need* a man to tell me what to do." Troy smiled like he thought what I was saying was cute, and I wanted to wipe the grin off his face. "What about Poppy? Does she get to ride on her own?"

Poppy sobered then and rolled her eyes, moving toward

Harriet. "Of course, I do. He's your Neanderthal, not mine."

Brantley stepped in front of her and slowly shook his head.

Poppy tried to sidestep him, but Brantley moved with her, so she spun around and scowled at Troy. "What did he say about me?"

"He said neither of you women had the sense God gave you, that you'd find a way to ride off a cliff."

Her eyes shot to mine, and I smiled sweetly. The shoe was on the other foot now.

"I say we stay single, Sienna. No man is worth this. We can be like Eunice and Bernice. We'll just have a bunch of lovers and play aunties to Cali and Devin's kids."

Troy and Brantley shook their heads as they climbed on top of the horses. Troy had strung a rope to Boris' horse and tied it off on Tiny Dancer's saddle, reminding me why we were in this position in the first place.

"Let's get back and see if we can help," I said. "We can decide later how to bury Bo's body so we don't get caught."

The return trip was slow and hot. By the time we reached the corral, my shirt was plastered to my back with sweat and I was in desperate need of water and shade. The ranch seemed quiet, eerily quiet. There were no hands baling hay. No cowboys working horses. Just the swirling sound of the windmills as they danced in the breeze; a reminder that life goes on even in the absence of man.

"Where is everyone?" I asked as Troy handed me down to the ground.

"Probably followed Boris to the hospital," he answered, then kicked Tiny Dancer and rode her into the stable.

"We should try to help in some way. Maybe we should check to see if the cows need milkin' again?"

I wasn't sure how often cows were milked, but I assumed if

they produced milk like women did, they'd need to be emptied several times a day.

"Cows have been milked," Brantley murmured as he kicked Harriet and followed Troy into the stable.

I scanned the yard, looking for a way to help, and noticed a five-gallon bucket sitting in front of an outbuilding that housed livestock. It looked to be full of food.

"Look," I said, pointing to the bucket. "I bet someone was in the middle of feedin' animals and never finished."

As we approached, I heard the distinct sound of pigs.

Poppy turned toward the pen and scrunched her nose. "Should we feed them?"

I scanned the pen. The trough was situated in the middle, which meant I'd have to enter it. Thankfully, the pigs were sunning themselves, oblivious to the world as they cooked their skin, so I figured it would be easy to get in and out.

"Yeah. Get the gate, and I'll pour this in the trough."

Poppy unlatched the wooden gate and opened it wide for me to enter. The bucket was heavier than it looked. I struggled with it, dragging it between my legs. Halfway to the trough, the bucket caught on something, causing my feet to slip out from underneath me. With an, "Oh, fudge," I fell to my knees, sinking into the muck and mud. Unfortunately, the racket I made when I fell caused the pigs to jump up, and they began heading for me, snorting and squealing as they came. That's when the melee began. One minute I was on the ground, trying to stand as the wet muck squished between my fingers, and the next I was knocked to the ground as the pigs raced for the open gate.

"Close the gate," I cried out.

Poppy managed to slam it closed before any escaped, trapping both of us inside the pen. I tried to stand to avoid the feeding frenzy, but each attempt found me on my knees again as one of the pink behemoths knocked me down like a prize fighter. Poppy joined in the fray then, tugging on my arm to help me to my feet, but she got sandwiched between two pigs and lost her own footing, face planting in the wet, muddy earth.

I scrambled to her on all fours before she was crushed, then we used the other for balance and stood, moving quickly out of the pigs' way.

"Water," I cried out when I got a good look at Poppy. "We need lots and lots of water."

We were a disgusting mess. Mud was in our hair, pig droppings were squished into our shirts like fecal art, and the smell was beyond horrendous.

Poppy turned her head and looked at the small lake bordering the property. "Follow me," she bit out.

We climbed over the gate, rather than risk the pigs escaping, and made our way toward the lake. Troy and Brantley walked out of the stables as we passed by, and stopped dead in their tracks. They scanned us from head to toe, both wearing incredulous looks.

"We only left you alone for five minutes," Troy said, shocked.

"You mean Bo didn't tell you I'm capable of causin' a world war in less than a minute?" I snapped, flinging mud from my hands at the two men. "We're headed to the lake to delouse, unless that's also against Bo's rules?"

Both men were smart enough to keep their mouths shut.

When we reached the small lake, I kicked off my boots and dove in. My shirt was already ruined from the raspberry bush, but my jeans might be salvaged if I washed them a hundred times.

"I'm pretty sure I got some in my mouth," Poppy whined. "If I die from pig poo poisonin', I'm gonna come back and haunt you."

Thankfully, the water was cool, which improved my mood by a half-degree, but I had no doubt a scalding shower was required to fully rid us both of the horrors we'd just endured.

"This is all Bo's fault," I groused. "I'm not sure how it is, but after a shower and a good slug of green magic fairy potion, I'll figure out how."

"Do we have any?" Poppy asked. "I'm open to forgettin' the last twenty minutes."

"I picked some up on the way home from Cali's," I grinned. "I was in need of forgettin' a certain gray-eyed cop."

"Speakin' of Bo . . ." Poppy said, as she tried to scrub her face clean. "Explain to me why you have reservations? Because yesterday, he made your heart race, your legs weak, and your breath leave your lungs."

I leaned back into the water and began to float, moving my arms and legs slowly to keep from sinking, and then asked Poppy a question rather than answering hers.

"If you met a man who reminded you of your father, would that keep you from datin' him?"

Poppy submerged for a moment, then broke the surface sputtering. "My father abandoned me when I was a baby," she answered, wiping water from her eyes. "If I met a man who would walk out on his kid, I'd run as fast as I could in the opposite direction."

"So you're sayin' if a man reminded you of your father, he would never make the cut?"

"I just said that," she mumbled before dunking her head and shaking her hair from side to side to rid it of mud.

I stopped treading water and let my body sink to the bottom like a rock, symbolic of my dashed dreams that I could have something special with Bo. I couldn't risk my heart. I was certain he would eventually get tired of the comparison and move on, just like my father had.

I could hold my breath for well over a minute without needing air, but I must have stayed under the water longer than Poppy was comfortable with, because she grabbed my arms and pulled me to the surface.

"Are you Aquawoman or somethin'?" Poppy chuckled.

"Somethin' like that," I gasped, filling my lungs with air.

"You're also the Queen of Avoidance," she stated pointedly. "Don't think I didn't notice you avoided answerin' my question about Bo."

I groaned and started swimming toward the bank.

"Jeez, Sienna. How bad could it be?" Poppy called out as I crawled up the rocky bank. My jeans were waterlogged, making it hard to walk, so I peeled them off and began to wring them out.

"You've got an audience," Poppy called out, pointing over my shoulder.

I turned and found Troy and Brantley standing at the edge of the meadow leading to the lake. They were watching us like the secret service stood guard over the president.

Guess they took Bo's threat seriously.

"They're far enough away, and my shirt hangs over my panties. I'll put my jeans back on after I wring the water out."

Poppy pulled herself out of the water, dropped to her back, raising her hand to block the sun from her eyes before pressing me for more information.

"Spill," she said. "What's the problem with Bo?"

The problem with Bo? *He's everything I want in a man, and I'm afraid I can't have him.*

"I remind him of his mother."

Poppy turned on her side and rested her head in her hand. "I'm sensing this is a bad thing?"

"It isn't unless you throw in the fact that she walked out on him when he was ten because she was addicted to drugs and then overdosed and died."

Poppy blinked.

"Oh, my God. His mother died from a drug overdose?"

"Yeah. Can you fathom losin' your mother so young?" I said, imagining a little Bo crying for his mother. I felt my bottom lip begin to tremble, so I turned hoping Poppy wouldn't notice. "And to lose her to a drug addiction makes it even worse."

Poppy didn't answer, so I took a deep breath to calm my emotions and turned back to her. She was staring at the ground, her forehead drawn in a taut line.

"What's wrong?"

"You said Bo was a jerk because you reminded him of his mother," she snapped. "How could he think you would ever leave your son?" she cried out, incensed on my behalf.

I sighed, then dropped to my knees and sat down next to her. "He didn't mean that. He said somethin' about her being headstrong like I am. I got the impression I reminded him of her in spirit, but that was all."

She nodded. "So I take it the obstacle you're concerned about is the comparison?"

I slowly nodded, then reached out and grabbed a wildflower that was growing near the shore, mumbling, "That . . . and somethin' else."

"What?"

I turned and looked at Poppy, but said nothing at first. I'd been lying to her for the past two years. Lying about my experience with men. I was still a virgin, and she didn't know. I don't know why I was embarrassed to admit I'd saved myself for Chase, other than the obvious—I'd been stupid. Stupid to put all my hopes and dreams in the hands of that douche canoe. But now I was faced with a decision. I had to tell her the truth, so she could help me decide.

Stalling for time, I began pulling the petals off a daisy-shaped flower, silently chanting; *he loves me, he loves me not.*

I ran out of petals on he loves me not.

"Sienna?"

I rolled my head, trying to find the courage to admit how big a fool I'd been.

"I was a virgin when I went off to college," I began. Confusion clouded her eyes, so I rushed through my explanation. "I had a romantic dream about saving myself for my husband, and then I met Chase. So . . ."

If it was possible, I swear her expression became more confused.

"Poppy, I've spent the last five years either obsessed with him or ruing the day I met him. Don't you get it? I'm still a virgin."

Her eyes grew wider, and she stared back at me for a moment before her face softened.

"I'm not afraid of having sex. Believe me; sometimes it's all I think about."

"Then what's the problem?"

Lord, she's gonna think I'm stupid.

"You promise not to laugh?"

Poppy sat up and crossed her heart. "Tell me."

"When I started reading historical romance in high school, one of the things I loved about them was how a woman's virginity was a gift to her husband. It meant that she belonged to him, and no one else. When Chase got engaged, I told myself to just sleep with a random guy and get it over with, but the one time I tried, I couldn't do it. I realized I still wanted to wait until I found the guy I would spend the rest of my life with, and that hasn't changed."

"And you're unsure about Bo, so you don't want to sleep with him?"

"How can I not be? You said yourself that you'd run in the opposite direction if you met a man who reminded you of your father. If I took a chance on him, and he changed his mind, I'd not only lose my heart, but a gift I can never get back."

Poppy stood up and started pacing in circles. "I need to think about this," she mumbled.

She worried at her lip as she concentrated on my situation. After a few minutes, I got dizzy watching her pace, so I stretched out on the soft grass and focused on the gossamer clouds moving slowly across the sky.

"What does your heart tell you about Bo?" Poppy asked, kicking my shoulder to gain my attention.

I squinted up at her. "My heart wants me to rip off his clothes and vow my undying love. It also says that if his mother wasn't an issue, I'd have to give up my Wallflower membership because I'd no longer need it. But how do I risk my heart when so much is on the line?"

She rolled her eyes. "Sienna, we've already been through this with Cali. *You* even pointed out to her that you can't hide from heartache. Guarding your heart is *not* an excuse not to explore things with Bo, and you know it."

Lord, I hate when my own words come back to bite me in the ass.

"However, losing your virginity to Bo is a big deal. You can't give it away unless he's the right man."

"So what do I do?"

"You don't have a choice. You have to tell Bo that you can't have sex with him until you're sure he won't turn tail and run."

"I'd rather join a nunnery."

"You already live in a self-imposed nunnery," she returned.

"And they'd throw you out when they saw your Helena Hunting collection."

"Her hockey players are hot," I defended. "Five minutes with Randy Balls and a vibrator keeps me warm at night."

"You're a sad little hymen lover," she sighed. "We need to determine if Bo is your Wyatt slash Iain."

"But how do I do that?"

"He needs to prove to you that you can trust him."

"Okay, but how do I do *that*?"

"By his actions, I suppose. He needs to prove to you that he will put you above all others. Even himself. Prove that he would, I don't know, jump in front of a bullet for you if need be."

A tingle ran up my spine. "Or jump from a ledge, risking bodily harm, to rescue me from a tree?"

A smile pulled across her mouth. "Or risk his job as a cop to threaten an asshole who was gonna get you drunk and have his way with you?"

I stood up, my heart pounding out a beat of hope. "He's already proven himself, hasn't he?"

The crunch of tires caught my attention, so I turned around. It was Bo. He'd returned in the Bullwinkle Jeep alone.

"He's back," I cried out. "What do I do?"

"What do you want to do?" Poppy asked.

"Rip off his clothes and vow my undying love," I answered and began walking toward the Jeep.

"Sienna?" Poppy called out.

I turned and looked at her.

"You're not wearin' any pants."

It had been two hours since Bo left Sienna. Two hours he figured she'd had to twist his admission about his mother into a reason to keep her distance. He would squash that idea the minute he saw her if she had. He wasn't letting her walk away from him. Not after he'd kissed her and the storm clouds shadowing his bleak life had lifted, shining a ray of light on his gray existence. She was his sun on a dark night, and she belonged to him now, whether she understood it or not.

Bo made the final turn into the ranch and came to a stop outside the main house. Troy and the other man he'd left in charge of returning the Wallflowers to the ranch were standing at the edge of the meadow watching something. Bo peeled out of the Jeep and started to head inside the house when he caught a glimpse of blond hair the color of spun gold, in the distance. He squinted his eyes against the sun until Sienna came into focus, and his lungs froze. She was bent at the waist trying to pull her jeans up, and the soft blue color of her panties glistened in the sun like a bull's eye for any man to see.

Bo's eyes shot to the ranch hands, and his legs began moving in their direction. When he was five feet away, he barked out in a low growl, "Eyes off her ass."

Both men went rigid in their boots, turned their backs on his woman, and walked away without a word. Bo tracked them with his eyes for a moment, then they shot back to Sienna who had managed to pull one leg up to her knee while she bounced around on one foot. He started moving again as a smile pulled across his mouth. She'd fallen in an attempt to right her clothes, landing in the water. She was now facing him with eyes the width of saucers because he'd pulled the T-shirt from his body as he walked toward her.

It was clear they'd been swimming in the lake, and right now the idea of cold water appealed to him. He would pull her in with him so she couldn't run, and get down to the matter at hand. She was his. He was hers. But more importantly, she needed to keep her fucking pants on unless she was alone with him.

He stopped a few feet short of Sienna and unbuckled his belt. She said nothing as she watched him slide the zipper down and then kick off his boots. Before pulling his jeans off, he turned to Poppy, who was standing still as a statue with her mouth hanging open, and said, "I go commando." Sienna gasped at his admission, and Poppy turned tail and headed for the house on quick feet.

Turning back to Sienna, he grinned. She'd thrown her hands over her eyes but was peeking out between two fingers.

"You're gonna skinny-dip in broad daylight," she squeaked out.

Bo dropped his jeans and stepped out of them, walked into the water, and picked her up, then kept walking until it was deep enough to submerge them both. As they broke the surface, he wrapped her legs around his waist, then covered her mouth with his. Despite the temperature of the water, he was instantly hard.

Her tongue danced with his, heating his blood as he ran his hands over her firm ass. Needing to feel her soft skin, he pushed one leg of her panties aside and kneaded the muscle as he deepened their kiss. Sienna responded to his touch instantly, melting into him further until no distance remained between them.

Ripping his mouth from hers, Bo buried his face in her neck and let her sun wrap around him like a warm blanket. "Never felt this before. Never felt this at peace," he mumbled, tracing the lobe of her ear with his tongue. "Swear to Christ, I won't fuck this up. You're nothin' like my mother, baby. Nothin'. You scared the shit out of me, is all, and I used the comparison as a poor excuse to keep my distance."

"I believe you," she whispered. "I've had time to think and

I realized you've already proven yourself to me. With Chase. Coming all the way out here to apologize. I don't know another man who would go through that much trouble if his heart wasn't pure."

"Jesus," Bo mumbled, tugging her hair back so he could see her face. Her eyes sparkled in the sun. *Her sun,* Bo thought. "Are you a dream?"

Her mouth pulled into a sexy grin. "Yes. I'm a figment of your imagination," she teased.

"Then I never want to wake up," Bo said low, pressing his forehead to hers.

"Tell me about your mother," Sienna asked, running a cool hand down the side of his face. "She must have had some good qualities to produce a man like you."

Bo squeezed his eyes shut. He never spoke about his mother. "I told you she had a voice like an angel," he answered. "I remember she would sing while she tucked me into bed."

"Do you remember the song?"

"'Your Song' by Elton John," he said, thinking back on how his mother would softly sing as she tucked the covers around his body to make sure he felt safe. "It's the only thing about her I can remember clearly. Her angelic voice."

Sienna's eyes softened, and her bottom lip began to tremble. He looked away to avoid seeing any pity she might feel, but he looked back when Sienna began to sing Elton John's ballad in a broken voice. He couldn't take the reminder of his past, so he crushed his mouth over hers, silencing the bittersweet memory.

Sienna's body began to tremble as he devoured her mouth, reminding him that the water was cold. "Let's get you into dry clothes," Bo muttered when she buried her face in his neck and held on tight.

"Tell me about Boris," Sienna asked as he began swimming

for the shore.

"He's in ICU. He needs a heart bypass."

She pulled her face out of his neck, turning worried eyes toward his. "Do you think he will live?"

"He's got as good a chance as anyone," Bo stated.

When he reached the bank, Sienna unwrapped her legs and slid down his body until she was standing in front of him. Her hands were braced on his chest, but her eyes were diverted over his shoulder. Bo grinned. His Wallflower was embarrassed to look at his naked body.

"Bo?" Sienna said, swallowing hard before continuing. "There's somethin' I need to tell you before we go any further."

He could see a pink blush spreading across her face, so he raised his hand and tipped her head back until he had her eyes. "You can tell me anything," he murmured, leaning down to brush a kiss across her mouth.

"I have towels!" Poppy shouted, interrupting them.

Bo looked over Sienna's shoulder to find her walking toward them. Sienna gasped and turned in his arms, throwing her arms out to shield him from her friend. Bo chuckled low in his throat at Sienna's reaction, which reminded him they needed to have a talk. Wrapping his arm around her shoulders, Bo pulled Sienna into his body and leaned down, whispering, "Love the color of your panties, baby, but so did the rest of the ranch. Keep your pants on unless you're alone with me from now on."

Sienna froze, then nodded. Poppy must have taken the action to mean come closer, because she kept moving toward them both.

"Stop!" Sienna shouted. "Drop them by his clothes and leave. He isn't decent."

Poppy threw her hands up and covered her eyes. "I thought he was jokin' about the commando thing."

"Well, he wasn't."

Poppy tossed a towel to Sienna and then turned her back. "Cover him. I want to know about Boris."

Sienna handed the towel over her shoulder, still avoiding his body, so Bo took it and wrapped it around his waist. "I'm decent now," he rumbled low. "Let's head to the house and take a shower, then we can talk about Boris."

"Is he alive?" Poppy asked.

"He is, but he needs surgery," he responded, grabbing the extra towel from Poppy and wrapping it around Sienna so she was covered from her chest to below the knee.

"How is Natasha holdin' up?" Sienna asked.

"She won't leave his side. I promised you ladies would bring her clothes to the hospital."

"What about the ranch? Can their son come here and run it for them while Boris is ill?"

Bo picked up their clothes and boots, then wrapped his arm around Sienna's shoulder and began heading toward the ranch house. "That's what we need to talk about. The son lives in China. He's an investment banker, not a rancher like his dad."

"So, he's not comin' to see his father?" Poppy asked.

Bo gritted his teeth and shook his head.

"Asshat," Sienna spit out.

"Boris' surgery is scheduled for tomorrow morning. Natasha won't leave until she knows he's gonna live, so she needs someone to oversee things for her while she's away."

"We could do it," Poppy jumped in. "We were plannin' on bein' here 'til Saturday anyway."

Bo nodded. "I told her you'd say that. If you ladies could handle the meals, I'll make sure the men get their work done."

"Did the other workers come back with you?" Sienna asked, looking around the yard as they walked up.

Bo's brow creased. "Come back with me? They were here when we left. There was an ambulance waitin' for us when we arrived back, and I drove Natasha to the hospital." Bo searched the compound until he saw Troy. He put his tongue to his teeth and whistled. Troy turned and started walking in their direction.

"Get inside, baby. Take a shower."

He expected Sienna to argue, but she shocked him and dashed up the steps with Poppy in her wake.

"About earlier," Troy said as he walked up.

Bo raised his hand and cut the man off. "Save it. Just keep your eyes off my woman, and we'll have no problems."

Troy jerked his head in agreement, and Bo let it go. He needed information, not a battle on his hands.

"How's Boris?"

"He's alive for now. He needs a bypass."

"He's a stubborn man. He'll live," Troy stated.

Bo nodded in agreement. "Where are the other workers?"

Troy looked confused, then scanned the yard. "I thought they followed you?"

"No one came with me but Natasha. Could they be out with the cattle?"

He shook his head. "Brantley and I handle the cattle with Boris. The other men are seasonal."

Bo rubbed his hands across his face as fatigue from the past week set in. "So they hightailed it out of here when they thought the old man was dead. Probably moved on to the next job. How many men do you normally hire on during the spring and summer?"

Troy thought for a moment. "Four, maybe five. If we had men with strong backs and good work ethic, we could get away with two, maybe three."

Bo dug his phone out of his jeans. "You've got me, and a man whose back is as broad as a barn and doesn't quit. Is that enough for a few days until Natasha can get Boris settled and hire some new men?"

"Can this man ride? We need to bring the cattle down tomorrow. There's a storm comin' in sooner than we expected, and we need them in the lower pasture where we can keep an eye on them."

"If he can't, I'll teach him," Bo stated, opening his phone and hitting 'Call Devin.'

"You ride like you grew up on a ranch," Troy said.

Bo put the phone to his ear and answered. "I did. My dad was a rancher."

"Is he still raising cattle?"

Bo shook his head. "Died when I was nineteen."

Devin's deep timbre cut across the line, pulling Bo from his thoughts about his father. The man never recovered from his mother's death and ended up drinking himself into a coma he never woke up from.

"You find her?"

"Yeah. Can you ride a horse?"

"I grew up in the country, what do you think?"

"I think you need to get your ass up here and help me bring in the herd, is what I think."

There was a pause, and then Devin began to chuckle. "They landed in a mess, didn't they?"

"Not of their own doin'. But yeah, I need your help."

"I'll be there in a few hours," was Devin's only response before the line went dead.

"He'll be here by tonight," Bo informed Troy.

"Appreciate the help," Troy mumbled, then turned to leave. He made it two steps before he turned back to Bo. "Just so you know, your woman . . . she's not stubborn, she's all bluster."

Bo raised a brow.

"She doesn't disobey like you think; she's like a dog that growls when you try to pet her, and continues to growl while she rolls on her back to submit. She doesn't want to appear weak. I got a friend who's the same way. Her parents praised her brother and showed her little attention. She came across as bull-headed, but the minute she met a man who respected her, she turned into a kitten."

"A kitten?" Bo asked in disbelief.

"More like a tigress, but the right man can tame the wildest of cats. Just ask Boris when he recovers," Troy chuckled, then jerked his head and left.

Bo smiled. He liked the idea of Sienna curled up in his lap like a kitten waiting to be petted.

Looking around the yard for a moment, Bo felt the familiar tug that comes with being in the country around livestock. Ranching was in his blood, but he'd turned his back on it in favor of law enforcement, just like his mother had turned her back on it. He figured he had a bit of his mother in him after all. She'd hated being isolated on the ranch and went out in search of excitement that didn't have to do with bulls and heifers. He had washed his hands of that life for two reasons: to gain the structure he needed after a childhood full of chaos, and to forget his past.

He knew you couldn't run from your past; it eventually caught up with you, and you had to face it head-on. Distancing himself had worked for a while, but falling for Sienna—a woman who looked like his mother—and now spending time on a ranch had brought him full circle. Facing them both was like playing chicken with a Mack truck . . . on a horse.

He looked up at the house and started climbing the steps. Knowing Sienna was inside quickened his steps and strengthened his resolve. He may be on a horse facing down a Mack truck, but he felt like he could leap any obstacle as long as Sienna's brand of sun kept shining down on him.

Five

ARE YOU REAL?

"DID YOU TELL HIM?" POPPY asked as we bounded up the stairs to our shared room. "Did you tell him you're still as pure as the driven snow?"

I spun around and shook my head. "No, not yet. And I'm not pure in thought, just untouched."

"How untouched?" Poppy returned with wide eyes.

"Bases wise," I said as I pushed through the door and began to unbutton my shirt. "One guy got his hand under my bra for about three seconds."

"Oh, my God. I don't even think that counts," she answered in awe. "You're like Snow White. I'm bettin' the seven dwarves saw more of her body than any man has seen of you."

I snorted, then grabbed a towel from the pile inside the armoire. Our bedroom was decorated with log pine everything. Pine bed, nightstands, and a pine rocking chair that sat next to a big bay window. "I'll have you know, that in my head, I could teach a porn star a few things."

Poppy crawled onto the bed and curled her arms around her

legs, smiling like a loon. "Wait until Cali hears how much of a Wallflower you really are. She'll have to give up her title as reignin' president."

"I think she lost that title when Devin took her on the dinin' room table, don't you?"

"You have a point," she laughed. "So, when are you gonna tell him?"

"As soon as we're alone again."

I looked out the window to see if Bo was still talking to Troy. I caught a glimpse of him as he turned and headed up the front steps.

"He's on his way up," I rushed out. "I need to take a shower and make sure the pig poo is gone."

Ripping open the bathroom door, I turned on the shower then stripped out of my bra and panties. When the water was warm enough, I stepped in and grabbed my shampoo. I'd just lathered my hair into a soapy ball, when I heard the bathroom door shut behind Poppy.

"What do you think Bo's reaction will be when he finds out I'm a virgin? I hope he doesn't keep his distance, thinkin' I'm not ready."

There was silence for a moment, then the shower door ripped open, and I gasped, turning around to ask Poppy what the heck she was doing. Instead of finding her peering in at me, I met gray eyes rimmed with long dark lashes, and I froze. I started to cover my breasts in embarrassment, but his eyes shot to mine, and I stopped. The look on his face was possessive, as if he owned every inch of my body, speaking without words not to cover what he deemed *his*. All the books I'd read, dreaming of the day a man would possess me physically, hadn't prepared me for the moment a man saw me fully naked. I was terrified he'd find me lacking.

I lowered my eyes and waited for him to say something. In my periphery, I saw the towel he'd been wearing drop to the floor, and then his bare feet stepped inside. The silence was killing me, so I began to raise my eyes. My attention stopped at the apex between his thighs, and I took a step back. I'd seen enough images on Google to know Bo was larger than most men. Suddenly, the thought of having something that large in an area so small scared the crap out of me.

Peeling my eyes off his cock, I took in the hard lines of his body for the first time, licking my lips as my mouth ran dry. He was beautiful. Far more beautiful than described in books. His skin was kissed by the sun, pulled taut over muscles that bulged naturally at rest. His legs were long and heavily muscled, his abs chiseled like a Roman statue, and his chest was so defined it could inspire flowery poetry of mythological gods.

He was simply magnificent. And I was scared to death.

"I'm a virgin," I whispered nervously, my voice shaking. "No man has ever touched me, so I don't know what I'm doin'."

When he didn't answer, I raised my eyes from his body and found his were closed, his nostrils flared as if he were fighting for control.

"You're angry with me?" I asked, puzzled.

Gray eyes popped open, and he moved instantly, pinning me against the wall. "Are you real?" he asked in a guttural tone.

"I . . . I don't understand?"

"I've spent most of my life wonderin' if I was cursed. Yet here you stand, a promise of somethin' beautiful that belongs *only* to me. Are. You. Real?"

In that instant of brutal honesty, I saw not only hope but also fear written across his face. The little boy who had lost so much needed reassurance that I wouldn't vanish like his mother did.

Raising my shaking hand, I ran the tip of my finger across his bottom lip. "I've spent my whole life dreamin' of a man who'd be worthy of my trust. A man I could give myself to without hesitation. Are *you* real?"

Bo covered my mouth with his own the moment the words were spoken, wrapping his strong arms around my back. I arched into him, eager to feel the scratch of his chest hair on my sensitive nipples. With a growl, he broke from my mouth, running his tongue down my neck, then further down my chest until he captured a pebbled nipple in his warm mouth, and began to drive me wild with a pulsing need. I'd never felt this white-hot sensation, and my legs buckled in response. I realized then, in that moment, that the dreams I had about being taken by Bo didn't do reality justice. Not in the slightest.

"You're so fuckin' soft," Bo growled against my skin. "I could bury myself inside you and never come up for air."

My clit began to throb, impatient for what I'd withheld from it the past twenty-five years. I instinctively rubbed my center on his leg as he continued his assault, moaning with a need I'd never experienced, didn't understand. Bo raised his head at the sound and pressed his forehead to mine. "I'm not takin' you the first time in a shower."

The pressure for release was so great that I whimpered at the thought of waiting another minute. "You can't leave me like this," I cried out.

His eyes grew stormy as I begged for release, and he dropped to his knees. "Spread your legs for me," he ordered. I complied without hesitation, anxious to feel his touch, and he covered my core with his mouth. My head hit the wall as lightning spiraled through my body. When he lifted my leg over his shoulder and continued his attack on my body, I grabbed his hair and held on.

Within moments, the lightning turned into a blazing-hot fire, followed by a burst of stars behind my eyes, and an orgasm rocked my body. My mouth opened, but no sound escaped, then a deep keening moan rose from my depths, and I fell off the precipice into mindless bliss.

Sienna slumped into Bo's arms as he stood, and he crushed her to his chest, the gift she'd saved for him still rioting in his mind. She was his reward for having survived the first twenty-eight years of his bitter existence, and he planned to savor each day of it for the gift that it was.

It hit him how close he'd come to walking away from her, and he began to shake with anger. "I could have lost you because I was stubborn," he hissed.

Sienna wrapped her arms around his waist and buried her head in his chest. He tightened his hold on her, then leaned down and kissed the silky skin on her neck.

He tasted soap mixed with her salty skin and moved her under the water, grabbing the body wash resting on the shelf.

"Let's get you clean," he murmured thickly, his own arousal affecting his voice.

He flipped the top off the soap, but Sienna snatched it from him before he could pour the liquid into his hand.

"Not yet," she whispered, then leaned in and kissed his chest. "I've dreamt about doin' this all week." Her warm hand wrapped around his cock, and he grit his teeth for control.

Her mouth began to blaze a trail down his stomach, nipping and kissing his abs experimentally, and his head fell back with a groan. When she kneeled and cupped his balls, and her tongue rimmed his sensitive head, he hissed and grabbed her hair for control.

"Open your mouth," he ordered between clenched teeth.

Her eyes flashed with excitement, then hooded as she opened her pink lips and took him inside her wet, warm mouth.

He sucked a breath deep into his lungs, tightening his muscles to keep from exploding down her throat when she took him all the way to the back of her throat on her first attempt. His shaft was too long for her to take all of him, so he grabbed her hand and wrapped it around the base, showing her what he needed. Her inexperience on how to please a man only made him harder.

She was a quick study—which had him fighting for control within seconds. She experimented with her technique as he surged his hips forward, moaning her own approval when he tugged roughly on her hair.

He refused to come in her mouth, so when he felt the burn deep within his balls, he pulled her off him then wrapped his hand around his cock. Sienna stayed on her knees as he ran his hand up and down his shaft, her breath coming hard as she watched him jack off.

"Touch yourself," he ordered. She didn't hesitate to reach down and sink her fingers into her slick heat.

When her head fell back and she moaned, Bo barked out a grunt as his seed pumped from his body onto her chest. He shuddered with his release, pumping his cock three more times until he was empty, then he reached down and pulled Sienna from the shower floor. Her eyes were glazed, her lips red from using them on his cock. She was sex personified. It was a sight he'd never forget as long as he lived.

"I gave you my cock since you seemed to need it, but I don't want you on your knees again. The next time you want me in your mouth, it's on a bed where I can taste your sweet pussy at the same time. Do you understand?"

She slumped into him and nodded. "You can wash me now."

Bo chuckled. She was back to bossy.

"If I can't kneel to take you, does that mean you can't either?"

"Nope. If I want to taste your heat, I'll do it kneeling in the kitchen if I have a mind to." She shuddered at his response, and he made a note to take her in his kitchen while she cooked for him as soon as he could.

After squirting a handful of soap into his hand, Bo turned her around so he could start with her back.

"Put your hands on the wall," Bo ordered. Sienna complied immediately. He rewarded her with a nip to her shoulder.

"I don't understand the difference. Why can't I, but you can?" she asked as he began to knead the muscles in her shoulders.

"Because your body was meant to be worshiped, not the other way around."

To explain his meaning, Bo ran his hand down her stomach, through the sexy thatch of curls covering her heat to her silken folds, then rolled her clit with his thumb until she arched her back into him. He surged his fingers deep inside her, grunting low at how tight she was, as his other hand wrapped around her breast.

"Do you get it yet?" he whispered. "Mine to touch. Mine to taste. Mine to fuck until you're breathless . . . Mine to worship."

She whimpered she understood, then her knees buckled as she reached for her climax, so he pinched her nipple hard until she exploded around his fingers.

Grabbing her hair, Bo pulled her head back and took her mouth as she rode out her climax. He moaned into her mouth as her taste overwhelmed his senses. She tasted like sex, like the most exquisite liquor money could buy. She also tasted like hope and forgiveness. But mostly, she tasted like home.

"I need to get back," Bo said hoarsely as she recovered. "All the men, except two, have taken off. Devin's headed this way to help until Natasha gets back."

Sienna turned in his arms and rested her forehead in his neck, still panting from her orgasm. "And I need to get a change of clothes to Natasha."

Bo cupped her ass and pulled her to him. He was hard again, aching to slip inside her heat. He knew until he did, she wouldn't truly belong to him.

"Tonight," he said—sucking in a breath when she rubbed against him—"you're mine."

Sienna tipped her head back and looked at him with hooded eyes. When she licked her mouth, he claimed her lips, pouring his need for her into the kiss, showing her without words how much he wanted her.

"Be good," he mumbled against her lips, then kissed the tip of her nose and left the shower, looking back once to wink at his Wallflower.

A knock on the bedroom door pulled my attention away from the window. Bo had left after our shower to help Troy and Brantley with the chores, and I was watching him work. I was still a riot of emotions as I stood there drinking in the sight of him. The strongest being hot and bothered. What had transpired in the shower left me wanting, for lack of a better word, greedy for more of what Bo could teach me.

Poppy opened the door before I could reach it and poked her head inside. "I figured the coast was clear since Bo was outside. So . . . how did it go?"

I rolled my eyes. "I'm still a virgin."

"Did you tell him?"

"In a roundabout way . . . I thought he was you when he came into the bathroom, and I asked him what he thought his reaction would be to my bein' a virgin."

Poppy's eyes grew wide, then she threw her head back and laughed. "What did he say?"

"Nothin'. He ripped the shower door open and then let it be known how much he liked the idea that I was unsoiled by another man. I guess bein' a virgin is a bonus for some men."

Poppy's eyes dulled suddenly, and her face fell, pulling into a mask of anger. "Men are such hypocrites," she spit out. "They screw anything with two legs, but they want to marry virgins. How are there supposed to be any left if they can't keep their *you know whats* in their pants?"

Her abrupt change in attitude caught me off guard. "You don't have to sleep with a man if you don't want to. It's just as much our responsibility to check our behavior as it is theirs."

"Even when they throw out pretty lines of love and happily ever after? Isn't that what's happenin' between you and Bo? You want him, so anything he says that sounds like a lifelong commitment has you ready to give up somethin' you've held sacred for twenty-five years."

I'd never seen Poppy like this. Her anger was palpable.

"Why are you so angry? Earlier you were all for me losin' my virginity," I questioned. "Wasn't it you who called me a 'sad little hymen lover'?"

Her eyes flared for a brief moment, then her bottom lip began to tremble. "I thought Blake was like Bo," she cried out. "I thought I'd found the man who'd be my happily ever after, but he lied. I'd saved myself like you have, and he took that from me on a bed of lies. While I was dreamin' of a white picket fence with two point five children, he was screwin' anything with two legs."

When she burst into tears, I followed suit. Her heartache filled the room as much as her anger. I wanted to find this Blake and cut off his third leg for using my friend that way. But she needed something to calm her down, not revenge on an appendage, so I ran to my bag and pulled out my bottle of green magic fairy potion and handed it to her. "Take a really good swig."

She took the bottle, then wiped the tears from her cheek with the back of her hand. "I hate cryin'," she said as she unscrewed the top. "And I swore I'd never cry over a man again."

"You'll feel better in a minute," I promised, pushing the bottle of Absinthe toward her mouth. "*Trust* me."

She looked skeptical but took a long pull on the bottle.

Then she choked on the green fire.

Then she went in for another swig.

"Good, right?"

Her eyes seemed to soften as the Absinthe worked its magic, and her mouth tugged into a grin. "Amazin'," she breathed out. "You're right. I feel like I could take on the world."

When she tried to take another sip, I pulled the bottle from her hand. "We have to head to the hospital *and* cook dinner," I explained as I screwed on the top and put the bottle back in my bag. "I can't have you loopy."

"I forgot about that. What should we cook?"

"We'll worry about that in a minute. I want to know why you never told me about Blake. I just thought he was a guy you dated for a short time."

"I don't know," she sighed, moving to sit on the bed. "I guess I didn't want to admit I'd been an idiot."

"So, he cheated on you?"

She looked down and began to play with a thread that had loosened itself from the quilt.

"Poppy?"

She sighed. "I caught him about a week after you and I met, with his ex-girlfriend. It was the typical trope; I stopped by his apartment and found him in bed with her."

"Why didn't you tell me, honey?" I asked softly.

She shrugged. I could feel the wall she'd built around her heart as if it were a tangible object.

"Jesus, you build walls just like Cali does," I pointed out.

Poppy nodded. "It's probably why I never told you."

I sat on the edge of the bed. "Well, it's not like I've been completely honest with you."

"That's true," she sighed. "I don't know why you didn't share your virgin status with us. It's not like we would have judged you."

I looked at my hands to avoid her prying eyes. "That's not the only thing I haven't told you."

"What else is there?" she asked softly.

Not once since I found out about my mother's affair had I told anyone the truth. I guess in a way I thought if I didn't speak the words, then the truth about my father was just a lie I could ignore.

"My mother had an affair twenty-six years ago. My father isn't Stephan Miller."

Poppy blinked. "Then who's your father?"

I shrugged. "My mother never told me. She said it was a guy who worked at her gym. That's all I know."

"Do you want to know?"

I nodded then shrugged again. "I was always the odd man out in my family. After my dad left, it got worse, so I let it go. It's not like I'm ten and need a father figure in my life."

Poppy nodded. She knew better than anyone what it was like to be fatherless. "We're two peas in a pod keeping stuff hidden. But I'm done bein' closed off, startin' today. You and Cali have taught me that there's strength in admittin' your shortcomin's."

"Wallflowers don't have shortcomin's," I snorted. "We just

see the world differently. And because of that, we need a certain type of man."

"You mean a blind man who's unable to see our faults?"

"Nope. We need heroes. Only the best type of men will do for Wallflowers like us."

"I need a hero, huh?"

A twinkle of humor had returned to her eyes.

"You're gonna start singing that damn song, aren't you?"

"Wouldn't dream of it," she deadpanned. "But now that you mention it . . ."

I slapped my hand over her mouth and dragged her off the bed. "Let's go see what Natasha has in the kitchen before you break the glass with your voice."

"I'm not that bad," she groused.

"You aren't that good, either," I laughed, dragging her toward the stairs.

The kitchen was located on the first floor just off the massive dining room. Like the rest of the ranch house, the downstairs was decorated with a western flare. Bronze sculptures of cowboys riding horses and bulls graced end tables and sofa tables around the great hall. The walls were covered in a log veneer, filled with family photos, giving the space warmth and a sense of home.

We headed to the back of the house where the kitchen was located and stopped dead in our tracks. Where the rest of the house was warm and inviting, the kitchen was stark and efficient. It was a chef's dream, filled with high-end stainless steel appliances, every innovative gadget a cook could dream of, with granite countertops in a warm taupe.

But no matter how efficient the kitchen seemed, it wouldn't help me. I sucked at cooking.

"Please, tell me you can cook?" I asked. "My culinary skills are limited to Lean Cuisine and microwave popcorn."

Poppy's head shook rapidly. "I can make sandwiches and soup like a pro, though."

I moved to the oversized, Sub-Zero refrigerator and opened the door. Inside was a huge plate of hamburger patties Natasha had already formed.

"Looks like hamburgers were on the menu tonight."

"Then we're set. Men deem grills as their territory, so all we have to do is handle the condiments."

I looked at the clock. "We have three hours before we have to light the grill, so let's grab some clothes and head to the hospital."

Ten minutes later, we were in Poppy's car heading toward town. We found the hospital and parked, then asked reception where ICU was. We found Natasha sitting on a couch, watching the afternoon news.

"How's Boris?" I asked, handing her the bag we'd packed.

"Orderin' the nurses around," she chuckled.

"He's that alert?" I asked, surprised.

She bobbled her head. "I should say, when he's coherent he's orderin' them around. But that's a good sign in my book. Means he has no intention of leavin' me."

The waiting room door opened on a whoosh of air and a man walked in, then stopped dead in his tracks. We looked up at him, and he stared back at the three of us, then said, "Need coffee," before heading to the kitchen area set up for visitors. He was medium height, decent looking, and had tattoos peeking out from under his shirt sleeve. I watched him walk into the kitchen, then turned my attention back to Natasha.

"When are they doin' the bypass?" Poppy asked.

"Not soon enough for me. I want him fixed now, but they're waitin' to see if he's stable through the night."

"Well, just know that Poppy, Bo, and I will make sure the ranch keeps goin' 'til you can get back. Our good friend is comin' up to help as well, so you're in good hands."

Natasha's brows pulled in confusion. "Why is your friend comin'?"

I looked at Poppy then back at Natasha. "Your seasonal workers took off, and they're short help."

Natasha closed her eyes, then cussed softly. "Of all the times for this to happen. We can't afford to lose a day of work," she bit out. "Is there no loyalty anymore? No sense of honor? In my day, we would have rallied around a family goin' through this. But not today."

I grabbed her hand. "Poppy and I were plannin' to stay the whole week, so you have us."

"You need muscle," she replied, standing up. "I need to run an ad in the paper."

"There's no rush. Bo and Troy have it covered for now," Poppy said.

"Excuse me," the man from the kitchen called out. "I didn't mean to overhear, but I'm lookin' for work."

Natasha turned and looked at him. "You from around here, Mr. . . .You seem familiar to me."

"Clint Black," he stated putting out his hand. "And no, ma'am. I'm passin' through on my way from Florida. I lost my job, so I'm headin' north hopin' to find somethin' permanent. Got an aunt the county over whose been hospitalized with a broken hip. I stopped in to see her."

"You don't say. How do you feel about shovelin' manure?"

He shrugged. "It's a dirty job, but somebody's got to do it."

Natasha snorted, and Clint looked at me and winked.

I blinked at his behavior.

"Can you follow the girls back now?"

"Yes, ma'am. I just finished visitin' with my aunt."

"Good. Payday is Friday. We take out taxes, so I'll need your social security number and a forwarding address for when you move on. We can settle all the paperwork when I get back."

"Appreciate it, ma'am. Workin' on your ranch is exactly where I need to be right now."

"You can call me Natasha. None of that ma'am stuff. You'll make me feel old."

Clint smiled, then turned to Poppy and me. "Are you ready to leave?"

"Um, sure. We're parked in the front. You can follow us down," I replied.

We hugged Natasha then left. Clint followed us to the parking lot, climbing into a truck, and then waited for us to lead him back to the ranch.

"Clint seemed nice," Poppy stated.

"He winked at me."

She snorted. "He'll stop flirtin' the minute Bo catches on."

"Am I supposed to tell Bo about that?"

"About the man winkin'?"

I chewed on my lip. "I'm not exactly sure how this works."

"How what works?"

"This whole relationship thing."

Poppy thought about it a minute. "My experience is limited, but what I know about Bo, I'd say no. If you tell him about every man who winks at you or stares at your boobs, he'll develop a permanent eye twitch."

She had a point.

"You're a wise grasshopper," I chuckled.

Poppy's phone began to ring, so I picked it up. "It's Cali." I swiped 'Answer' then put it on speaker. "Miss us already?"

"Bo Strawn drove all the way up to the ranch, and you didn't call me?"

Whoopsie. "We've been kinda busy."

"Wallflower code specifically states that if a man drives through the night to declare his feelin's, you must inform all party members."

"I'm thinkin' there's a codebook out there I don't know about," I mumbled under my breath.

"You can apologize when I get there," Cali announced.

"You're comin' with Devin?"

"He enticed me to come."

"The hell I did," Devin growled.

". . . He asked me to come."

"Jesus," Devin sighed.

". . . He ordered me to come. Said I'd end up dead without his supervision," she groused.

"That's not all I said."

"I can't repeat the rest," she whispered. "And they don't need to know about our sleepin' habits."

"Baby, there's no sleepin' involved in what I said."

Cali gasped.

Poppy and I snorted.

Devin chuckled low.

"Ignore Devil, I certainly do when he's not bein' a gentleman."

They were like an old married couple after less than a week.

"How soon 'til you arrive?" I asked.

"We'll be there in thirty. We just stopped to top off the tank," Devin replied.

"Got it," I returned. "We just pulled into the ranch. See you then."

Bo was in the corral with Troy and Brantley when we pulled up. He was manning some sort of an enclosure with a cow inside. When I climbed out of the car, he turned and smiled at me. The effect was heart-stopping.

"Pinch me," I mumbled.

"You're droolin'," Poppy chuckled.

"Give me a hundred years, and I'll stop."

"Lordy, you're gonna be worse than Cali."

I shrugged. If I ended up as happy as Cali, she could rib me as much as she wanted.

"Is that the boss man I need to talk to?" Clint asked from beside me, making me jump. I'd forgotten about him.

I turned and looked at him. He was staring down at me with a wolfish grin.

Hmm.

A piercing whistle broke through the air, and my eyes shot to Bo.

He crooked his finger at me.

Hmm again.

"I'll be right back," I said, heading for Bo. "I've been summoned."

I dodged cow patties as I made my way over to Bo. He kept his eyes trained on me as I approached, with his warrior's mask in place.

"You crooked—I mean called?" I snipped.

Bo raised an arrogant brow. "Climb up here," he ordered.

"Why?"

"Climb. Up. Here," he repeated low.

I wanted to say no because he had a funny look on his face, but dammitalltohell, I obeyed.

Once I reached the top, I started to snap at him for calling me over like a dog, but Bo snagged me around the neck and claimed my mouth roughly, cutting off my retort.

"Who's the guy?" he whispered against my lips.

Holy cow! Poppy was right. Bo clocked the guy's flirting from fifty paces.

"Natasha hired him when she found out all the men

disappeared."

"For what?"

"Natasha said somethin' about shovelin' manure."

Bo loosened his grip on my neck, then ran his hand down my back so he could pull me closer. "I can still taste you," he whispered low. "Best fuckin' taste in the world."

"Oh, my God," I whooshed out.

"Plan on tastin' even more tonight."

"You're tryin' to kill—"

"Then I'm gonna bury myself so deep—"

I slapped my hand over his mouth.

"I'm gonna go chop condiments now. I'll be in the house if you need me."

His eyes crinkled at the side, and he kissed my palm.

"You're a very bad man," I whispered, then tried to move out of his arms. He snatched me back and kissed me soundly again.

"Now you can leave."

"You're also a very bossy man."

He grinned.

"Bossy and naughty."

He grinned bigger, and my foot slipped from the effect.

"Turn that thing off," I huffed, then climbed down and headed back to Poppy and Clint.

"He wanted me to tell you to start in the barn," I lied.

Clint looked back at Bo, then down at me. "I take it that's your man."

"Yep."

"I'll get to work," he mumbled, then turned on his heel and left.

"Told ya Bo would handle it," Poppy chuckled.

I looked back at Bo, shielding my eyes from the sun. "He's a very naughty man. You wouldn't believe the things he said to me."

"Nope, no way. I don't want to hear it," she snapped, backing up. "Just keep all the good stuff to yourself. I can't look at Devin now, what with Cali and her 'no recovery time needed' comment. In fact, I'm writin' a new Wallflower code. A non-disclosure code. You break it, and it's an automatic divorce."

I bit my lip. I couldn't lie to save my life. I may not have slept with Bo yet, but his recovery time in the shower was remarkable, and I knew she'd read between the lines.

She narrowed her eyes. "Not him, too?"

My eyes widened. Apparently, I couldn't lie through facial expressions either.

"You both suck," she groused, then turned to leave. "First time out of the gate and *both* of you land Superman."

"Poppy, come back," I called out.

She flipped me off.

I sighed and went to follow her. Looked like it was time for more green magic fairy potion.

Six

THREE OF A KIND BEATS A PAIR

THE ROAR OF A HARLEY announced Devin and Cali's arrival. Poppy and I rushed outside, thankful for the break. I'd amassed two cuts while chopping lettuce for the salad, and the tomato up next seemed to be laughing at me. I'd be lucky to make it through the meal prep with my fingers still intact.

"Together at last," Poppy cried out as we ran to Cali's side.

Devin shook his head and rolled his eyes.

"What?" I asked.

"We came here to help, not burn the place down."

"What's that supposed to mean?" Cali snapped.

Devin snagged her around the shoulders and drew her close. "Exactly what I said. The three of you together are a lethal combination."

Cali snorted, then kissed him soundly on the mouth. "Go play cowboy while the girls and I handle the rest."

Grinning, Devin turned and headed toward the corral, where Bo and Troy were presently wrestling with a calf.

Cali sighed as he stalked across the yard, his masculine form graceful like a panther's. "I could watch that man walkin' away from me all day."

"Get a room," Poppy grumbled.

"Yes, yes, you have great taste in men, but can you cook is the better question?" I asked hopefully.

"Devin will say no. But I make mean eggs."

"Explain how we made it this far without culinary skills," I commented as we took the back steps to the kitchen.

The moment we crossed the threshold, Cali stopped dead in her tracks and took in the chaos. "It looks like a war zone."

"The lettuce is winnin'," I chuckled, picking up a knife. "It won't be satisfied until all ten of my fingers are wrapped in Band-Aids."

"Maybe between the three of us, we can avoid losin' a digit."

The kitchen door swung open behind us, and Clint stepped through. He scanned the three of us and smiled. "Fringe benefits," he muttered, heading for the fridge. "I haven't been around this much beauty in a while."

Then he winked at Poppy.

I looked at Cali, and she bugged out her eyes.

"Did you need somethin'?" Poppy snapped, stepping in front of the fridge.

Clint raised a brow. "I was hopin' for a bottle of water. The barn's hotter than Haiti."

Poppy opened the door and snagged a bottle, shoving it into his gut. "You've got it now, so back to work."

Clint didn't seem perturbed by her behavior in the least; instead of getting angry, his mouth pulled into a sly grin. "You've got a temper on you. I like it."

"And you've got a lot of nerve winkin' at any of us. And before you make the mistake of winkin' at Cali over there,"—Poppy jerked her head in our direction—"her man, a very big, badass man, will tie you in a knot if you so much as glance at her. So, take your roamin' eye and get back to the barn."

Clint continued to grin at Poppy then took a long pull from his bottle of water. His attention turned to Cali and me, dismissing Poppy. "Ladies," he said, inclining his head before heading for the door and leaving.

"Poppy needs to blow off some steam," Cali whispered.

"Poppy needs a man who isn't an asshole," I returned under my breath.

"Poppy can hear you," Poppy snipped.

"Do I need to break out the green magic before you go postal?"

Poppy grabbed a tomato and picked up a knife, then began mutilating the poor thing. "Winkin's the same as catcallin' in my book. He started with you, then moved to me when he saw you had a man. He's not choosy. He's just flirtin' with whomever he thinks he's got a chance with. Typical man!"

With each word she bit out, her knife made mincemeat out of the villainous tomato.

"Step away from the vegetable," Cali said cautiously like a negotiator talking down a potential jumper.

"Technically, a tomato is actually a fruit," I said.

"A fruit is sweet. Tomatoes are not sweet. I don't care what anyone says, it's a vegetable."

Poppy looked down at the mess she'd made and grimaced. "Perhaps I'm a little on edge."

"Devin's less on edge when he's lecturin' me about biker bars. What gives?"

I looked at Poppy and waited to see if she would confess to Cali about Blake.

Sighing, she grabbed another tomato and slowly began cutting it into chunks, then she recounted the entire tale from the beginning for Cali.

"I need a knife," Cali groused when she'd finished. I handed her one, and she grabbed a cucumber and began chopping away with vigor. "Anything else I missed?"

"Sienna's a virgin, and she doesn't know who her dad is," Poppy blurted out.

Cali's eyes shot to mine. "First Poppy and now you?" She shook her head. "And you all gave me heck for not lettin' you in."

I glared at Poppy. "You're like a little sister who tattles without givin' all the facts."

"What facts?" Cali asked.

"I didn't tell Poppy until today. I was keepin' it from both of you."

"But why did you keep it from us?"

I shrugged. "I suppose the same reason Poppy didn't tell us about Blake. I waited for the wrong man, and now I feel like an idiot."

"And your father? Why wouldn't you tell us about that?"

I pulled out a stool and sat down. "My whole life I was different from my family, the odd one in the bunch. Admitting to anyone that my mother had an affair, and that I was the product of that mistake, made me more so. My father barely speaks to me, and my brother and sister look at me like I'm a leper."

Cali laid down her knife and took my hand. "Different means special, not the other way around. If they can't see what a beautiful person you are, then they're the odd ones, not you."

I nodded. I knew she was right.

"And Bo?" she questioned. "Are you really ready to lose your virginity to him?"

I opened my mouth, then shut it, then opened it again. "I know I want him. That he's everything I've been lookin' for in a man."

"And if it doesn't work out between the two of you? Will you feel like Poppy? Will you feel like you've lost something precious you should have saved for another man?"

I started to say no, but I hesitated. "The only thing I know for sure is that when Bo touches me, I feel safe, wanted, worshipped. I ache deep within my bones for what you have with Devin; the intimacy that comes with being close to a man, closer than anyone else in your life. I also know that Bo is the kind of man I could, without reservation, fall deeply in love with. And that he would never intentionally hurt me. The rest I'll figure out when it happens."

Leaning against the wall, just outside the kitchen, Bo lowered his head. He'd seen Clint enter the back door while he was talking with Devin, and he'd gone on red alert. Something about the guy pushed all his buttons, so he'd jerked his head toward the house and Devin followed. They'd walked up just as Poppy gave Clint the lay of the land, confirming his suspicions, so they'd waited for Clint to exit. He made it two feet outside the door before Devin had him by the collar. "Eyes to yourself, or you'll deal with me."

Clint nodded, so Devin shoved him back, growling, "Back to work like the lady said."

Before he and Devin could check on the Wallflowers, the conversation inside had turned abruptly to matters of the heart. He'd paused, not wanting to interrupt, so he'd stepped back and waited for them to finish, unable to tear himself away from their conversation.

A myriad of emotions coursed through him as they talked about Poppy's history, Sienna's family, and her feelings toward him. He felt possessive when she said he made her feel safe, wanted, worshipped. And felt hope when she admitted she could fall deeply in love with him, solidifying his resolve to do whatever it took to make that happen. She trusted him not to hurt her, to do what was right for her, and he was determined to earn that trust. He wouldn't take her virginity until she was ready, until he'd earned the right to possess her fully. Until he'd proven to her that she'd trusted the right man with her innocence. And he'd do that by being patient, by giving her control when she'd lost so much of it in her lifetime, by simply waiting for her to come to him when she was ready.

Pushing off the wall, he looked at Devin then jerked his head toward the corral.

"Someone needs to find this Blake and teach him some manners," Devin bit out.

Bo nodded in agreement. Poppy deserved better than the cards she'd been dealt in life. "You got someone in mind?"

"I'm thinkin' the man who needs to hand him his ass is the man who takes on the woman," Devin stated.

Bo cocked his head. "She got someone on the hook?"

"Yeah. He just hasn't come to terms with it yet."

Bo started to ask who, but his phone vibrated in his pocket. He pulled it out and saw a text message from John William, the man in charge of his cases for the week.

Daniels was found in an abandoned warehouse. He'd been beaten within an inch of his life. He's in a coma.

Bo's blood ran cold. His case involving the Wallflowers turned from bad to deadly.

"Jesus."

At his tone, Devin turned, his eyes on full alert.

"Larry Dwayne Daniels, the Serpents' prospect who chased the Wallflowers, he's been beaten and is in a coma."

Devin's jaw ticked. "Tell me this is unrelated to the Wallflowers."

"No clue. But my gut says no."

Devin looked back at the house, and Bo's eyes followed. Laughter rang out from the open kitchen door. Three women who'd done nothing but stop for a drink were now caught up in some unknown danger, and Bo couldn't fix it as long as he was here.

"They're safe here. We'll figure this out when we get back. In the meantime, as a precaution, they aren't out of our sight unless another man we trust is here."

"Only one other man I trust besides you," Devin growled.

"He's not here," Bo pointed out.

"He will be," Devin stated, pulling out his phone. "He'll need time to cover the bar, so until he arrives, the herd stays up the ridge."

"Then we keep them with us at all times until he arrives."

Both men turned and headed for the house.

"You think we'll survive this?" Devin muttered.

"If we keep them away from horses, pigs, and small machinery, we might stand a chance."

Laughter broke the air again, and both men smiled. "We're fucked," Devin sighed.

"That we are," Bo agreed.

"How in the hell did we end up with unpredictable women?"

Bo didn't hesitate to answer. Once he'd stopped fighting his feelings for Sienna, the blinders came off. Their unpredictable personalities were what made them unique. And also, he suspected, what drew men like Devin and him to them.

"Their inner light drew us in. They're like a beacon shinin' the way in the darkest of nights. Once you've seen it, there's no fuckin' way to change course."

Devin stopped and looked at Bo. "Jesus. All that and looks to boot?"

Bo's lip twitched at his own words being thrown back at him. "Yeah. And then some."

"What about your other problem?" Devin asked. "You sure enough about the woman to go there before she's ready?"

"I'm sure enough. But I'm not goin' there until she is."

Devin nodded and began to walk again. "Should make stickin' to her like glue interestin'."

"I make it through this without killin' anyone, it'll be a fuckin' miracle."

Devin flashed Bo a smile. "You do, I'll nominate you for sainthood."

The object of his desire walked out the kitchen door and smiled at him. His own mouth pulled into a grin as he climbed the steps and stopped in front of her. He wanted to take her into his arms and kiss that smile right off her face until she was frantic with need for him. He started to reach for her, then remembered his promise to earn her trust, so he dropped his hand. "We need to talk."

"First, light the grill," Sienna announced, holding up a lighter. "Hamburgers are on the menu for dinner."

Devin snatched the lighter from her hand, mumbling, "Grillin's a man's domain."

Sienna's eyes lit up, and she rocked back on her feet, swinging her arms behind her back with a huge grin. Then she looked over her shoulder at the window and winked like a child with a secret.

She was so damn cute, so damn happy at that moment, Bo hated to ruin her mood, but he didn't have a choice. He needed to set things straight before it was time for bed.

"Walk with me," he muttered, grabbing hold of her hand. She peered up at him as they headed down the steps and around the house. Bo kept his face neutral as he led her back to the meadow near the lake. Once they were far enough away, he pulled her into his arms and rested his chin on her head. He didn't know how else to say what he had to say, so he didn't beat around the bush.

"I think we should slow down."

Sienna stilled in his arms, then started to pull away. "I knew the resemblance to your mother would be an issue," she whispered, stepping back. "It's fine. I get it. No harm, no foul," she choked out, then turned her back on him and let out a sob.

Bo reached out and turned her back to him, crushing her to his chest. "That's not what I meant," he whispered. "I don't want to rush you into sleepin' with me. I don't think you're ready, and when I take you for the first time, makin' you mine in every way possible, I don't want there to be any regrets."

Sienna buried her face in his chest but didn't reply, so Bo wrapped her tighter in his arms and leaned down until his mouth was next to her ear. "I take it my slowin' things down doesn't sit well with you?"

She shook her head, then shrugged.

"So you're okay with my decision?"

She nodded, then shook her head, then nodded again, confusing Bo.

"Which is it?"

She tilted her head back and cried out, "Both. I want to, but a part of me is still afraid you'll change your mind about us. But I'm also afraid you'll get bored with me."

Bo blinked.

"You think I'll get—"

He threw his head back and laughed.

"This isn't funny," Sienna snapped. "Men like you can have anyone you want, so why would you settle for a borin' virgin?"

Unable to contain his laughter, he buried his head in her neck and continued to laugh, tightening his hold on Sienna until she was breathless.

"Can't. Breathe," she gasped.

Bo loosened his hold and tipped his head up, choking on a chuckle. "Baby, you gotta know, you couldn't be borin' if you tried."

"I couldn't?"

"No," he answered, then leaned in and brushed a kiss across her lips. "You save your friends from killers, climb trees to save a calf, and take on a dangerous biker with a Yeti. A fuckin' Yeti, for Christ's sake. You're far from borin'. And the virgin part? Jesus. Just the thought another man hasn't touched you drives me to distraction. I'm fuckin' hard knowin' I'm the *only* man who'll ever hear you moan while I taste your sweet heat. Over the fuckin' moon I'm the *only* man who will use his hands, his mouth, his cock to make your body burn." Her eyelids grew heavy as he spoke, and she began to pant as he described what he planned to do to her. Then Bo made the mistake of looking at her lips. "And I'm fuckin' thrilled I'm the *only* man who'll ever watch you take his cock into your mouth. *You* are my desire," he rumbled low, wrapping his hand in her hair to pull her closer to his mouth. "My ideal. My fuckin' wet dream," he rasped out, claiming her mouth with a possessive need.

Heat spiked instantly between them. He chased her tongue, tangling it with his own until desire burned away into the purest hunger he'd felt in his life. When she began to lead the kiss, he pulled back, trying to ebb the flames sparking between them. But she wouldn't let him retreat. If they'd been alone in a room, he'd have been in trouble, but the sounds of the ranch around them kept him grounded in reality. With a groan, he ripped his mouth from hers and took a step back.

"Go," he bit out.

"Go?"

He closed his eyes and counted to ten, trying to rein in his need to claim her on the spot.

"Go before I drag you inside and break my promise to give you more time."

"You're serious?"

Bo's gray eyes shot to her face, and he narrowed them. "About this? Yes. I want you, but only when you're ready. You're not, so give me a minute to calm the fuck down."

She started to say something, but he shook his head. "Don't."

With one last look at him, Sienna turned and began heading to the house. Bo turned his back on her and stripped off his shirt, heading for the lake. He needed a cold shower, but he wasn't going anywhere near that house while she was in it. "Fuck sainthood. I've gone straight to hell."

"He wants to wait?" Poppy said incredulously.

I nodded and then scowled. I still didn't know what to make of Bo. I hadn't even known I was hesitant to take the next step until Cali asked, so how had he known?

"Do you think he's havin' second thoughts about us?" I asked the girls.

Both looked at the other and shrugged. "We're Wallflowers, what do we know about men and their thought processes," Poppy answered.

"What exactly did he say?" Cali asked.

I replayed the conversation over in my mind, then answered. "That he didn't want to rush me until I was ready. He said I was his desire, his"—I looked at them both and grinned—"his wet dream."

Poppy snorted. "He's not havin' doubts."

"No, he's not havin' doubts," Cali agreed.

"Then how did he know I had any at all? We, you know, fooled around in the shower, so he should have thought I was all systems go."

Cali cocked her head. "Are you all systems go?"

"I thought I was, but then I hesitated."

Poppy pushed the bottle of green magic across the table and smiled. "Go on," she said cheerfully.

I rolled my eyes. "I'm not upset."

At least I didn't think I was.

"Mmhmm," Cali hmm'd calmly, pushing the bottle even closer to my hand.

"I don't need it. I just need answers to my questions. Answers I'm not sure I have."

"About?" Cali asked.

"Why the sky is blue. Why the Kardashians are even relevant. Why Taylor Swift dumped Tom Hiddleston, because, hello, he's *lush*."

"My granddaddy would say you're avoidin' the question with drivel."

"How is dear old granddaddy, by the way?"

"Still an asshole, but he's stopped tellin' me Devin's not good enough, so answer my question. Why did you hesitate?"

I bit my lip.

"Sienna?" Poppy said with a long, slow drawl.

I huffed and hung my head. "What if I'm not good at sex? Bo's experienced, and if we don't mesh sexually, he'll know immediately."

A growled "Jesus," sounded from behind me, and I swung around. Devin was standing at the door with a lighter and charcoal in his hand.

"Tell me you didn't hear that," I gasped.

Devin's eyes shot to Cali then back to me.

"I heard it," he grumbled, walking further into the kitchen, "and it's bullshit. Bo's a man, not some idiot who doesn't know how to treat a woman. Trust me, if he cares about you, it won't matter to him."

I should have been mortified to have this conversation with Devin, but for some odd reason, I wasn't. Devin was family now, and family talks about anything, I was learning from watching Cali and her aunts.

"But how will I know what he likes or dislikes?"

Devin looked a wee bit horrified by my question. "You just will."

Oh, this was too good to pass up.

"He'll tell me, or will I know by the sounds he makes?" I asked innocently.

Devin's jaw grew tight, and then he turned on his heel and walked right back out of the kitchen, mumbling as he went, "I've landed in hell."

I turned back to Cali and grinned from ear to ear. "That'll teach him to knock before entering a room."

Poppy stood and looked out the window, then shut the back door. "He's gone," she chuckled. "I almost feel sorry for him."

"Devin's right, you know," Cali laughed. "If Bo cares about you, it won't matter what you know. He'll just teach you how to please him. Men like that don't pussyfoot around. He'll just drag you where he wants you then play your body like an instrument until he's memorized every curve."

The front door slammed shut, startling us. Moments later, Bo walked in with dripping wet hair. He scanned the kitchen, taking in our stunned expressions, and raised a brow. "Why do you three look like the cat that caught the canary?"

Poppy snickered, and he narrowed his eyes.

Cali jumped up and grabbed my hand, pulling me from my seat. "Nothin' untoward. We were just discussin' if it was time to milk the cows. Come on, ladies, let's go grab some tits and squeeze."

Bo froze solid at her comment, dropped his head back, mumbled something about sitting at the right hand of God, then he turned abruptly and left the kitchen the way he came.

We headed out the back door laughing, then burst out louder when Devin saw us and turned in the opposite direction. By the time we made it to the barn, I felt more relaxed than I had in months. I didn't feel pressured by Bo, and between Devin and Cali, I wasn't scared about the unknown. If Bo cared, he'd wait. And if he cared enough to wait, then he'd take the time to teach me.

As we entered the barn, Clint stepped out from a stall holding a pitch fork. We jumped in response, then skirted around him and kept going.

"Hey, look at that," Poppy said, pointing inside an open stall.

Inside were five four-wheelers of various sizes.

"That doesn't have four legs," I mumbled.

"And it's not a tree," Poppy smiled.

Cali looked between us. "Am I missin' somethin?"

"Bo ordered her to stay off anything with four legs, and to stop climbin' trees."

Cali blinked and scrunched nose. "I swear these men are autocrats. They need to get with the times."

"So?" Poppy asked, her eyes gleaming. "Do we buck the system and have some fun?"

"What about the cows?" Cali jumped in. "Shouldn't we milk them first?"

"I milked the cows already," Clint said from behind us. "If you ladies want help with the four-wheelers, I'm your man."

Poppy turned and glared at him. "Have you learned some manners? Or do I need to use that pitchfork on you?"

Clint smiled sheepishly. "Yes, ma'am. I apologize for my wicked behavior."

"All right, then pull out three of these beasts and check for fuel."

Clint actually bowed at Poppy, then he walked past her and began moving the four-wheelers out. He checked the gas, the tire pressure, then started each one for us.

"We should go out the back entrance so we avoid the men," Poppy shouted over the noise.

Cali and I agreed and jumped on, then one by one we made the wide turn and exited out the back, opening up the throttle as we cleared the gate Clint had opened for us and flew across the pasture kicking up dirt. Once we'd cleared the gate on the opposite side of the pasture and drove up the rise, we stopped and looked across the valley below, taking in the ranch.

I could see Troy and Brantley in the corral looking up at us, pointing. I scanned the courtyard and found Devin and Bo running toward the barn.

"We've been ratted out," I cried out.

"Do we wait for them?" Cali asked.

Poppy gunned her four-wheeler and took off.

I grinned at Cali and followed Poppy.

Seconds later, Cali flew past me laughing.

The game was afoot.

After realizing there was no escape from our predicament, Cali and I hid behind a mulberry bush watching breathlessly as Bo and Devin rode on horseback up to the rise. Poppy had sped off toward the lake as a diversion, stating her ass wouldn't be in trouble if she was caught. Our half-assed plan was simple on the surface: get Bo and Devin to chase after her while Cali and I snuck back to the ranch, avoiding an unwanted confrontation with the brooding men. But Bo and Devin didn't fall for it. They were currently scanning the hillside we were on. We were trapped like rabbits in a briar.

"Why are we hidin' exactly?" I asked Cali.

"We don't want a lecture about misbehavin'."

"Then why didn't we go back when we had the chance?"

She shrugged. "I was followin' you. You seemed to have a plan."

"I didn't have a plan. I was followin' Poppy."

"Followin' Poppy? Poppy doesn't have a man who'll give her crap about takin' chances with her safety."

"Then why didn't you stop me?"

She opened her mouth, then snapped it shut.

"Well?"

"I'm thinkin'."

I peered through the branches until I caught sight of Devin. His face was drawn taut, his eyes wild. He wasn't pissed; he was worried.

"Cali, Devin doesn't look pissed; he looks worried."

Cali pushed me aside and looked through the bush. She closed her eyes slowly, shaking her head, and then mumbled, "Stupid. I'm so stupid. I should have known better. I got kidnapped four days ago, and now Devin watches me sleep like he's afraid to take his eyes off me."

She stood immediately and started making her way through

the brush. I followed quickly on her tail, tripping over rocks as we slid down the hill. When we broke through the clearing, Devin shouted, "There," and kicked his horse, racing toward Cali. I moved out the way to give him room and then faced Bo. His reaction was a little different. He crooked his finger at me again.

"I'm thinkin' that's a bad idea," I whispered. "I'll just get the four-wheeler and meet you back at the ranch."

He was too far away to hear me, but the sinister grin that pulled across his mouth said he'd read my mind.

I picked up my pace.

He kicked his horse.

I started running.

Goliath snorted loudly at my puny attempt to outrun him.

I made it within five feet of the ATV when my feet left the ground on a shriek. One second I was running, and the next I was laid out across Bo's lap, facedown.

"Put me down," I cried out, struggling to raise my head.

He kept riding.

And riding.

All the way back down without saying a word.

Troy met us at the barn, sporting his own version of a scowl, so I ignored them both on principle.

I tried to slide off on my own when Bo stopped, still sporting the silent treatment, but Bo threw Troy the reins before I could. He pulled me up without a word and slid off Goliath, taking me with him as he went.

I was ready to do battle at being manhandled like a child, but my feet never hit the ground because he threw me over his shoulder and headed toward the house.

"I can walk," I bit out. "I can also ride an ATV without supervision. I'm not incompetent."

He continued to ignore me and kept walking until he'd entered the kitchen. Then he deposited me unceremoniously with a thud into a chair, caging me in with both arms until we were eye to eye.

I chanced a glance to gauge his anger and swallowed hard. His gray eyes were tweaked, his nostrils flared, and a tick had returned to his eye. A spark of fear shot through me, and I swallowed.

Danger, Will Robinson. Proceed with caution.

"I may not be fuckin' you yet, but that doesn't mean I don't have rights as your man. I *asked* you not to put yourself in danger again. What if you'd been hurt? Or worse?"

What anger I'd stored up over being manhandled like a child evaporated immediately. He'd been worried as well, but he showed it differently than Devin. My own family never showed that much concern for me, so I didn't recognize Bo's concerns for what they were.

Guilt flooded me like it had Cali, and I reached up and grabbed his face, pulling his mouth to mine. I whispered, "I'm sorry. It won't happen again," against his lips and watched his eyes turn from stormy gray to ink.

On a hiss, Bo pulled me from the chair and claimed my mouth, then he leaned over until he'd deposited me on the table, and I wrapped my legs around his waist. The kiss turned wild after that. Bo never broke from my mouth. We exchanged air as he ground his erection against the inseam of my jeans, and his hand moved to my waistband then inside my panties. I gasped when he found my clit and threw my head back.

"Lift your hips," Bo growled low and husky, and I obeyed, not caring if anyone walked into the kitchen at that moment. All I cared about was the man making me feel alive, and what he was doing to my body.

He slipped a long finger inside my core, then curled it up and pressed in while he rolled my clit with his thumb.

Sensations flooded me, and I arched my back as millions of nerve endings spiraled out of control.

"Give it to me," Bo hissed. "Come all over my hand."

I groaned low in my throat as the pressure built, reaching out to grab the edge of the table to anchor myself to reality. This is what I read about in books. The deep pulsing that comes with an orgasm so powerful that your atoms split at the point of release, only to merge again as you float down from heaven.

"Bo," I whimpered, terrified of what I was feeling but still wanting more.

Grabbing the front of my shirt, Bo yanked it up until my breasts were exposed. He leaned down and sucked a nipple into his mouth, growling around it, "Imagine my cock pounding into you," before he bit down on my nipple.

I erupted into a kaleidoscope of color as every nerve ending fired at the same time. Bo crushed his mouth over mine to silence my scream, his thumb unrelenting as another orgasm followed on the tail of the first.

His mouth was everywhere at the same time, coaxing the second orgasm to its crest. Needing a connection to Bo, I reached down and grabbed him through his jeans, and he thrust into my hand. "I want my cock inside your mouth, in your sweet pussy,"—one of his fingers found my ass and pressed in—"and I'm claiming you here, too."

I gasped at the pressure. Anticipation and longing for the pleasure he promised directed my hips to press down against his finger. Bo hissed his approval, rubbing his cock against my hand once more. Then he claimed my mouth and groaned as his finger pressed all the way into my ass, and I exploded around them both.

I convulsed from the overload of sensations pouring through my body and cried out, arching my back off the table as the orgasm claimed my body. As I rode the waves, reveling in the beauty of the physical touch on a body, my bones became liquid and I slumped into a pile of mush against the table.

As I lay there panting, Bo pulled his hand out from inside my jeans, running his tongue around each of my nipples before pulling my shirt down. Then, without a word, he picked me up from the table and headed up the stairs to my room, placing me on the bed. He brushed a kiss across my lips as I watched through hooded eyes, still exhausted, and unable to form a clear thought, and then moved to the bathroom, turning on the shower.

I was too sated to move or contemplate what had just happened, so I lay there and listened as he undressed and jumped into the shower. Moments later, I heard the telltale sound of a man grunting and sat up. I moved to the bathroom door with my heart beating out of my chest and found Bo standing in the middle of the shower, running his hand up and down the length of his cock. It was the most erotic thing I'd ever seen.

He pinned me with his eyes the second I cleared the doorway. He'd been waiting for me to come watch. My gaze drifted down the length of his body, and I licked my lips. His breathing increased as I touched each inch of his body with my eyes, and when mine came back to his, he bit his lip, moaned deep in his throat, and threw his head back as his release pulsed into the water.

My knees went weak at the sight. I was tempted to throw caution to the wind and strip out of my clothes, but I didn't. Instead, I lifted my hooded eyes back to his, licked my lips, and then turned and left the room. I needed to think. I needed to figure out what the hell was holding me back from Bo.

I needed the Wallflowers.

Seven

WHAT IF

A SOFT BREEZE LIFTED MY hair as I stared silently at the stars. The moon shone in the gloom of the night sky. The old man's face hid behind a sliver of shadows as the stars danced around it, peeking out like fireflies at twilight. I'd always preferred the darkness of night to daylight. The vastness of the universe made most feel small and insignificant, but for me, it was a time to dream. A time to plot the course of my life away from my family. I'd lie in my bed trying to find the constellations, wondering if there was a man out there staring at the same night sky, thinking about me as well. I'd try to picture him. His hair color, his eye color, whether he was tall or medium height. His face would never come to me, but his presence was always there somewhere between dusk and dawn. He'd appear in that place between consciousness and dreams, a shadowed figure reaching out his hand for me to take hold, beckoning me to trust him.

Looking over my shoulder where Bo sat with Devin, I wondered if I'd finally found that man. "Men at some time are masters of their fates. The fault is not in our stars but in ourselves,"

I whispered. The abbreviated quote from Shakespeare's Julius Caesar seemed apropos. I was master of my fate if I chose to follow it. If I didn't, it wasn't fate's fault, but my own.

Had fate led me to Bo?

I'd accepted Bo as the man in my life with little argument, but I was holding back from the one aspect of a relationship that brought a man and woman closer, and I wasn't sure why anymore.

I wasn't a child, a fresh-faced college student with stars in her eyes, but a woman. So why was I acting like the virgin I was?

"How did you know that Devin was the one for you?" I asked Cali.

She and Poppy were sitting on the top railing of the horse corral, silently taking in the beauty of the night as well.

"I knew he was the one when I jumped on the trolley. I was prepared to turn my back on us to protect him from my granddaddy, but I couldn't breathe at the thought of what I was leavin' behind."

I closed my eyes, wondering what it would feel like if Bo were to change his mind. I drifted back to earlier in the evening when he'd said he wanted to slow down, and how my immediate reaction had been emptiness. I'd turned my back on him to hide my tears, but I remembered a pain in my chest, as if I couldn't fill my lungs. The thought of being so close to what I'd always wanted had tumbled around in my head, then extreme relief had pulsed through me when he'd clarified his statement.

"You said that you thought fallin' in love happens by chance. Serendipity. That it's like walkin' into a room and *bam*, you just know when you lay eyes on them that they're the one. Is that how it happened to you?"

Cali looked down at me a smiled. "*Bam*," she muttered. "It was like the planets aligned when I finally reached out and took hold of his hand."

"*Bam*," I whispered to myself.

"What's runnin' through your head?" Cali asked, looking down on me.

"A bunch of what-ifs."

"Such as?" Poppy asked.

"What if I take a leap of faith and give myself completely to him and it doesn't work?"

"There are no guarantees in life, you said so yourself."

I smirked. "Always easier to give advice than to take it."

"Well, to quote you further, if you're lookin' for a life free from pain and heartache, you won't find it. You just have to trust your instincts. What does your heart tell you?" Cali said.

"My heart wants him,"—an impish grin pulled across my mouth—"and so does my body."

"So, you're holdin' back because?" Poppy questioned.

"I guess I'm holdin' back that one aspect of our relationship as a way of protectin' my heart."

"Well, there's no reason to rush if you're not sure," Cali said, jumping down from the railing. "But I can tell you that the bond that forms between a man and a woman once sex is introduced is a whole other level. The connection you'll have with Bo will be deeper than what you're feelin' already."

I rolled my lip between my teeth and looked back at Bo again. As if he could sense I was watching him, his head turned toward me and our eyes locked. I barely noticed when Poppy and Cali walked back toward the house; I was caught in Bo's invisible web. I could feel his eyes burning a trail from my head to my toes, and my body reacted. The intensity in his gaze reached across the courtyard and pinned me in place, sucking air from my lungs. Holding back from him was almost physically painful, leaving my body battered and bruised without him landing a single blow.

I knew all about the scars from emotional neglect, but now I was the one inflicting them on myself. Life was about experiences. About falling down and getting back up to fight another day. It was about collecting scars that proved you'd lived it to the fullest, and I realized I was being a coward. I wanted him with every fiber of my being, and the only reason I was holding back from him was to protect myself. That wasn't living; that was hiding from life.

Holding Bo's eyes, I turned toward the barn, mumbling Sonia Ricotti's words of wisdom. "Surrender to what is, let go of what was, have faith in what will be."

When I reached the opening, I looked back at Bo. He was leaning against a post watching me. I turned fully to him and stared back. His relaxed stance became rigid, and he pushed off the post, facing me, watching. Neither of us moved. My heart began to trip a beat of anticipation as I willed him to follow with my eyes. In the pale moonlight, I saw the moment he read my thoughts. His jaw tightened, and then he moved. I turned without looking back, then disappeared into the inky blackness of the barn, and waited.

Bo's muscles strained for control as he followed Sienna into the barn. His baser needs were howling at him to hunt her down and make her his completely. To fill her body with his, spilling his seed into her as a warning for all other males to back off.

The need to claim her was so powerful, he stopped at the opening and took a deep breath to control the burning need running rampant through his blood.

Movement caught his eye, and he looked toward the hay loft.

Sienna was climbing a ladder, carrying a wool blanket across her shoulder. Without a word, he followed. When he reached the ladder, he paused and took another deep breath so he didn't scare her. He felt wired, out of control, and he needed his hard-fought control at that moment.

He took each step slowly, patiently, until his heart slowed to a steady beat. On the top rung, his heart skipped a beat. Sienna had shed all of her clothes and was standing at a window, gazing up at the moon. Pale silver light highlighted her curves, leaving others in shadow. She looked ethereal in the heavenly light seeping through the window, and his breath caught for a moment before he moved.

Stripping his shirt from his body as he approached, he could feel his hands shake in anticipation. He'd left his boots off after he'd taken a shower, so the only thing between them now were his jeans.

Standing behind Sienna, Bo didn't touch her. Afraid he'd move too fast, he leaned in, ran his nose down the side of her neck, and breathed in her unique scent of sweet almonds and sex. Lust ran rampant through his blood, and his lungs froze, trapping her essence inside.

His fingers itched to touch her soft skin, so he released the button on his jeans as his tongue snaked out and tasted her neck, and he stepped out of them. Reaching around her shoulders, Bo cupped her chin and nudged it sideways until her neck was bared to him. He ran his teeth gently across her tender flesh, then whispered, "You're sure? No doubts?" as her body trembled. Sienna answered him by rubbing her ass against his throbbing cock.

Bo hissed at the contact and grabbed her hands, forcing them to the window. "Keep your hands on the window," he rumbled low. His control was wrung tight, if she touched him again, he'd lose it. "Don't move."

Running his hands down her body to her legs, Bo spread them until he had full access to her slick, wet heat. With more patience than he felt, he ran a finger across her silken folds and hissed. She was dripping already in anticipation, and his control slipped further from reach. "This is mine," he growled, making sure she understood exactly what was about to happen. "Once I slip inside, you'll belong to me completely."

Sienna sucked in a breath on a whimper and nodded.

Inch by inch, Bo caressed and played her body until a fine sheen of sweat covered her. He worked her core with precision until she was moaning with the need to orgasm, but he wouldn't let her find release. He was teaching her. Teaching her to feel with her body and to follow his lead. Teaching her body to know only him, and what he could do to her.

Sweat trailed down her neck as she writhed on his hand. Bo leaned in and swept it off with his tongue, growling, "Do you want my cock?" When she arched into him, trying to reach for the precipice, he wouldn't let her. He'd given her all he was going to give her with his hands. Her next orgasm would be around his cock.

"Yes," she whispered, out of breath.

In one fluid motion, Bo picked her up and moved to the blanket she'd spread out on the hay. He placed her gently on top of it, then dropped to his knees, crouching between her legs. "Ride my face first," he growled, then covered her core with his mouth, anchoring her in place with his hands. His tongue danced across her slick flesh, building the embers he'd fanned with his hand. She buried her hands in his hair, arching her back with the sensations playing across her body. When she began to moan with a coming orgasm, Bo slid up her body, took her mouth, and then gently slid inside her warm heat until the barrier that held her innocence stopped him. Sienna ripped her mouth from his and looked up at him. He expected to see fear of the unknown, but lust reflected back at him. He pulled out and slid back in until he couldn't go any further, gritting his jaw to keep from slamming into her. When he slid out from inside her again, he paused at the entrance and held her eyes. He was waiting for her to give him a signal. Waiting for her to give him permission to take her innocence.

She wet her lips and stared back at him. Then in a burst of passion, Sienna grabbed his ass and impaled herself on his swollen cock, shredding her innocence in a single thrust. Bo moaned at the sudden heat wrapping fully around him, and Sienna gasped at the intrusion.

An emotion he couldn't describe spread through Bo like warm honey, and he slammed his mouth over hers as he held still, waiting for her to adjust to his size. Sienna wrapped her arms around his neck and kissed him back with equal intensity, and then began to move against him, unable to stop the riot of sensation flooding her system.

"Slow," Bo whispered in her ear. "Slow and steady. Let me bring you with me."

Clutching his shoulders, she held on as he pulled out, then pushed back in slowly, easing into her so he didn't hurt her. He increased his tempo gradually until she arched her head back, and moaned. Gritting his teeth to keep from exploding, he kept at her body until they were both wrung tight with need. When she was ready, he pulled her leg higher on his hip and slipped inside her body to his root. Sienna gasped at being completely full of him. Wanting his name spilling from her lips as she came, he rolled his hips, causing her to cry out, then thrust back in. He reached down when her moans began to sound like pleading and rolled her clit. Her back arched and her mouth opened as he stimulated her, and he surged in on a groan of his own as her hot walls squeezed him, milking his cock instinctually. She was a fucking natural. The hottest woman he'd taken to bed in his life, and she belonged to him completely, no one else. Possessiveness raged through Bo, and he vowed that he'd do whatever it took to keep it that way.

"Bo!" Sienna gasped, clutching his shoulder. She was frantic for release.

He rolled her clit faster and watched her eyes roll back in her head. When she began gasping his name, and her body began to shudder with her climax, he thrust hard twice more and then exploded deep within her, covering her mouth with his as they both moaned through their orgasm.

Once the shudders stopped, Bo rolled to keep from crushing Sienna, taking her with him, wrapping her tightly against him while his stampeding heart tried to slow.

She was limp against his chest, while her breath came in pants.

Tilting his head up, he brushed his lips against her forehead, asking in a hushed voice, "Did I hurt you?"

She shook her head in answer, then brushed a kiss across his chest.

He heard her tears before he saw them, and froze. Pulling her further up his body until she was eye to eye with him, he searched her face. "Talk to me."

She bit her lip, then shook her head.

Bo rolled again until she was pinned beneath him, then ran a hand through her hair before brushing a kiss across her mouth. "Did I rush you?" he asked, praying to God he hadn't misread her.

"No," she hiccupped. "I'm…It's just…It was everything I hoped it would be. Better than I could have imagined."

"But?" he asked, trepidation setting in.

"I'm just afraid it will end. I've wanted this for so long that I'm scared to lose it."

Bo blinked, then pulled her up and crushed her to his chest. "I'm not goin' anywhere."

"Don't make promises you can't keep."

He was treading in dangerous waters now, and he knew it. After hearing about her situation with her family, he knew she had insecurity issues. Her family had led her to believe she was worthless in their eyes. It was his job to repair the damage they'd caused.

Bo rolled a third time until Sienna was perched on his chest. Then he grabbed her face with his hands.

"You think I lived twenty-eight years without knownin' a fuckin' great woman when I see one? You think I lived through what my dad endured without learnin' a thing or two about women in general?"

She shook her head.

"I told you before you're my desire, my fuckin' wet dream. My life was gray before you entered it. I woke up the day I laid eyes on you, baby. You made the sun shine for me for the first time in fuckin' years. I'm not lettin' that go without a fight. I want you in my life, and I don't see that changin' . . . Ever."

Her bottom lip began to tremble, then she crushed her mouth against his. He opened for her and poured every ounce of emotion he could into the kiss until Sienna was whimpering with need again.

He knew he should hold off taking her again, but he needed to show her how much he wanted her, so he slid back inside her as she lay on his chest and surged deep. Sienna moaned in his mouth at his intrusion, and pushed up to her knees and began riding his cock with enthusiasm, her body hot and pliant under his hands. She was hungry for what he could give her after suppressing her needs all these years.

Reaching down, Bo found her clit and began working her, bringing her closer to release as he met her downward thrust with his own. When her head fell back, he reached up and grabbed her shoulders and pounded harder until a low keening noise broke from her throat. He lost all control then and jackknifed up, rolling her to her back and sliding back in deep.

"You're mine," he hissed.

She whimpered.

"I'm not lettin' you go," he vowed.

Her back arched as her mouth opened in a noiseless cry of passion, and Bo drove in deeper and held, throwing his own head back as he pulsed inside her, making her his again in every way.

When her eyes opened, still hooded with residual passion, he brushed a kiss across her mouth. "Do you understand now?"

Her eyes softened, and she nodded. "I'm not letting you go either," she whispered back.

"Good," he returned, kissing her thoroughly once more.

Bo collapsed to his side, exhausted, and wrapped her in his arms, tucking the blanket around them both.

"Sleep," he ordered.

She didn't answer, and he looked down at her. Her eyes were closed, her face slack, and he smiled. He'd fucked her into submission.

As Sienna's breathing evened out, it hit Bo that they hadn't used protection. The thought she could be carrying his child hit him like a ton of bricks, and he clutched her tighter to him.

Then an arrogant smile pulled across his lips.

With heavy lids, I opened my eyes slowly. Still wrapped tightly in Bo's arms, I smiled. Then I frowned. The moon was still up in the night sky, but there was a bright light spilling into the hay loft.

Blinking to clear my eyes from sleep, I stared at the light. It seemed to move, dance across the courtyard like children chasing each other in a game of hide and seek. I squinted my eyes against the light and then sat up in a panic . . . "Fire!"

Bo sat upright, then stood and grabbed his jeans, completely alert and in control. "Get dressed," he ordered.

I fumbled in the darkness for my top and jeans as Bo pulled on his shirt.

He rushed to the window and looked out. "The main house is on fire."

"Go!" I cried out as I fumbled with my jeans. "You have to get everyone out!"

Bo hesitated for a moment. He seemed torn between leaving me alone and waiting for me to dress.

"I'll be right behind you! Go!"

Nodding, he disappeared down the ladder and out of sight. I ran to the window and watched as he tried to open the front door of the house. He stepped back, shaking his hand. The fire was too hot. Grabbing a chair from the porch, he smashed in a window near the side of the house and disappeared inside.

"Please, God. Let him get them in time."

Throwing on my shoes, I climbed down the ladder and met Troy and Brantley in the courtyard. They bunked in cabins on the opposite side of the ranch and must have seen the fire. They looked wired as they grabbed hoses and tried to tame the blaze crawling up the side of the house, bursting windows on both levels.

I was frantic to help, but my cell was inside, so I couldn't call

911. All I could do was stand there helplessly and wait for Bo to emerge from the inferno with Devin and the Wallflowers.

What seemed like hours passed before Poppy ran out the front door with a towel covering her head, then Devin ran outside carrying Cali over his shoulder, followed by Bo carrying his boots.

I ran to Bo and leaped into his arms, overcome with emotion. He could have died. They all could have died.

"I'm okay," he mumbled in my ear, then squeezed me once before letting me go to help Troy and Brantley.

The fire department arrived ten minutes later, but it was too late. The fire had engulfed most of the structure.

I huddled together with Poppy and Cali. They'd escaped in nothing but a T-shirt, so the fire department had given them blankets to cover themselves with. We watched in horror as the power of the flames destroyed everything in its path.

It took the men and the voluntary firefighters more than an hour to control the blaze. By the time the last flicker of fire was doused, all that was left was a charred shell of memories forever lost.

"How do we tell Natasha?" Poppy whispered.

"I don't know. But we don't tell her until after Boris is out of surgery. She has enough to worry about this mornin'," I replied.

"We need clothes," Cali stated, then looked around at the destruction. "And more help."

"Are you thinkin' Bernice and Eunice?"

She nodded. "They can help Natasha with Boris while we handle the cleanup here."

"What about work? Don't you have to be back tomorrow?"

"I'll call Jolene. The only book I'm working on is the one with family connections to Poe. They can wait another week. This is more important."

I'd been Alexandra Poe's right-hand woman for the past three years, so it was natural for me to start prioritizing the cleanup.

"We'll need to call the insurance company first," I explained. "They won't want us touching anything until they've investigated the fire. I'll head to town as soon as the stores are open and get clothes and food for all of us, while you call your aunts and rally the troops. Once we know Boris has made it through the surgery, we can break the news to Natasha."

"Bernice can handle that. She's been friends with them for over twenty years," Cali said.

"We'll need phones," Poppy pointed out. "Ours were lost in the fire. I plugged them all into chargers in the kitchen."

"Devin's wasn't," Cali announced. "I felt it stickin' out of his jeans pocket when he carried me out of the house."

I turned and walked over to Devin. I could see his phone peeking out from his back pocket just like Cali said, so I snatched it out and turned back to the girls, grinning when I heard Bo chuckle.

I handed it to Cali. "Call Bernice so we can get the ball rollin'."

A strong hand wrapped around mine and tugged me to the side and kept walking. I quickened my step to keep up with Bo. When we were far enough away from the girls, he turned me into his arms and kissed me. Thoroughly.

"This is not how I envisioned wakin' up with you this mornin'," he whispered. "How are you feelin'?"

With all that had happened, I hadn't had time to process the night before. A blush began to spread up my neck and settled in my cheeks. I'd slept with this man, and now I had to look him in the eyes.

"I'm fine," I told his chest.

"Look me in the eyes."

"I'd rather not."

"Why?" he asked hesitantly.

"You've seen all my bits, and I'm embarrassed."

His body shook as a low rumble of laughter filled my ears. "I've tasted all your bits, too."

I buried my face in his chest. "You're a very naughty man."

"And you're cute."

I peeked up at him, and he winked at me.

"Was I any good?" I whispered, then held my breath. I would die a thousand deaths of humiliation if he said it was just okay for him. It had been . . . otherworldly, fantastic, perfect for me.

Bo blinked, then a sexy grin pulled across his mouth. "If you'd been any better, you would have killed me."

It was my turn to blink. "You did most of the work. How could I have killed you?"

Bo pulled me in closer, then leaned in to whisper in my ear. "I've never wanted a woman the way I wanted you. Every touch, every whispered word drove me wild. As long as you're responding, I'll keep giving you what you want. Even if it kills me."

"So I almost killed you by enjoying myself?"

He grinned.

That wasn't exactly otherworldly, but he did seem pleased.

I rolled my lips between my teeth and thought about what he'd said. He loved the way I responded? Hmm. "You'll probably need some rest if that's the case, because I don't anticipate disliking anything you do to me in the foreseeable future."

His grin turned arrogant.

I rolled my eyes.

"Time for a serious talk," he said, pulling me deeper into his body. "First, we didn't use protection last night. That's on me. I should have been lookin' out for you."

"That's not on you. I'm just as responsible for my own body," I sighed. "But it's not an issue since I'm on the pill."

"All right. Then I need to tell you that the man who tried to rob you two days ago was found beaten. He's in a coma, and my gut tells me it's connected somehow to you three women. Now we have this mysterious fire on our hands, and I'm on red alert. I don't want you or the girls out of our sight until we know different."

I felt the blood drain from my face. "You think the fire was on purpose. That someone set it to kill us?"

"I'm sayin' I don't like coincidences, and until the fire marshal gives me the cause for the fire, I don't want to take chances with any of you ladies."

"You're scarin' me now."

Bo hugged me tighter. "Good. Bein' scared will keep you on guard. And I need you on guard right now. So, no more takin' off on four-wheelers. No more ridin' horses unless it's under my or Devin's supervision. We've got a lot of work to do here, and I don't have time to keep huntin' you women down when you get a wild hair up your ass. So I need you *not* to be unpredictable until we know what the fuck is goin' on."

I nodded, but added, since he was disparaging me and my friends, "We aren't unpredictable, just so you know. We spent years keepin' to ourselves, so now we're just makin' up for lost time."

"Don't kid yourself." Bo grinned. "You're as unpredictable as a hornet, and the three of you together is like a swarm."

I narrowed my eyes. "Careful, or you'll get stung."

Bo snagged me around the neck and pulled my mouth to his. "You won't sting me," he mumbled against my lips. "You like what I do to your body."

"Arrogant," I mouthed back.

"Truthful," he answered and then kissed me hard, wet, and deep to prove his point.

Eight

I *LIKE* ALL OF YOU

"THE GRILL?" DEVIN BARKED OUT.

"That's what the fire marshal's sayin'," Bo sighed, rubbing his face. The whole weekend was turning into a clusterfuck.

Devin looked over his shoulder at the Wallflowers. "Which one of them pulled the burgers off last night?"

Bo cringed. "Calla did."

Devin closed his eyes and hung his head. "I predicted this when I arrived. But I sure as hell didn't think my woman would burn down a house."

"We can't keep the truth from her," Bo stated. "It's gonna come out."

Devin stood and cracked his neck, rolling it on his shoulders. "I need a vacation from my new life."

"Nate said it best," Bo chuckled, "There's never a dull moment in Savannah."

Devin shot Bo a look that suggested a dull Savannah would be fine with him. "At least we don't have to worry this is related to Daniels."

"Yeah, but I'd rather err on the side of caution until he wakes up and tells us if the beatin' he took has anything to do with the girls."

"I've already read Calla the riot act after she took off on the four-wheeler. She'll toe the line."

Bo raised a brow.

Devin grinned. "She'll toe the line as best she can, I should say."

Clint Black drove into the courtyard, his mouth gaping wide as he took in the smoldering remains of the ranch house.

"Black's here," Bo said, jerking his head in the man's direction.

Devin stood and glared. "I'd send him packin' if we didn't need the help more than ever."

"If you do, we'll be shovelin' shit for the next week. I'd rather brand cattle than clean out the stalls."

Black made his way over to Devin and Bo, shaking his head in amazement. "What happened?"

"Grill was left on, and it caught the house on fire," Bo replied.

"Jesus. It looks like a total loss. Do you still need me?"

"Nothin's changed," Devin returned. "The ranch still needs runnin' until they hire more men and rebuild."

Black looked shocked. "If you say so," he said, looking back over his shoulder at the destruction. "Can't imagine they'll be able to recover from a loss like that."

"They will," Bo bit out. "So, clean the stalls and milk the cows or hit the road."

Black raised his hands in surrender and backed away, heading for the barn. Both men watched him disappear inside.

"I don't trust him," Devin grumbled.

"You gettin' a vibe other than ladies' man?" Bo asked.

"A gut feelin'."

"I trust your gut. If he steps out of line again, he's gone."

"Girls are headed our way," Devin said.

Bo turned and watched the Wallflowers make their way slowly across the graveled courtyard. Two were barefoot due to the fire and, except for Sienna, draped with blankets to cover their lack of clothes.

"I need to run to town and get clothes and supplies. Bernice and Eunice are on their way up to take care of Natasha and Boris. When can I go?" Sienna asked.

Bo looked at Devin. "Fire was an accident, but I'm still uneasy about lettin' her out of my sight. I need to deal with the police, so you'll have to go."

"Y'all act like she'll cause trouble," Calla chuckled.

Devin looked at Calla then at the burnt ranch house. "Hurricane-force winds don't stand a chance against any of you. Someone needs to go."

"Very funny," Calla snapped. "It's not like *we* set fire to the house."

Both men rolled their lips between their teeth.

Calla looked between them both. "We didn't, did we?"

"It was the grill," Devin finally admitted.

Calla blinked. "But I…I turned it off."

"You're sure?" Bo asked.

Calla's brows drew together in concentration, and she shook her head. "No. I'm not sure. There were so many dials, I may have left one . . . Oh. My. God. I burnt down their home."

"Baby, it was an accident," Devin drawled, pulling her into his arms.

"I know it was an accident, but they lost all their belongin's, their history. I . . . I have to make this right."

"Calla, you've got that look in your eyes," Devin said, looking ready to pounce. "The last time you looked at me that way you jumped on a trolley and took off. What are you thinkin'?"

"Give me your phone," she bit out, raising her hand, palm up, ignoring him.

Bo shook his head. He knew determination when he saw it. Devin didn't stand a chance in hell of talking Calla out of whatever was running through her head.

"What are you gonna do?" Devin asked, suspicious.

"Never you mind. This is my fault, and I'm gonna fix it."

Devin shot Bo a look that suggested there would be a fight, so he grabbed Sienna's hand and mumbled, "Time to go."

Poppy caught on just as quickly and followed them as Bo walked Sienna to Poppy's car. "Troy's gonna have to go with you since Devin's"—he turned back and looked at his friend—"gotta contain Calla now. I trust Troy as much as I can, but I want you to be on the lookout. If you see anyone followin' you, tell him."

"Why the caution if the fire was an accident?"

"I'm wired that way, and you three have already proven you have bad luck, so humor me."

"I'll be insulted for the three of us, since you're sleepin' with him now," Poppy said.

Sienna grinned at Poppy. "Just say 'Bite me, lawman.' That one pisses him off."

Bo opened the car door and whistled between his teeth at Troy, ignoring them both.

"I'll leave the bitin' to you," Poppy continued as he kissed Sienna good-bye and helped her into the car. Knowing she wouldn't be able to help herself, he shut the door on whatever salty retort Sienna had for Poppy and turned to glare at the other Wallflower. She snorted, completely unfazed by his scowl, then turned on her bare heel and walked away.

"The man who takes on that woman will need balls of steel," Bo growled.

The sound of a bike roaring up the drive turned his attention away from Poppy. Nate Jacobs pulled to a stop next to Devin and pulled off his helmet, grinning.

"New bike?" Devin asked casually while he wrestled with Calla for his phone.

"I missed yours," Nate responded, chuckling when Calla pulled the phone from his hand, threw her hands up in victory, and stormed off.

A gasp caught Bo's attention, and he looked back at Poppy. She had stopped in her tracks at the sight of Jacobs, then began turning in circles, looking for something, then settled on the barn and took off. Bo followed her retreat with fascination, then looked back at Jacobs and caught him watching Poppy with a scowl.

Then he threw his head back and laughed.

Three hours, a trunk full of groceries, four new cell phones, clothes, purses, shoes, and a variety of toiletries for the Wallflowers and our men later, Troy and I were finally heading back. The road leading to the ranch wound around the hillside like a roller coaster, so I let him drive since he knew the roads better. I was just settling into the passenger seat for the drive back when my new phone began to ring. I looked at the caller ID. Crap. It was my mother.

Sighing, I answered. "Mom?"

"I've been tryin' to reach you all mornin'," she stated accusingly.

"My phone was destroyed in a fire. I had to get a new one."

"A fire? Where are you?"

"On vacation."

"On vacation? Where?"

Oh, Lord.

"Bullwinkle Ranch."

"You're in Canada?"

"Why would you think I'm in Canada?"

"Sienna, I'll never understand you," she sighed.

Ditto.

"Is there somethin' you needed?"

"I just hadn't heard from you in a while and thought I'd touch base." Her tone of voice said she was lying.

"Okaaay," I drawled out. "Nothin' new to tell you."

"Nothin'? No new man in your life?"

Oh, there was, but I had a feeling she knew that already. I had no doubt my brother had relayed Chase's versions of events two days prior. And now that I understood what was running through Bo's head, I'm sure my brother had already put two and two together and knew Bo's interference was based on his feelings for me. He wouldn't be able to stop himself from filling my mother in on all the details. However, letting her in on my new relationship wasn't gonna happen. I didn't have the energy to play twenty questions.

"Nope. No new man in my life."

Troy turned his head and looked at me, raising a brow. I mouthed, "My mother," and he grinned.

"Then who was this man who manhandled poor Chase? David said he punched him."

Poor Chase, indeed. He'd be poor Chase the next time I saw him.

"He's a friend," I lied.

She sighed dramatically. "I hope you're not stirrin' up trouble for poor Chase *again*,"—I felt the blood run from my face. She knew about what happened with Chase in the bathroom—

"because he didn't feel comfortable comin' by the house for the longest time because of you."

"Mother—"

"You know, you're just like your father," she went on, cutting me off. "You can't let things lie. Why can't you be more like your sister? She never causes problems."

I felt like I'd been slapped across the face, and I reacted. "Which father? The one who ignores me or the one I've never met?"

Mother gasped at my response. "You only have one father," she retorted. "Let that go."

"How can I let it go when every time I look at my father, I'm reminded of what you've done, that I don't belong anywhere? Who is he, Mother? Why is it such a big secret? Who the hell is the sperm donor?"

There was no response to my question, only a dial tone for my trouble.

I didn't realize I was crying until Troy handed me a handkerchief. I glanced at his outstretched hand, then at his face. He looked terrified I might burst into tears. I grabbed the offered piece of linen, mumbling, "Thank you," before drying my face.

As we rounded the next corner, the entrance to the ranch came into view, so I blew my nose to hide the fact I'd been crying from the girls and Bo, but the tears wouldn't seem to stop. Years of frustration and loneliness rushed to the surface, and I couldn't control the onslaught.

When Troy came to a stop in the courtyard, facing the burnt-out shell of Boris and Natasha's home, the dam broke, sending me bailing out of the car and into the still smoldering ruins.

Boris and Natasha had memories of a happy life in that house that I envied. Memories of a happy family that cared for each other rather than pass judgment, and I was determined to save what I could. If I had to, I'd turn over every timber to find a single photograph or keepsake that meant something to them.

As I began climbing what was left of the front porch, I heard Troy call out Bo's name. I ignored them both. I was on a mission.

Water and soot covered every surface, clinging to what remained like a black plague. Stepping over what was left of the living room, I tripped on a hard object and looked down. One of the bronze cowboy statues that had graced a table in the living room was lying on its side like an abandoned doll. I reached for it and began wiping off the soot with the tail of my shirt, ignoring the heat emanating from the metal.

Footsteps on the porch alerted me to someone coming, but I didn't look up. A crystal bowl had caught my eye. It twinkled in the sun like a diamond. I lowered the statue and reached for it, but a pair of large boots stopped in front of me, blocking my way. I tried to dodge them, but Bo squatted in front of me and grabbed my shoulders.

"Baby?" he rumbled low.

"We have to save their memories," I explained, shrugging off his touch.

"We will once I'm sure the structure is safe."

I shook my head. "No. There's water on everything. It will ruin the photographs. We have to save them now!"

A charred picture frame peeked out from under a fallen truss. I lunged for it, tugging on the end to pull it free.

Bo moved to my side and laid his hand on mine, grumbling, "I'll get it. You'll hurt yourself."

The strength in his hand made my bottom lip quiver. My mother's call had unnerved me, reminded me how unwanted I was even in my own family. Would he eventually see what everyone else did? That I was a thorn in his side, not the sun he claimed I was in his gray existence.

My stomach dropped at the thought he'd eventually see the real me, and I pulled my hand away, distancing myself from him.

Bo's eyes popped to mine, his brow creasing as I stumbled back.

"I need to leave," I whispered, panting as if I'd run a mile.

"What?"

"I need to leave. I need to go home. I—"

Bo moved swiftly, wrapping his arms around my body until I was crushed to his chest. Then he leaned in and whispered, "Breathe, baby. In and out. In and out."

I began to shake my head in protest, pushing at his chest. "This isn't gonna work between us. You'll figure out I'm not worth the trouble."

Bo squeezed me tighter and then shook me once to gain my attention. "I'm not lettin' you walk away from me because your mother's a bitch. Whatever she said to make you doubt yourself, I'm tellin' you right now, she's wrong."

"I don't belong . . ." I hiccupped.

"You don't belong?"

"Anywhere. I'm different. My mother had an affair, and I don't know who my father is. The man who raised me barely looks at me, and my brother and sister avoid me at all costs. I don't belong anywhere."

Bo searched my face, then brushed a kiss across my mouth. "You belong to me," he whispered. "That's all that matters."

I hiccupped again and buried my face in his chest. My mind was bouncing around in so many directions I was suddenly weary. "Why do they hate me?" I whispered.

Bo went solid and tightened his arms, growling, "Sienna, if your family is blind to the beauty that is you, then they're the ones who don't belong in your life. Not the other way around."

I looked up at him to argue. "But—"

"No. Fuck 'em," Bo hissed. "You don't need that shit in your life. You have your own family now."

"My-my *own* family?"

"Yeah. A family of Wallflowers who would risk their lives to keep you safe, and a *man* who would step in front of a bullet for you."

I gasped, disbelieving. "You'd step in front of a bullet for *me*?"

His face softened, and his eyes turned from stormy gray to shining silver as he scanned my face. "I'd do worse to keep you safe. So would the girls."

I turned my head to look at Cali and Poppy. They were watching us with concern etched in the lines across their faces. He was right; I did have a family I could depend on.

"Look at me, Sienna," Bo whispered. I turned my attention back to him and stared into his penetrating eyes. They were filled with tenderness as he ran his hands up into my hair and tilted my head back until he could meet my gaze head on. My heart quickened in response to his gentleness. "You're not defined by who your parents are. We all come into this world pure of heart; it's how we live our lives from that point forward that defines who we are. And your heart's so fuckin' pure, baby, that it radiates from you like the sun."

After years of feeling like a dirty little secret within my family, and the reason they broke apart, Bo's words poured over me like a cleansing shower and filled me with hope that just maybe I was worth loving. "You barely know me. How are you so sure I'm pure of heart?" I whispered, wanting more than anything to believe him.

"Because my gut's never wrong, and it tells me I wanna be the man who makes you smile. The man you turn to when your mother pisses you off. The man who makes your body shudder while you're callin' out my name," he drawled low and sexy. "But mostly because you make me want to be a better man."

Hope grew brighter, and warmth settled in the pit of my stomach. "But why do you want to be that man?"

Bo drew me further into his embrace, wrapping me in his strength, and then rested his forehead against mine. "Why?" he muttered. "Because your smile is like the sun, and when I look at you, I see a future with laughter, headaches, passion . . . and love. Any man would kill for that; work hard to keep it. Strive to make sure he didn't give a woman like you any reason to look elsewhere."

My breath escaped in a whooshing rush, and my heart began to race. The way he talked about me, I almost believed him.

Pressing in closer to Bo, I drank in his confidence in me. I'd been filled with despair just a few short moments before, and now I felt . . . Safe . . . Loved—and just like that, it hit me so forcefully that if he hadn't been holding on to me, I would have dropped to my knees. I was falling in love with him. May already be in love with him.

"Bo, I . . ." I started to panic again. I was in too deep to turn back. If he changed his mind about us, I would never recover.

"Yeah?"

I think I love you.

I looked down to shield my face. I was afraid he'd see the truth written across it and run for the hills.

"What's runnin through your head?"

When I didn't answer, he pulled back and looked down at me. "Eyes on me, Sienna."

I shook my head. I wouldn't be able to hide my panic.

Bo grabbed my chin and forced my head up.

I closed my eyes.

"Baby, *look* at me."

I took a deep breath to rid myself of the panic, then opened my eyes like he'd asked, praying he couldn't read the truth in my expression.

"Talk to me," he whispered, brushing a kiss across my mouth. "Tell me what's goin' on in that head of yours?"

That I love you.

Bo searched my eyes for a moment, then his face softened, and he leaned his forehead against mine, whispering, "Jesus," before he crushed his mouth to mine, pulling me deeper into his body.

The panic I'd experienced drained fully from my body. He'd read my thoughts and hadn't run.

"I promise to earn that look every day," he mumbled against my mouth.

I shuddered in relief. "You already do," I whispered. "Thank you for what you said. For reminding me it's okay to be different."

"It's the truth. If they can't treat you with the respect you deserve, then scrape them off, baby. You're not defined by them, you're defined by you. No one else."

God, I loved this man.

"I promise not to drive you crazy," I blurted out. I wanted to be a better woman for him as well.

Bo smiled slowly. "Babe . . . baby steps."

"Pardon?"

Bo curled his arm around my shoulders and started leading me out of the wreckage.

"Are you gonna answer me?"

"Nope. I just vowed to earn that look. Answerin' you wouldn't be earnin' it."

I snorted. "Ass."

"I thought I was arrogant," he chuckled, lifting me over the front door.

I shook my head. "No, you're not arrogant, or an ass for that matter. You're just you, and I . . . *like* all of you."

Bo grabbed my neck, pulling my mouth back to his. His eyes had turned stormy gray again. "Ditto," he whispered softly. "I *like* all of you, too. Every fuckin' inch of you."

"Even the crazy part?"

His eyes crinkled at the side.

"Is that a yes?"

He smiled wider and then kissed me silent.

Devin whistled, drawing our attention, so we broke apart and joined the others.

"We need to head up top to bring the cattle down," Devin said as we walked up.

Bo nodded, then turned to me. "Nate's here to help. I don't want you out of his sight while I'm gone."

I rolled my eyes and then turned to look at the big man. Nate was taller than both Devin and Bo by an inch, maybe two. He was built like a wrecking machine, and completely out of his league if he thought he could contain the Wallflowers. It was one thing if you were one of our men. But an unattached badass? No way. He'd never stand a chance against the three of us. He'd be putty in our hands.

I smiled brightly, going for sweet and innocent. "Hey, Nate. Who's watchin' your bar?"

A slow grin pulled across his mouth. "My Aunt Martine."

"Welcome to Bullwinkle Ranch," Cali stated, just a sweet as you like.

His grin pulled wider across his face.

"Why's he smilin' like that?" Poppy whispered.

Nate's gaze shot to Poppy. He clearly had bionic hearing. "I'm smilin' 'cause I see the wheels turnin' in those gorgeous heads of yours. You three are as predictable as the sun risin' and fallin', so if you think for one minute you can control me, think again." Poppy started to argue, but he stopped her cold in her tracks. "If you say 'Dilligaf,' we're gonna have problems."

Poppy looked at me and asked smugly, "If I refrain from killin' him, does that count as savin' someone's life?" Then she scanned Nate from head to toe, pfft'd, and turned to leave.

"Hold on, spitfire," Devin called out. "I want your word you won't get into trouble while we're gone."

Poppy's back stiffened at the question, and she wheeled around. "I never get into trouble," she answered sweetly.

"This is serious," Bo jumped in. "The man who tried to rob you is in a coma. I don't know what the hell is goin' on, but until we do, we have to assume all three of you are in danger. We want your promise to behave while we're dealin' with the cattle."

"Yes, yes, I'll be on my best behavior," she sighed, flipping her hand out. "It's not like any of us try to get into trouble, you know. It just seems to find us."

"They'll be fine," Nate stated, crossing his arms. "I have this under control."

Devin chuckled. "We'll see."

"You got balls of steel?" Bo asked with a grin.

Nate raised a brow. "Yeah. Why?"

Bo looked at Poppy for some reason and grinned. "Just checkin'."

The sun was hot as Bo and Devin made their way to the high country, made even hotter by the fact that when they reached the spot where the herd should be, they were gone.

"Where would they go?" Devin asked as they searched the horizon.

Troy pulled a pair of binoculars from his saddlebag and began searching. A minute later, he barked out, "There," pointing toward a lower valley. "Fence is down."

"Down?" Bo questioned. "Have you checked the fence line recently?"

"Not that section."

"Whose land is that?" Devin asked.

"Ebenezer Craig," Brantley grumbled. "He's as mean as they come."

"Ebenezer?" Bo questioned.

"His momma loved Charles Dickens, according to Eb. I reckon she knew he'd turn out to be an old coot and named him that on purpose."

"Is he likely to pull down your fence?" Bo asked.

"Not likely. He's in his seventies. Lives alone, no family to speak of except for a granddaughter who comes around from time to time. Only livestock he's got is an old goat that eats everything in sight."

"Is his land secured?"

"He's got a fence around his property, so the herd should still be intact."

Bo rolled his neck, then looked back at Devin. "You think Nate can hold down the fort? This is gonna take longer than we thought."

Devin grinned. "It's high time he had his turn keepin' track of them. Maybe he'll pull his head out of his ass sooner rather than later if he deals head-on with Poppy."

"Throwin' him in the deep end? He'll drown."

Devin grinned wider. "Let's go find the herd so we can get back and see how he's doin'."

Troy and Brantley looked between the two, both with identical expressions. Expressions of disbelief.

“Remind me not to piss them off,” Brantley murmured. “If this is how they treat a friend, I don’t want to see what they’d do to someone they hate.”

Bo chuckled. “We’d do the same thing. There’s no punishment worse than wranglin’ three high-spirited Wallflowers.”

Nine

MY CHILDHOOD DREAMS WERE NOTHIN' LIKE YOU

NATE LIFTED A FALLEN TRUSS as the girls and I rummaged through the debris of Boris and Natasha's home. The insurance company had come and gone, and the electric company had finally disconnected the live wires, so it was safe to enter. The timbers were now cool enough for us to touch, so we dug in with both hands, determined to rescue what we could. The second floor was still somewhat intact, but the staircase was questionable, so Nate made us promise, under penalty of no beer or food for a week at Jacobs' Ladder, we'd only search the first floor. Since none of us wanted to fall through the ceiling, we decided we'd cut Nate some slack and obey. In appreciation of our willingness to listen, he braved the stairs and found what was left of our purses and clothes. We were thrilled when he came down with our wallets still intact.

"How did it go last night?" Cali whispered, looking over her shoulder at Nate to make sure he couldn't hear.

I looked up from a box of pictures I'd found, and smiled. "Hot. Magical. Kicking myself for hesitating."

"So I take it you're not having buyer's remorse?" Poppy chuckled.

I started to answer, "Not in the least," but Nate grunted, interrupting my train of thought. He was straining with a beam, lugging it over to an interior wall to brace it.

"Do you think he was a bouncer before he turned bar owner?" Poppy asked. "He looks like he could crack heads for a livin'."

There was something in the tone of her voice that was just this side of awe. I looked at Cali and grinned. Somebody had a crush on Nate. She wasn't wrong, though. Nate looked like he could punch through a concrete wall and dodge bullets with ease, and when he was angry, he oozed menace.

"Devin said he's smart. That he pulled himself up from poverty and earned a full-ride scholarship to UG, but no mention of bustin' heads for a livin'."

"He does seem smart," Poppy mumbled absentmindedly as she watched him.

Nate finished bracing the wall and then turned. He caught all three of us watching him, and he narrowed his eyes suspiciously. "What?"

"Were you a bouncer in a former life?" Cali inquired.

His brow creased and he shook his head slowly.

"Did you take human growth hormones to get that big?" I questioned.

His mouth pulled slightly into a smirk. "No."

"Train with the Russian weightlifting team?" Cali threw out.

One brow rose on his handsome face. "No."

"Eat your Wheaties?" Poppy asked innocently, and his eyes shot to hers, and he grinned, in my opinion, somewhat sexily at her.

"No," he responded yet again.

"You're a man of few words, aren't you?" I asked.

"No." He full-on smiled then, crossing his arms. "Can I trust you three to stay out of trouble long enough for me to walk to the barn and grab a hammer and nails?"

"No," we chimed in unison.

He shook his head, chuckling, then moved to an opening in the wall and disappeared around the corner.

I stood, arched my back to work out the kinks, then picked up the box of photographs I'd found in the living room. They'd been inside an entertainment console, which had protected them from the heat.

"Are you ladies hungry? I picked up a loaf of bread and peanut butter."

Cali and Poppy nodded and stood as well.

"The fridge is still standin'; I'll see if there's any bottled water," Poppy said.

We followed her to what was left of the kitchen. The sink was still intact, so out of curiosity, I turned the faucet on. Water streamed out, and I laughed.

"We can set up food prep in one of the cabins," Cali said.

Poppy tried to open the refrigerator, but it was melted shut. "There're only three cabins. How is that goin' to work?" she asked. "Natasha will be home tonight now that Boris is out of surgery, so that leaves two cabins."

"Boys in one and girls in the other," I replied.

"That should go over well," Cali snickered.

"Why?" I asked.

She smiled, then giggled. "I don't know about Bo, of course, but Devin needs *you know what* before he sleeps and *you know what* when he wakes up."

I looked at Poppy. "She still wins hands down as president of this club. She can't even call it sex, yet."

Cali rolled her eyes. "I'm just bein' polite."

"Say *sex,*" Poppy dared her.

"I can say the word," she grumbled. "You're bein' ridiculous."

I saw Nate heading for the kitchen and smiled. *This should be good.*

"Then say Devin and I have hot, sweaty sex before we go to sleep each night."

She glowered at me.

"You can't, can you?" Poppy dared.

Cali squared her shoulders like she was getting ready to do battle, then spit out quickly, just as Nate stepped through the wall. "Devin and I have hot, sweaty, mind-blowin', off the charts, sometimes *deviant,* SEX before bed each night. Are you happy now?"

"Good to know," Nate stated as he walked through the kitchen and into the living room, unfazed by our conversation. "Thanks for the update."

Cali whipped around on Nate and turned beet red, then whipped back around on Poppy and me, scowling as we burst into laughter. "You did that on purpose," she bit out.

I doubled over, holding my stomach, cackling loudly. Fortunately, Cali couldn't seem to hold a grudge. She snickered and snorted, then began laughing along with us. At the commotion, Nate popped his head around the corner and smiled, winking at Cali.

"Time…"—I gasped for air—"Time for lunch," I said between giggles, stumbling out of the kitchen, heading for the trunk of Poppy's car where I'd left the food.

I searched the yard as I went, looking for Clint to ask him if he wanted a sandwich. He was nowhere to be seen.

"Have you seen Clint?" I asked the girls.

"He must be in the barn," Poppy said, "I'll check."

"He might be in the pasture," Cali added. "I'll go look there."

I nodded, then loaded my arms with the bags and headed for the guest cabins on the other side of the barn.

The cabins were situated in a secluded area far from the main house. The first cabin was bigger, meant for a large family or gathering, the other two were smaller, perfect for an intimate getaway. I chose the larger one and went inside.

Like the main house, the cabins were decorated in the same log furnishings with tribal print rugs and pillows. The warm honey-colored wood was welcoming, the furniture large and comfortable looking. Boris and Natasha clearly had spared no expense when it came to the comfort of their guests.

I put the groceries on the counter as Poppy walked in behind me and began unloading the sacks.

"He wasn't in the barn."

I noticed a dining room chair was lying on its side, and the rug beneath the table was flipped over on one side, so I walked over and righted the furniture. "He must be in the pasture, then," I answered.

"He wasn't in the pasture," Cali called out as she walked through the door.

I turned and looked at them both. "Is his truck still here?"

Cali turned back around and walked outside, then shouted, "Truck's still here."

I shrugged. "Maybe he went with Bo and Devin."

Five minutes later, we had sandwiches ready. "Grab that bag of chips," I mumbled to Cali as I grabbed three plates and headed outside.

As we rounded the corner of the barn, I could hear a vehicle heading up the hill from the main road. We paused to see who it was. As the dust settled, I swallowed hard. Natasha was in the passenger seat of Bernice Armstrong's Jeep, and she was staring at the burnt-out shell of her home.

"Oh, God," Cali whispered, "she's never gonna forgive me for burnin' down her house."

"It was an accident," Poppy stated. "She knows that."

"Accident or not, it's still my fault, and I plan to make it right," Cali vowed, then set the food down on Poppy's car, squared her shoulders, and headed for Natasha.

Poppy and I hung back to give Cali privacy for what came next. And what came next made my throat hurt. Natasha turned her head when Cali tapped on the window, then opened the door and got out, pulling Cali into a deep bear hug. I could see Cali's shoulders shake as she cried on Natasha's shoulder, all while Natasha ran her hand down Cali's back in motherly comfort, further emphasizing what a decent human being Natasha was.

When Cali pulled back, Poppy and I moved forward and offered hugs of our own.

"How is Boris?" I whispered.

"He's good. Out of surgery. He's groggy and will probably sleep most of the day, but the doctors seem to think he'll make a full recovery."

"That's good news," I said, smiling.

"He's too bullheaded to leave me just yet," she replied, then looked back at the house. "But just in case, let's keep the fire to ourselves until he's stronger."

"We've been searching for anything that made it through the fire," I explained. "I found a box of photographs that was shielded from the heat in a cabinet."

"There's nothin' in there worth worryin' about," Natasha said. "I uploaded my photos to the cloud a few years back, and the furniture is easily replaced. As long as you girls are safe, that's all that matters."

"We're fine," Poppy stated. "Bo got us out in the nick of time."

Natasha turned and looked at me. "He's a fine piece of manhood. I take it he belongs to you?"

"He did the pursuin'," Bernice commented, smiling. "Just like I thought he would."

"Just as it should be," Eunice Armstrong muttered from behind her sister. "My Odis Lee could teach all these young men a thing or two about goin' after what they want."

Bernice scoffed. "The man should count his 'Lucky Star' you're even speakin' to him."

Odis Lee was in the dog house with Bernice. He'd spied on their family for Cali's grandfather, feeding the man information for years, and in the process, fell in love with Eunice.

"I don't have to 'Justify My Love' to you."

"Here they go," Cali muttered. "They love Madonna," she continued. "They use her song titles in most arguments."

"That's so cool," Poppy said, then threw out, much to my dismay, "Sienna was 'Like A Virgin' 'til last night, but Bo was all 'Give Me All Your Luvin'', so now she's 'Burning Up' for him."

All three older women blinked, then looked at me.

I blurted out, "'Papa Don't Preach!'" when their mouths opened in retort.

Nate took that moment to step out of the house. He scanned our group and shook his head, mumbling, "They owe me big time for this," then turned and walked back inside.

Natasha was the first to speak. "Who was that, and can I keep him?"

"THAT is Nate. Devin's best friend," Cali answered.

"Who is Devin?" Natasha asked.

"Devin is my man," she replied, proudly.

"Is he here, too?"

"Yep. He and Bo are up the mountain bringin' down the cattle with Troy and Brantley."

"They'll be lookin' for a while. I saw the herd on old man Craig's land as we came up."

"How'd they get there?" Poppy asked.

Natasha shrugged. "I imagine the fence came down again and they moseyed on over. It's happened before."

"Would Troy and Brantley know this?" Cali asked.

Natasha cocked her head and thought for a moment. "Doubtful. Last time they got out was before they hired on. I'll radio them and tell them where to look."

I shook my head. "Radios were in the house. Do the cell phones work that high up?"

"It's a crapshoot. Sometimes they do, sometimes they don't."

I pulled out my phone and tried Bo. It rang, but no answer. "It's not goin' through," I sighed.

"How about that Clint Black I hired?"

"He must have gone with them. We haven't seen him in a few hours."

Her shoulders sunk on a deep sigh. I could see the exhaustion written in the lines of her face. Boris and the fire were taking a toll on the woman.

"We'll go find them," I said.

"What about the promise we made not to leave Nate's sight?" Cali whispered.

"Sometimes promises have to be broken for the greater good," I whispered back, jerking my head toward Natasha. "Nate won't leave to go find them because he can't keep an eye on us if he does, so that leaves us. We'll have to sneak off."

"How do we get past him?" Poppy asked.

"Easy. I'll sic Eunice and Bernice on him," Cali chuckled.

"Four-wheeler or horse?" Poppy asked.

We looked toward the corral. "ATV," I answered, remembering

my previous attempt on Tiny Dancer. “It will take less time to get situated, and we can make a quick getaway when Nate’s not lookin’.”

“*Or* we could wait for Bo and Devin to return,” Cali threw out.

I thought about that for a moment, then remembered a storm was coming in that night. It was one of the reasons they wanted the herd in the lower pasture. “Storm’s comin’. They need to move the herd before nightfall.”

Cali nodded, then looked over her shoulder toward Nate. “He’s watchin’ us with one eye while he works.”

“I’ll keep him occupied,” Poppy blurted out. “It doesn’t take all three of us to hunt them down.”

I looked at Cali and smiled. Poppy definitely had a thing for Nate.

“Okay. Let’s grab the food and take it into the kitchen, then Cali and I’ll make an excuse we need to grab bottled water.”

“Why are you whisperin’?” Bernice whispered.

I popped my head up and raised my finger to my mouth in a ‘shhh’ sign, then pointed to Nate. “We need a distraction. Bo and Devin left Nate in charge, and he’s watchin us like a hawk. If there wasn’t a storm comin’ in tonight, we’d let it go, but Bo and Devin need to know where the cattle are so they can get them down quickly. Can you help us?”

“Why not send Nate?” she questioned.

“He would never leave us. He promised to keep us safe.”

“Why do they think you’re not safe?” she asked.

“Because they’re Neanderthals,” I answered. “They don’t think women can take care of themselves.”

Bernice’s feminist side curled a lip. “Is that so?”

Bernice being Bernice winked at me, then started for the house. “Nathaniel!” she hollered, as Eunice and Natasha followed. "Natasha had the cutest little pig statue on the first floor. Did you find it?"

"That's my cue," Poppy whispered, then turned and headed up the steps.

Cali and I took the food inside and cleared a spot on what was left of the countertop. Then Cali said loudly, "We need more water."

Nate looked over his shoulder at the food, studied us for a second, then turned back to Bernice and shook his head at whatever she'd said.

"We'll be right back," I shouted as we headed for an opening in the wall. "We left the water in the large cabin."

We looked back at Nate as we hit the courtyard and found him engrossed in something Poppy was saying, so we took off running.

The ATVs were parked outside the horse stall, so we put them in neutral and pushed them out of the barn and through the open gate that led into the pasture.

"He'll come for us the minute we start them up, so we need to hit the ground spinnin'," I said, closing the gate as a barrier between us and Nate.

Cali nodded and climbed on, then turned the key to start.

"Ready?" she asked.

"Let's do this," I answered, climbing on the back of my ATV. "On the count of—"

"Don't even think about it," Nate thundered, running toward us. He looked ready to kill.

I looked at Cali and mouthed, "three," then started my ATV and gunned it. She followed suit, and we were flying across the pasture as a litany of expletives echoed loudly in our ears.

We made it to the upper pasture thirty minutes later and found it empty. Scanning the horizon, Cali found the downed fence and pointed. We gunned the ATVs and headed to the opening and through it. Pausing on the other side, I switched off the engine so we could talk.

"If we found the downed fence, then they did, too. Do you think they already located the herd?" I asked Cali.

"Probably, but I think we should head down there and make sure."

Nodding, I started my ATV, and we took off toward the road.

Twenty minutes later, we could see cows dotting the landscape. They were grazing on bright green grass, leisurely meandering around the flat land, but Bo and Devin were nowhere in sight.

As we approached the herd, I could tell from the size there were more than a few missing. Most were clustered in one area, but a few were scattered here and there, so out of curiosity, I turned left and headed toward three. Just like I thought they would, the cattle turned toward the safety of the herd and trotted after them. Cali hooted loudly and headed for another four that were near a tree. As she came up behind them, they, too, ran toward the herd.

Smiling, I waved Cali over.

"This isn't too hard," she laughed.

"Right? If there were a gate on this side, we could have them home in half an hour. I can see the top of the barn from that rise."

"We could make an opening in the fence," Cali suggested.

I looked at the fence line. It was an old split rail fence aged to a light gray by the sun, with barbed wire curling around it.

"Check your toolbox and see if you have a cutting tool," I said, turning in my seat and opening mine. The inside was stuffed full of tools. I dug through and found what looked to be wire cutters. "Think these will work?"

Cali pulled out a pair of gloves and tossed them to me. "Use these, so you don't cut your hands."

We climbed off the ATVs and made a wide arc around the herd until we reached the fence. I picked a section that was right in the middle of the grazing cattle and pulled on the gloves.

"Lift up the rail, and I'll cut the wire."

Cali tugged until I had enough room to get the wire cutters underneath. I clamped hold with both hands, grunting as I put pressure on the wire. They bit into the hard metal, but I wasn't strong enough to sever it completely.

"Give me a hand," I said.

Cali lowered the rail and grabbed hold of the end of the cutters. With a deep breath, we both squeezed hard. My muscles began to shake just as the wire gave under our force. With a ping, it snapped, burying itself into my left forearm.

I let out a scream and yanked out the sharp barb without thinking.

"Please tell me you've had a tetanus shot recently," Cali said on a gasp.

"I have no clue," I groaned. "Probably."

The cut stung more than it bled, so I ignored it and began unwinding the wire from around the top rail. Five minutes later, we pulled the top rail out of the post and followed it with the bottom one.

Then we turned and looked at the herd.

"ATVs?" Cali asked.

"Yep."

I glanced up the hill as we climbed on, looking for Bo. There was still no sign of him. "I think the guys must be hunting down the missing cows."

"How do you know there are missin' cows?"

"We were checkin' on them when Boris had his heart attack. I'd say half the herd is missin'."

"Then let's get these steaks home so they don't have to worry about them," she said and gunned her ATV to life.

She pointed to the right side of the herd, and I nodded, pointing to the left as I started mine up.

We moved slowly toward the cattle, pausing as they moved closer together. When the front cows started to move to the left, I took off to discourage them. It took a good ten minutes, but finally, with the prompting of hooting and gunning the engines, the herd began flowing through the opening in the fence. Once the others saw an escape from our noise, they took it as well, and within ten minutes of the first crossing the property line, the whole herd had passed through quickly, fleeing our torment for the pasture.

Cali and I hooted with triumph when the final cow trotted across, high-fiving each other on a job well done, then drove the ATVs through the opening and climbed off. We were picking up the bottom rail to secure the fence when a shout came from up the hill. We both looked up and saw four men on horseback pushing cattle down the hill. Two broke from the herd and raced down the hill, came to a sliding stop in front of us as we covered our eyes with our hands.

I smiled brightly at Bo as he approached, but it faded when I took in the thunderous expression on his face.

"What the fuck are you doin' out here?" he bellowed.

I looked at Cali and swallowed hard. "Natasha saw the herd when she came home, so we came out here to tell you. We couldn't find you, so we took down the fence so they could go home."

"And Nate let you?" Devin bit out, looking equally murderous.

"Um," Cali stuttered. "We kinda—"

"Snuck off," Devin finished for her, raising a brow.

I chanced a look at Bo and caught him staring at my arm.

"You're injured," he snapped.

"It's nothin'."

His eyes shot to mine. "It'd be nothin' if you'd stayed where we left you. Christ, you could have been killed if a bull had been around."

"Well, he wasn't, and we're fine," I defended.

"Yeah, you're fine this time, but that's twice I've asked you not to take a risk, but you can't seem to help yourself. You're too impulsive and headstrong for your own good."

I could almost hear the words *just like my mother* in his accusation, and I turned my back on him and picked up the fence rail, shoving it into the joint, securing the opening so he couldn't follow me quickly.

"I'm heading back," I told Cali without looking at Bo.

"I want you to wait for me," Bo ordered.

I stopped, looked back at him, saying "I don't think waitin' is gonna solve this problem, do you?" then kept on walking to the ATV and climbed on.

I heard Bo cuss under his breath, but I ignored him and started the ATV. I was done. I should have trusted my instincts and kept my distance once I learned about his past and why he'd held me at arm's length. I would always remind him of his mother. Better to end it now before I lost my heart so completely I'd never recover.

Cali called out to me as I gunned the engine, but I took off. I held on to my anger as I pushed the ATV to its limit. I could break down later when I was alone. I'd have Poppy drive me to the nearest bus station and get the hell out of Dodge, maybe head to Atlanta for what was left of my vacation.

The tears began to fall as the burnt-out shell of Boris and Natasha's home came into view. How could I leave them when they needed my help? But how could I stay and suffer through being around Bo?

Nate must have heard the ATV as I approached, because he was standing with his arms crossed over his chest, waiting as I arrived. He took one look at my face as I pulled up and his anger fled, followed by worry.

"What's wrong? Where's Calla?"

"She's with Devin," I choked out, then jumped off the ATV to look for Natasha. I figured I had at least thirty minutes before Bo made it back here with the rest of the herd. By then I could have begged Natasha's forgiveness for bailing on her and be on the road to the bus station.

I'd made it halfway through the barn when the thundering sound of hoofbeats broke through my heartache. I turned to find Bo hot on my heels. He flew past Nate and came to a halt inches in front of me.

"We're not done," he rumbled low, then slid off the back of Goliath.

"Yes, we are," I said, swallowing hard to control my tears. "I can't change who I am, Bo. If I could, I would have done it years ago and saved myself years of heartache."

His brows pinched together in confusion and he cocked his head to the side. "Why the fuck are we talkin' about you changin'?"

"You don't want me to act like your mother. You don't want me to act like *me*. Newsflash, I'm not gonna change."

"I never asked you to change," he sighed, pinching the bridge of his nose for patience.

The action tweaked my anger, and the heartache I'd been feeling fled. My father used to pinch the bridge of his nose when he was tired of dealing with me.

"Don't," I bit out. "Don't stand there and lie to me. We had a great night and took a chance it might lead to something, but we both know this isn't gonna work. I'm leavin', so you don't have to pretend any longer."

His eyes narrowed, and he took a step closer, leaning in a hairsbreadth away. He scanned my face for a moment, searching for something. "I never saw you as a quitter," he mumbled.

I sucked air into my lungs. I felt like I'd been slapped.

"I'm not a quitter!" I shouted, shoving him in the chest.

He didn't move back an inch. Instead, he moved in closer.

"You're a quitter if you walk away from me over a stupid fight."

"Stop callin' me a quitter!" I shouted louder.

"Then stop actin' like one and fight for us instead of throwin' in the towel the minute I lose my temper."

"You lost your temper because I remind you of your mother, and you don't like the comparison."

On a "Jesus, Christ" Bo grabbed my arm and began pulling me out of the barn. I stumbled over my feet as I tried to tug my arm away, grousing, "Let me go," as we went, but I stopped struggling when I saw we had an audience. Natasha, Eunice, Poppy, and Bernice were watching us from the courtyard with varying degrees of hilarity written across their faces.

Bo didn't say a word until he'd opened the door to the first cabin, then locked it behind us, pressing me into the door with his body to keep me in place.

I turned my head so I wouldn't have to look into his piercing gray eyes. That didn't stop Bo from getting his point across, though. He ran his fingers into my hair and tugged gently until my neck was open to him. He laid soft kisses up my neck until he reached my ear, then nipped my lobe, causing my body to shudder in reaction.

"I don't give a fuck who you act like. I was pissed because the thought of you being injured brings out the worst in me. When I saw you on the ATV and realized you'd moved the cattle, I became irrational with what could have happened."

"You don't shout at someone you're worried about. You don't point out their flaws if you don't want them to change."

Bo pulled back and met my eyes. He looked confused. "You don't shout at . . . Baby, didn't your parents shout at you when you put yourself in harm's way?"

"My parents didn't talk to me unless they had to. And most of the time it was to tell me everything I was doin' was wrong or that I needed to change."

"Jesus, that explains a lot."

"Good. I'm glad one of us understands them. As for us, I still don't think—"

"Then think again," he growled. "You're not walkin' out of my life because you haven't got a clue what it feels like to be loved."

I blinked, then whispered, "What did you say?" on a whoosh of air.

"You heard me. My mother may have left me behind 'cause she was selfish, but in the short time I had her in my life, I knew she loved me. Knew what it felt like to be loved. It's clear you don't."

I swallowed. He was right. I didn't. "What does it feel like to love someone?"

"It feels like warmth, anger, passion, and an uncontrollable need to protect. You feel scared at the thought the other might get hurt. It makes you argue over stupid shit and laugh at the ridiculous. Keeps you from quittin' or lettin' the person you care about quit in the heat of the moment. You fight to keep it, 'cause you have no choice." He raised my hand and put it to his chest. I could feel his heart beating out a rapid beat. "I don't want to change a single thing about you, baby," he said gently, then brushed a kiss across my mouth. "'Cause in *my* eyes, you're perfect just the way you are, flaws and all."

My bottom lip began to tremble. I was in so deep with this man.

"Wallflowers don't have flaws," I choked out. "We just see the world differently. And because of that, we need a certain type of man."

Bo brushed a tear from my cheek, then leaned his forehead against mine. "And what kind of man is that?" he asked softly.

"Only the best kind of man. A hero," I whispered. "One who can save us from our pasts."

Both of his hands came up and cupped my face, and he closed his eyes, breathing out, "Christ, you're killin' me."

"You asked me once if I was a dream," I continued. "Well, you are to me. A dream I've had since I was a little girl. The man who would slay my dragons."

Bo sucked in a breath. "My childhood dreams were nothin' like you," he whispered. "They were never this beautiful."

"Bo, you have to know I'll probably screw up—"

"I don't care. Screw up all you want, I can take it. But right now, no more talkin'. I need to be inside you," he rumbled low, hot and angry, cutting me off. "If you're too sore from last night, you need to tell me now, because once I start, I won't be able to stop."

My heart began to pound in my chest. Soreness be damned. I wanted Bo inside me more than I wanted the air I breathed, so I grabbed the hem of my shirt and pulled it from my body.

Bo let his eyes drop to my chest, then they came back to my face.

"Take the rest off and lie on the couch," he ordered then grabbed the back of his shirt and pulled it over his head.

With shaking hands, I unbuttoned my jeans and began to kick off my boots. Bo wasn't touching me, and it left me feeling empty. I needed the connection to his skin, so I leaned in and brushed a kiss across his chest. In a flash, I found myself pinned against the door, with my hands held above my head.

"If you do that again, you'll find yourself bent over the back of the couch with your ass in the air. I'm wound too tight right now for games."

I'd like to say I listened, but my body reacted to the threat, and I rubbed my breasts against his chest, reveling in the feel of his hard lines against my softer curves. His reaction was instantaneous. One moment I was pinned to the door, the next I was backed into the couch and Bo was kissing me wet, deep, and thoroughly intoxicating.

When he broke from the kiss, my head was spinning and unable to process the speed at which he was moving. My jeans were gone before I knew he had his hands on them, then I was bent over the couch, grabbing hold of the edge for balance. I expected Bo to strip out of his jeans and enter me, but he spread my legs wider and then kneeled to the ground instead, putting his mouth on me. I jerked at the contact, still adjusting to having a man touch me so intimately, only to gasp when a firm hand landed on my ass, squeezing the muscle to the point of pain as I moaned at the sensations flooding my system.

"Don't move," Bo growled, then began working my clit with his tongue.

I moved against his mouth instinctively, clawing the couch with my nails when another sound slap landed on my backside.

"You like being disciplined?" Bo husked out, nipping at the inside of my leg.

I guess I did, because I wiggled my ass in answer.

A low chuckle sounded through the room before he stood between my legs and pulled my head back.

I looked back at him with hooded eyes, then reached for his

neck and pulled his mouth to mine. I could taste myself on his lips, and I moaned as he worked his jeans off, then I let go and grabbed the edge of the couch, lifting my ass in anticipation. I needed him inside me as soon as possible, so he could quench the desire ravaging my system. Seconds later, the tip of his cock brushed against my opening, only to disappear. I turned and looked back at Bo, ready to protest. He was staring between my legs, his hand wrapped around his cock, gently running up and down the shaft.

"Bo, please," I begged.

His eyes rose to mine. "You're fuckin' beautiful," he growled, then leaned down and took my mouth again as he positioned himself and then entered me slowly.

I whimpered as he filled me, sore from the night before, but I pushed through it and relaxed into his rhythm, pushing back until he was fully seated deep within my walls.

His pace increased as I lost all control, ramming down hard on his upward thrust, looking for that place where time stood still for a brief, beautiful moment.

I was reaching for the precipice, concentrating only on the feel of Bo's hands on my breasts, when he let go and found my clit, rolling it while a finger entered my backside. I ignited from the pressure and called out in a raspy voice as I hurtled over the edge. Bo kept at me, rebuilding a spark into a flame until I was ready to explode again, but he stopped suddenly and pulled out. I looked back at him, hungry for him to finish what he'd built, and my breath stole from my body. Bo was looking at me with such want that a knot caught in my throat.

"I want your ass," he growled. "I want to claim every inch of your body."

I swallowed hard at the thought, then nodded, excited and scared of the unknown.

Moving back between my legs, Bo lifted my ass higher, then leaned down and nipped it, running his hand over the muscle. His hand disappeared between my legs, and then fingers entered my core, pumping twice before flicking my clit and retreating. I took a deep breath to relax, but tensed when he ran the wet digits around my back entrance.

"We need to work up to my cock. I'll hurt you if we don't, so I won't take you there today."

On a shaking breath, I asked, "How do we work up to that?"

He circled my entrance again and then pushed in slowly. It felt fuller than before and my breath caught at the heightened sensation. So I pushed back against the intrusion and swiveled my hips.

"You like that?" Bo asked huskily, and I nodded.

He pulled back, then slowly entered me again, and I whimpered. The fullness had doubled, and I began to shake with need. Instead of hurting like I thought it would, the pain amplified my arousal, causing my clit to pound.

"Bo!" I moaned low.

"I could come just watchin' you writhe on my hand," he hissed, then pulled out and pushed back in.

"I need you," I cried out.

"I'm right here," he answered, then slid his cock back inside me and swiveled his hips. I erupted again instantly, my atoms splitting in an orgasm so powerful that I forgot to take a breath. I slumped forward like a noodle once my release was spent and Bo's hand left my backside. Moments later, he pulled my limp body from the couch and picked me up. I slumped against him as he headed for a bedroom and lay me down on cool, crisp sheets.

I opened my arms and legs immediately, and he settled between them, sliding back inside me as he claimed my mouth.

He moved slowly this time, touching every nerve as he glided between my walls, building yet another orgasm. I held on tight, my nails biting into the skin on his back as his pace increased.

I tensed as my third orgasm hit me, throwing my head back in sweet surrender, and Bo followed on a deep thrust, burying his face in my neck, groaning low with his release.

Sanity hit me within minutes, and I turned my head to hide the blush creeping up my face. I was addicted to Bo. Addicted to what he could do to my body. I was a wanton woman, as Cali had said, but a dirty one at that. I'd heard stories from other women about how much anal sex hurt. That no woman could possibly love it. But all I could think about at that moment was how long it would take to train my body to accept him, and how soon we could try again.

Poppy and Cali would kick me out of the club if they knew how kinky I really was.

"You okay?" Bo mumbled in my neck, tasting the skin before trailing a line with his tongue up to my ear.

I nodded, then wrapped him tighter in my embrace. He was still inside me, and I didn't want to lose the connection.

"Are you just sayin' that or are you really okay? Don't keep shit from me, babe. I need to know if I'm hurtin' you in any way."

I nodded again, so he pulled back and looked at me.

A slow grin pulled across his mouth. "She's okay," he chuckled, then kissed me slowly and thoroughly. My body responded instantly to his mouth, and my hands began to wander. But they stopped when Bo began to shake with laughter.

"What?" I asked.

"I've created a monster," Bo replied, rolling to his side.

I turned and rested my cheek on his chest.

"Are you complaining that you turn me on?"

Bo closed his eyes with a smile. "Not hardly."

"Did you not enjoy yourself?" I asked, poking his chest.

One eye opened, and it looked insulted, then he pulled me up his chest and kissed me soundly. "What do you think?" he whispered against my lips.

I wiggled my brows, then pushed up from his chest on a giggle, announcing, "Then you'll love this," as I rolled and dashed from the room, heading for the bathroom.

I heard Bo groan, "She'll kill me within a year," as he exited the bed. Grinning, I turned the knob to the bathroom door and pushed it open, stepping inside.

Then I let out a bloodcurdling scream as the room began to spin.

Ten

CLINT BLACK

FROZEN IN PLACE, I MOVED when I heard Bo shout my name and fled the bathroom right into a solid wall of muscle. Strong arms wrapped around me, followed by Bo's whispered, "I've got you."

"Clint," I gasped out, "in there"—I pointed toward the bathroom—"he's dead."

Bo didn't register surprise at my outburst; he just tried to push me behind him and growled, "Go back to the bedroom and wait for me."

I shook my head. I wasn't going anywhere without him.

"Baby, I need to look at the body, and you need to get dressed."

He had a point. The police would be called, and naked Sienna wasn't a good look. "Come with me to get our clothes, and then you can lock me in the bedroom," I begged.

Nodding, Bo wrapped his arm around my shoulders and led me back into the living room, where he pulled on his jeans. I quickly threw his shirt on to cover my nakedness, then grabbed my clothes from the floor and pulled him back to the bedroom.

"I'll give you your shirt back in a minute," I said as he started to shut the door. He scanned my body, mumbled, "Keep it. I like it on you," then shut the door. I locked it behind him and rushed to get dressed. Then I remembered I had my phone in my back pocket and called Devin.

"Yeah?"

"Clint Black is dead. He's in the bathroom in the large cabin," I blurted out. "Bo needs you."

"Jesus Christ," was his response, then, "on my way," before he hung up.

When I heard raised voices heading toward the cabin, I unlocked the bedroom door and shouted, "Devin's here," as I ran to unlock the main cabin door.

Devin came rushing in, dragging Cali behind him, with Poppy and Nate right on his heels. The cabin exploded in a frenzy of questions, and Bo exited the bathroom looking grim. I tossed him his shirt and he pulled it back on, then got right to the point. "Black's dead," Bo bit out.

"This situation keeps escalatin'," Devin growled.

Bo reached for my hand, turning me toward him. "I don't want you out of my sight, but I need to check the scene thoroughly with Devin and Nate. Can you ladies stay right here and not touch anything?" I nodded, and he squeezed my hand once before letting me go.

Moving to Cali and Poppy, I huddled with them, watching all three men as they disappeared into the bathroom, trying to keep from freaking out.

"I can't believe Clint's dead," Poppy whispered. I turned to her and nodded, then closed my eyes, trying not to picture him as he lay on the floor. It was no use. He'd died with his eyes open, a shocked look still present on his face, as if his attacker had snuck up on him or someone he trusted had surprised him.

"Was there blood?" Cali asked nervously. "I don't think I can handle another bloody body this week."

I shook my head rapidly, trying to push down the panic I felt. "He had a bruise around his neck. Like someone strangled him," I answered.

Minutes later, Bo exited the bathroom with a furious look on his face. "Window was open, and there's a dirty footprint on the toilet. Whoever killed him was probably inside when you came in to make sandwiches. They snuck out the window to avoid bein' seen."

Cold fear trickled through my veins. "How do you know he was in here when we came in?"

"Because Nate saw Clint when he went into the barn for a hammer. He said it was five minutes tops before you headed here, and he hasn't seen him since."

"Then we walked in right after he, he . . ."—I swallowed to keep from crying—"died."

Bo nodded. "He probably heard you comin' and dragged Black into the bathroom to hide the body, then crawled out the window to escape."

"That's why the chair was tipped over," I gasped. "Oh, God. He *was* in here when we made the sandwiches."

"First the fire, and now Clint?" Poppy gasped. "How do we end up in these situations?"

"And the cattle," Devin added.

"The cattle? What happened to the cattle?" Cali asked.

"Someone pulled down the fence. That's how they got out. We assumed it was the old man who lives next door, but considerin' Black is dead, I don't believe it now."

"This is crazy. It's nuts," I blurted out. "Who'd want to hurt Boris and Natasha like this?"

Bo's eyes shot to mine. "What did you say?"

"I said, who would want to hurt Boris and Natasha. You can't tell me all these things aren't related. It's too much. It's frankly unbelievable at this point. The fire. The cattle. Now Clint . . . NUTS!"

He swung around and looked at Devin. "She's right. We've been lookin' at this all wrong. This doesn't have anything to do with Daniels or the Wallflowers, and I'd bet my paycheck that the fire wasn't Calla's fault either."

"You're sayin' someone is tryin' to ruin Boris and Natasha, and what? Black stumbled across them or was involved, and it got him killed?" Devin asked, incredulous.

"That's exactly what I'm sayin'," Bo answered and then waited for Devin to come to the same conclusion.

Devin mulled it over for a moment and then nodded. "Would make more sense than some punk biker followin' the girls up here. That never fit."

"Wait, then I *didn't* burn down their house?" Cali asked, looking hopeful.

Devin shook his head. "Someone's watchin' us closely. They used the fact we grilled last night to cover their tracks."

"But who?" I asked. "Who would want Boris and Natasha ruined enough to commit murder?"

We all looked toward the bathroom, where poor Clint Black was lying on the cold tile floor.

"That," Bo growled as he grabbed my hand and started leading me out of the cabin, "is what I'm gonna find out. But first, we need to make sure you ladies are safe."

"I thought you said we were safe as long as we're with you?"

"You are. But I can't be in two places at once. We'll head to town and book rooms at a hotel. You'll be safe there while we're figurin' this shit out."

I nodded. I was fine with being as far away from the ranch

as possible. "We'll bring the aunts and Natasha as well, right?"

"Yeah," he growled. "I need to speak with Natasha. Someone has it out for them, and I need to know why."

"I'll call the sheriff," Devin said, pulling out his phone.

"I'll call Aunt Martine and let her know I'll be a few more days," Nate stated, pulling out his own phone. "She'll be thrilled, since she loves teasin' the college boys who come into my bar."

We rounded the corner of the barn and found Bernice, Eunice, and Natasha waiting for us. They were on alert, watching the six of us anxiously.

"We have a situation," Bo announced.

"Well, spit it out. It can't be any worse than what I've been through in the past twenty-four hours."

Bo glanced at me, then got right to the point as usual. One thing I've learned about Bo, he doesn't mince words. "Clint Black is dead. Murdered. We think someone's tryin' to ruin you."

Natasha sank down on a step as Cali's aunts gasped. "I was wrong," she muttered. "You *were* able to top the last day."

Bernice and Eunice sat down next to her, and each took one of her hands in comfort.

"Can you think of anyone who would want to hurt you?" Devin asked.

Natasha shook her head. "We've never harmed a soul, keep mostly to ourselves. It's just Boris, me, and the ranch hands."

"Has anyone come around recently inquirin' about the place?" Bo asked.

She shook her head again. Worry pulled at her features, and I became concerned that the stress might be too much.

"We should get them to town. Settle her into a hotel room so she can rest," I said to Bo.

He nodded in agreement, then turned and looked toward the barn. Then he put his lips to his teeth and blew a sharp whistle.

Troy and Brantley emerged from the shadows as if Bo had trained them to follow his command, and made their way over, looking at us with interest.

"Is somethin' wrong?" Troy finally asked.

"Black is dead. Murdered," Bo answered.

Both men blinked, then bit out, "By whom?" at the same time.

"That," Bo growled, "is the question of the day. We'll get to that as soon as we settle the ladies into a hotel. Grab two of the vehicles and start loading up their stuff, yours, too. The whole ranch is a crime scene until further notice."

Catham County Sheriff, Justin Moore, peeled out of his SUV and stretched, then he scanned the front of the hotel where Bo, Sienna, and the rest were staying. Bo looked at Devin just as his jaw tightened for control. Five days earlier, the same sheriff had interrogated Devin and Calla in the death of Charles Taft, a reporter who was keeping tabs on Devin for Calla's grandfather. His interrogation of Calla didn't sit well with Devin, nor did the card he gave her with instructions she should call him *any* time, no matter the reason.

"Is this gonna be a problem for you?" Bo asked with a grin.

"Nope. 'Cause he's not gettin' Calla alone again."

Bo rolled his bottom lip between his teeth to keep from smiling.

Moore entered the conference room they'd sequestered for the meeting and scanned the space. Instead of coming straight to Bo and Devin, he walked up to Calla and smiled. Then he turned to Poppy and Sienna, and his smile widened.

"Ladies," Moore drawled smoothly, then looked back at Calla. "I was more than a little surprised when I saw your name as one of the witnesses."

"I don't mean to keep findin' bodies," Calla rushed out.

Moore raised his hand to stop her. "I said, surprised, not suspicious."

"Is he purposely ignorin' us?" Devin asked.

Bo didn't answer. He was too busy watching Moore flash his million-dollar smile at Sienna.

"Player," Bo mumbled.

"Not a player," Devin answered. "Just cocky as hell."

Done with introductions, Moore finally turned his attention to the men and put out his hand.

"Detective, good to see you again," Moore said, then turned his attention to Devin. "Hawthorne, how's Armstrong treatin' you these days?"

"Like shit, so I think he's warmin' to me," Devin answered, shaking Moore's hand.

Moore flashed his smile at both men, then, done with the niceties, ordered, "Run this down for me from the top."

Devin turned to Bo and raised a brow. "I'll let you cover this."

Bo raised a brow in response, then turned to Moore and laid out what he knew.

"Black was found by Sienna Miller," Bo started. "He'd been dead two hours when she found him. No intruders were seen on the property. Everyone who was supposed to be on the ranch was accounted for. No one had the means or opportunity at the time they were alone. We suspect the fire and release of cattle onto the neighbor's property are also involved. Either the unknown perp has a score to settle with Boris and Natasha Winkle, or Black was runnin' from someone, and the rest is pure coincidence."

Bo expected Moore to ask further questions, but the man turned instead and looked at the table where the Wallflowers were sitting. "Is Miller the blonde or brunette?"

"She's the taken one," Bo clipped matter-of-factly. "The brunette's her friend Poppy Gentry."

"Poppy's taken as well," Devin added quickly when he saw Nate enter the room, "just like Calla."

Moore grinned, looked back at the Wallflowers, and shrugged. "A man would have to be blind not to notice."

"Noticin' is one thing; handin' out your card in an attempt to keep in contact with her is another. Not when you know she's got a man."

Moore raised his hands in surrender. "An oversight on my part. It won't happen again."

"What won't happen again?" Nate asked as he joined them.

"Moore here was just askin' about Poppy," Devin lied.

"What about her?" Nate replied, leveling Moore with a look of steel.

Moore turned, then sighed when he realized his eyes were level with Nate's jaw. "Jesus, Hawthorne. Your point was made," he grumbled.

"What point was made?" Nate asked, crossing his arms.

"That Moore here is barkin' up the wrong tree," Bo said. "Now, do you want to take each of our statements as a group or separate?"

"He wants to take our statements as a group," Devin rumbled low.

Moore looked at Devin and nodded. "Group is fine. I have no reason to suspect any of you. I've spoken with Mrs. Winkle on the phone, and she explained that Black approached her about a job at the hospital. It seems that, once again, you and your friends are at the wrong place at the wrong time."

"Or we're exactly where we're supposed to be," Bo argued. "Seems to me that a lot of harm would have come to these good people if we hadn't come."

"That's another way to look at it," Moore agreed. "Let's get the formalities out of the way so you can be on your way."

Devin shook his head slowly. "We're not leavin'."

Moore glanced at Bo. "Are you steppin' on my investigation?"

Bo crossed his arms. "We're here on vacation. Five days of horseback ridin' and campfires."

Moore's mouth twitched. "Right. Then let's get you back to singin' Kumbaya under the night sky."

Nate watched Moore head back to the Wallflowers, then looked at Devin questionably. "Asshole?"

"He's the sheriff who gave Calla his card," Bo informed Nate, reminding him of the night at Poe Publishing when Calla had dropped that tidbit of information.

"So, asshole," Nate replied.

"That about covers it," Devin grumbled, then moved to sit by Calla, slinging his arm tightly around her shoulders.

"He's in deep, isn't he?" Nate said, watching Devin.

Bo caught the smile Moore flashed Sienna as he handed her a pen, and his gut clenched.

"Yeah. He's in deep. Can't help but be," Bo stated as he moved past Nate, ready to pound his chest while he threw Sienna over his shoulder.

"Why's that?" Nate called out.

Bo turned and decided he'd give Nate a heads-up. "Wallflowers burrow under your skin and wrap around your heart. There's no escapin' them once they grab hold. Think about that."

"Gin," Poppy said, grinning.

"What? But you've only drawn two cards," Cali cried out.

I snorted, rolling to my side. I was lying on the bed in Bo's and my room, chatting with the Wallflowers while he, Devin, and Nate were off hunting down information that would shed light on Black's murder. Hamburger wrappers littered every surface of our room as the scent of onions mingled with air freshener. After spending two days on the ranch, being shut in a room with one window and no ventilation made me a tad claustrophobic and feeling antsy.

"We need to do somethin' to help," I said, sitting up. "I'm not meant to sit around and do nothin'!"

Poppy shuffled the deck, ignoring me, and started dealing out cards.

"Remember what happened the last time we took matters into our own hands?" Cali asked as she picked up each card she'd been dealt.

"We saved you from a mad woman hell-bent on endin' your life?"

Cali shuddered and shook her head. "I meant the most recent attempt to help."

"You mean when we found the cows and got them home with nary a scratch?"

"That's the one," she answered, picking up a card from the deck. "Didn't you end up in a fight with Bo for taking chances with your safety?"

I flopped back on the bed. "Yeah."

"So you're willing to risk his wrath again?"

"No. But that doesn't mean we can't help in a *non*-life-threatenin' way. We could, I don't know, go to the local diner and ask around. Wouldn't the locals know if someone had it out for Boris and Natasha?"

"Gin," Poppy called out triumphantly.

"Bullocks," Cali shouted. "Do you have another deck hidden in your lap?"

I sat up and glared at my two friends. "Aren't you the least bit curious what the heck is goin' on?"

Poppy rolled her eyes. "Of course, I am. I'm just waitin' for you two to grow some twiddle diddles and quit worryin' about what Bo and Devin will say."

"Good use of the word *twiddle diddles*," Cali smiled.

"Thank you. I've been waitin' to use it in the proper context."

"As for my twiddle diddles, they're big enough," Cali stated, standing from her chair.

"So, you're in? You'll go with me to the local diner and see if we can stir up any dust?"

"It beats gettin' my derriere kicked."

Poppy snorted. "Let me guess. You can't say *ass*?"

"We aren't startin' this again," Cali sighed.

I smiled at Poppy. "She can't say it."

"Oh, I can say it," Cali replied, grabbing her purse.

"She totally can't say it," Poppy chuckled, opening the hotel room door.

I started to leave, but thought a note saying where we'd gone might smooth things over with Bo, so I grabbed a sheet of paper from the desk drawer to write him one.

"Two seconds," I called out. "I'll just leave Bo a note so he won't worry."

"We could call and let him know," Cali said.

"No. They'd tell us to stay put, and I'll go stir-crazy if I don't get out and do somethin' productive. This way we can't go against them if they cause a fuss."

"I'm pretty sure I heard Bo say not to take any risks. Aren't you goin' against him now?"

I looked at her, then looked at the note. Then I put X's and O's under my signature for good measure, hoping the affection would appease him if he came back before us. Then I wadded it up. He was going to be pissed either way.

"I'll just tell Natasha where we're goin', to be safe. Besides, he told me he didn't want to change a thing about me, so I'm just bein' me."

The thing about small-town Georgia is . . . people find any reason for a celebration. The church got a new roof, have a barbecue. Little Timmy finished kindergarten; throw a graduation party. It seemed this night it was a wedding. Buck married Bill, so they threw a huge-ass party to celebrate love in all its beautiful forms.

Normally, this kind of celebration would be held at the local church, but seeing as the church was still coming to terms with gay marriage, they held the celebration at the local diner.

This was good news for the girls and me for two reasons. For one, most of the men were gay, so we didn't have to worry about being hit on. And two, the crowd was large, so our chances of finding someone who could shed light on Boris and Natasha's situation were good.

Twinkle lights wound around every surface, giving the once chrome and red diner a magical glow, while signs congratulating the happy couple hung from the windows. The cake, featuring two cowboys in denim jeans and western shirts, was a towering feat. Chocolate layers with raspberry filling stood nearly as tall as the happy couple.

The locals pegged us for outsiders the minute we walked in. They eyed us with curiosity and smiles as we pushed our way through the crowd to the cash bar for a glass of wine.

"We aren't dressed for a weddin'," Poppy yelled over the music.

"They won't care," I shouted back. "Half the people here are in jeans."

"So, who should we hit up for gossip?' Cali asked.

A cute teenage girl was walking past us as I scanned the crowd, so I tapped her on the shoulder. "Excuse me."

The girl turned and looked me up and down. "Yeah?"

"If we wanted to know everything there is to know about this town, who would we talk to?"

She crossed her arms in adolescent defiance, then asked suspiciously, "Who wants to know?"

I looked at the girls and bugged out my eyes. "Um, friends of Boris and Natasha Winkle."

That must have been good enough for her because she pointed to a woman with shrewd eyes. She looked to be in her late sixties, with silver hair braided into a bun. She was sitting in the corner watching everyone.

"She looks like she doesn't miss a thing," I told the girl.

"She doesn't," the girl replied, then smiled and walked away.

"Come on," I said, then pushed through the crowd past the towering cake and the two grooms who were shoving cake into each other's mouths. We dodged partygoers as they toasted Buck and Bill, and made our way over to the woman.

She looked up from her phone after taking a picture of the happy couple and smiled at us. "Hi," I shouted over the music. "I'm Sienna Miller and these are my friends, Poppy Gentry and Cali Armstrong. Do you mind if we ask you a few questions?"

"I know who you are," the woman answered. "You're the gals helpin' out Boris and Natasha. Sit a spell and take a load off."

Poppy grabbed a chair and pulled it to the booth, while Cali and I squeezed into the seat opposite the woman.

"We're sorry to bother you during a wedding celebration, Ms.?" I said loudly.

"Name's Irene. Irene Ledbetter. How can I help you?"

I wasn't sure if the town knew about Clint Black's murder, or if the sheriff wanted the news spread, so I went with who would want to hurt Boris and Natasha.

"Boris and Natasha have had some trouble at the ranch. We think someone is tryin' to hurt them, so we thought we'd ask around and see if any of the locals might have information that would shed some light on the situation."

"You're speakin' of the fire and the murder of that drifter."

"You heard about that?" Cali asked.

"I'm the dispatcher for the volunteer fire department. We got the call on the fire *and* the murder."

Bingo. We'd hit pay dirt. I had no doubt she knew where all the skeletons were buried.

"So, do you have any thoughts on who would try to hurt Boris and Natasha?"

"Other than their no-good son?"

"The banker who lives overseas?"

"That's the one. He left town and never looked back, other than to encourage them to sell the ranch to some friend of his."

"When was this?" Poppy asked

"Maybe a month ago. He wanted them to liquidate their holdings and retire to Florida. Asked them if he could have his inheritance sooner rather than later, so he could invest in some brokerage firm. He went as far as to have the land surveyed and the boundary markers set to make sure the total acreage was accounted for. It cost him a pretty penny, considerin' they're sittin' on fifteen hundred acres."

"I take it they didn't agree?" Poppy asked.

"Nope. They told him they'd think about it, but in the end, Boris said he wanted to be buried on his land. They haven't heard from him since."

"What an asshole," Cali spit out, then gasped and covered

her mouth.

Irene let out a cackle of laughter. "No need to worry I'll be offended. I agree. He is an asshole."

"Well, we learned two things for sure," Poppy shouted with a gleam in her eyes. "The son could be involved, and Cali can, indeed, say *ass*."

"Hardy har har," Cali snipped. "But I think you're wrong about one point. It doesn't make sense for the son to burn down the house and set the cattle loose. Those are assets. If he wanted money, then he'd be cutting his nose off to spite his face."

Dang it. Cali was right. Which meant we had nothing.

"Good point," Irene answered.

"Can you think of anyone else?" Poppy asked.

Irene shook her head. "Not a soul. Boris and Natasha are as kind as they come. I can't think of anyone who'd want to hurt them."

"Looks like we're back at square one," I sighed. "We can go back to the hotel if you want."

"Might as well stay and have some cake," Irene said. "It's rainin' now, and the wind's kicked up. You'll get drenched."

I glanced outside. Tree limbs were being blown back and forth as rain swirled around them.

"She's right," Poppy said. "We should wait out the storm."

"This must be the storm Troy was talkin' about. The reason they wanted the cattle moved."

"It's that hurricane that's been sittin' off the coast for days," Irene stated. "It finally came inland. If invitations hadn't already gone out, Buck would have cancelled, but it was too late to call off the weddin'."

"Should we be worried?" I asked, staring out the window.

Lightning streaked across the sky like tiny fingers and we jumped. The storm had come out of nowhere. One minute the air was muggy, the next all hell had broken loose.

"Nothin' to worry about. There's a shelter beneath the diner. If the sirens go off, we'll just head downstairs."

I looked at Cali. "Maybe we *should* call the men, so they won't worry."

She nodded in agreement and pulled out her phone. "The call's not goin' through. It says there's no cell service."

A resounding *crack* echoed through the night air, and then the lights went out, covering us in inky darkness. Everyone went still, hushed voices filtering throughout the diner as we waited to see what would happen next. A low moan that increased in intensity and volume broke the silence and everyone began to scatter like cockroaches. A tornado siren was warning us all to take cover.

Cali and I scooted out of the booth, grabbed Poppy and Irene's hands, and began moving with the crowd as they headed toward the back of the diner. Minutes later, we filed into a concrete bunker with muted lights. We were sandwiched in together like sardines in a can, waiting for the storm to pass.

Fifteen minutes later, when the sirens stopped blaring, we began to filter out from beneath the bowels of the diner with flashlights leading the way. Tree limbs were scattered about the streets willy-nilly, but no damage to the surrounding buildings could be seen. The storm had been all bluster, like a child throwing a tantrum.

"Should we risk it?" I asked the girls.

"Let's give it ten more minutes and make sure the worst is over," Cali said.

The lights came back on in a blinding light, causing everyone to cheer as the music blared.

"Generator finally kicked in," someone shouted. "Took it long enough."

"Beer's on the house," another voice added. "Let's get this party started."

The crowd began moving toward the bar in a crush, so I pulled the girls to the other side so we could watch the storm.

"If all the streets are littered with limbs, we might have a hard time driving back to the hotel," I stated.

"How far is it on foot?" Poppy asked

"Less than a mile," Cali said.

I shook my head. "Too far to risk. Let's wait it out and then try to drive there. If we're lucky, the guys won't even know we were gone."

I felt a tap on my shoulder and spun around. Three women stood behind us smiling.

"Can I help you?"

"Take a turn on the dance floor with us," one with bright red hair said. "Now that the storm has passed, it's time to have some fun."

"Take a turn . . . are you askin' us to dance?" I squeaked out.

"Oh, boy," Poppy mumbled.

"But we're not, you know, lesbians," Cali stuttered.

One of the women, who looked like she pumped weights on a daily basis, grinned knowingly. "We know you aren't . . . yet."

Yet? Oh, dear Lord.

"Then why do you—"

"'Cause we like to dance," the redheaded woman interrupted, grabbing my hand and pulling me to the dance floor.

This was a first for me. I was uncomfortable, but didn't want to cause a scene. I also wasn't sure where I was supposed to put my hands. Was she leading, or was I?

Red decided for me, then began leading me around the floor to Jason Aldean's "She's Country. " I tripped a few times, giggling nervously and repeating, "I'm so sorry," before I got the rhythm of the two-step. Cali and Poppy were laughing, too, enjoying the lighthearted atmosphere as they were spun around the floor. On the third pass around the dance floor, I stopped dead in my tracks. Bo, Devin, and Nate were standing at the front of the diner, and Bo's eyes were locked on me.

I started to wave, relieved to see him, but he shook his head slowly and began making his way through the crowd. When he stopped in front of Red and me, Red scanned him from head to toe, then asked, rather grumpily, I might add, "Is this your man?"

Bo scanned Red from head to foot and back, then took my hand and drew me closer, locking his arm around my neck to keep me close. "I'm her man," he answered low. "Thanks for keepin' an eye out."

Red jerked her head at Bo, then looked at me with a slow, heated smile, and winked. "If you get tired of flyin' straight, you know where to find me."

I blinked, and my eyes grew wide. "Right. Good to know. Thank you for the, ah, dance."

I could feel Bo's chest shaking, so I looked up. I expected him to be angry, but his eyes were glittering with laughter.

"What?"

"Only a Wallflower would have both sides chasin' after her."

Whatever.

I stepped back and crossed my arms. "We told them we were straight, I'll have you know, but they didn't listen."

Bo reached out and snagged my hand with a tug. I slammed into his chest, and he began to dance me around the floor. "You didn't stay put," he accused, keeping perfect rhythm with the music. To say I was shocked he could dance was an understatement.

"We didn't think askin' questions in a crowded diner was life-threatenin'. Besides, I'm capable of takin' care of myself."

"That remains to be seen," Bo murmured. "Evidence suggests the opposite."

I narrowed my eyes. He was so damn arrogant, I wanted to, well, kick him hard enough that he'd know he'd been kicked.

"You know, before you came along, I did a pretty good job. I don't understand why you think I'm some feeble woman who cowers at the slightest noise."

"You? Cower?" Bo chuckled. "Not likely."

"Then why do you insist on keepin' me in a corner while you battle the world?"

"Because I'm a man," Bo bit out. "It's my job to keep you safe."

"Even if I don't need you to?"

"I need you to," was his cryptic answer.

"I'm lost," I replied. "You need me to what, exactly?"

"It's who I am. I need *you* to let *me* be the one who stands between you and everyone else."

"You're sayin' that whether or not I can take care of myself isn't the point. That because of the type of man you are, you need to be the one who protects me?"

Judging by the look on Bo's face, you'd think I'd asked him a trick question. He watched me for a moment, taking in my measure, then nodded sharply, replying, "That's about it."

I opened my mouth, then shut it. I didn't know how to respond to such a caveman attitude.

"So, you don't think I'm feeble?"

"Feeble? No. A magnet for trouble? Hell, yes!"

Considering the past few days, he may have a point.

"Okay."

"Okay, what?"

"Okay, you can protect me."

"Babe . . . it wasn't a choice."

And I was back to wanting to kick him again.

Bo must have decided the discussion was over, because he asked, “Did you learn anything tonight?” as he moved his leg in between mine and spun us around, grinding me down on his thigh.

I gasped and looked up at him. He raised a brow, waiting for me to answer. “We, ah, we spoke to an Irene Ledbetter, who said the only person she could think of who would want to ruin Boris and Natasha was their son.”

With another quick flick, Bo dipped me back fully, then snapped me around until I crashed back into his chest. “But you don’t think it was him,” he rumbled low into my ear. His hot breath on my neck caused my concentration to wander. It was clear he was trying to keep me off balance for some reason, and it was working.

“What?” I asked breathlessly.

Bo ran his nose down the side of my neck, then tasted the skin near my shoulder, asking again, “The son. You don’t think it was him?”

I shook my head. “No,” I groaned out. “Cali pointed out if he’d burnt down the house and set the cattle free, he’d be devaluing the ranch. He’d lose the money he wanted for his investment.”

“Makes sense,” Bo muttered, then undulated his hips, keeping mine pressed close to his. I could feel him hardening through his jeans, and my breath caught. “But it could be it’s the land he wants, not the assets attached.”

It hit me then he already knew about the son. “You already knew, didn’t you?”

Bo dipped me back until my neck was bared, then he leaned down and kissed his way back to my ear. “Yeah, I already knew. But it took diggin’ into records at the courthouse to find out. You got the information in half the time.”

Wrapping my arms around his shoulders, I nuzzled his neck until I heard his own breath catch. Two could play this game. Flattery worked better on men than honey drew bees to a hive. "You're very resourceful gettin' into the courthouse after hours. That's impressive. Did you *find* anything else?"

He paused for a moment, contemplating his answer, then rumbled low, "Yeah. A geological survey was performed by a company based out of Florida last month. It was filed with a real estate company for any future sale."

Florida? Something about that clawed at my memory. Then it hit me, and I burst out with excitement, "Clint Black said he was from Florida. That can't be a coincidence."

Bo disengaged from me and scanned the room, calling out, "Hawthorne!"

Devin was dancing with Cali on the other side of the floor, so he pushed through the crowd, dragging Cali behind him.

"Black was from Florida," Bo announced when Devin stopped beside us. "Moore left out that tidbit of information when we called him."

"The pieces are comin' together," Devin replied. "I bet if we dig deep enough, we'll find a connection."

"Let's get the Wallflowers back to the hotel, then head over to the station. We can dig into Shelton Geological and see if Black worked for them."

"Where's Nate?" Devin asked, ready to go.

I turned and found him in a corner surrounded by several men, and bit my lip to keep from laughing. He looked ready to bolt.

"Does he know this is a gay weddin'?" I asked, pointing him out for Devin.

"He does now," Devin chuckled, then whistled between his teeth and waved him over.

"Poppy's still dancing," Cali shouted over the music. "And we've got our own car. We can find our way back to the hotel. You go on without us."

Bo looked over his shoulder at the downed limbs on the road, then back at me. "Remember what I said about being a magnet for trouble?"

"You can't blame us for Mother Nature."

"With your luck, you should have known somethin' would happen."

I bobbled my head back and forth, then nodded. "Your argument does have merit."

"Do you promise to go straight back?" Devin asked Cali.

She rolled her eyes, then crossed her heart, grinning. "I promise."

Devin looked suspicious, but nodded, then turned to Nate as he walked up. "We're headed to the station to see what we can dig up on Shelton Geological."

"Thank, Christ," Nate grumbled. "I've been hit on three times and got two phone numbers in my back pocket."

"Were they cute?" Cali asked, then burst out laughing when Nate growled at her and then stormed off toward the door.

Bo watched him leave, chuckling, "It's the hair. If he cut it, he'd have less trouble."

Cali and I snorted. "Don't kid yourself. Hair or not, that man will turn heads," I shouted over the music.

Bo raised a brow at me, and I smiled innocently. I might be his woman, but I wasn't blind.

Shaking his head, he curled me into his body, drawling low, "Be safe," before brushing a kiss across my lips.

"You, too. Remember, you're the one chasin' a killer. We're just fendin' off women."

Bo bit his lip to keep from laughing.

"What?"

"Never thought I'd hear you say that."

"What? Be safe?"

"No. That you're fendin' off women with romantic intentions."

I shoved his arm, and he kissed me again, laughing against my lips.

I watched him leave, wondering how late he'd be, then turned back to Cali. As I searched the room for Poppy, my eyes landed on Red, and she winked at me again. Leering almost.

"Um. Did you see that? The woman is definitely persistent."

"Oh, yeah. I'll get Poppy so we can leave," Cali stated.

"I think I'll meet you in the car."

Bo might have thought it was funny I was being pursued by a woman, but Red left me feeling vulnerable.

So vulnerable, the hairs rose on the back of my neck.

Eleven

WALLFLOWERS DON'T LEAVE A WOMAN BEHIND

HEAT HIT MY BACK SOMETIME before dawn, and I relaxed into Bo's chest. Arms like steel covered with warm flesh pulled me deeper into his body, then hands that had only known hard work began to bring me to life. I arched my back when a single finger brushed seductively over my warm heat, teasing, stoking a need in me until I shook, so I grabbed Bo's hand to keep it where I needed it most.

Lacing his fingers with mine, Bo slipped them inside my panties and urged me without words to touch myself. Anxious to please him, I ran a finger through my wetness, then found my clit and rolled it, moaning as prickling sensations rocked my body. My panties disappeared moments later, then Bo lifted my leg as I kept working my clit. With a muffled groan, Bo slid inside me, burying himself completely in a single thrust. I almost came instantly from the beauty of it.

"Been waitin' my whole life for this," he breathed into my ear. "Been waitin' my whole life for you," he continued. "With you, I feel whole again. Like the past doesn't matter," he groaned, then turned my head and claimed my mouth. Our tongues danced frantically as he worked my body into a shuddering mass.

Moments later, light exploded behind my eyes, the colors swirling together as I ignited for him, and I called out his name into the inky darkness of our room.

Bo didn't follow me into the sweet abyss; instead, he kept at me, ordering, "Say it again," as he drove deeper inside me.

I gasped out, "Bo," like he asked, but he grabbed my shoulders, anchoring himself deeper inside me, thrusting harder as he hissed. "Say it again, goddamnit."

With each thrust, I was coming apart at the seams. I was on the precipice again, but Bo wouldn't let me fall. I needed to release the building orgasm before I split in two, so I shouted, "Bo!" louder this time, hoping he'd finish me off.

With a frustrated growl, Bo jerked up, rolled me to my back without a word, and sank back inside me, caressing my walls with his cock agonizingly slowly. I was confused and frustrated to the point of screaming.

"Bo, please," I cried out, bucking hard, trying to find relief as my eyes welled with tears.

"Not 'til you say it again," he hissed as I scored his back.

"I did!" I shouted.

"You said my name," he whispered, laying his forehead against mine, "I want the other words."

My breath caught in my throat at his tenderness, and I thought back to what I'd said. I began to shake with awareness. I hadn't said his name before, I'd begged him to *love* me.

There was no turning back now. No shielding myself. I'd said it, and he wanted me to repeat it.

Reaching up, I cupped his face and brought his mouth to mine, begging once again like I had before. "Please *love* me."

Bo's eyes flashed with heat, and he drove in deep until he

was buried to the hilt, vowing in a hoarse voice full of emotion, "Every fuckin' day for the rest of your life," before slamming his mouth over mine. What my parents had broken inside of me, after years of neglect, sealed shut with Bo's uttered vow.

They say time heals what reason cannot, but I think the Bible said it best. Love bears all things, believes all things, hopes all things, endures all things. Or, simply put, love conquers all.

Time ceased to exist as we rolled around the bed, touching and tasting each other. Bo moved slowly this time, building the heat again until a thick sheen of sweat covered my body. We were both shaking with need when he thrust deeply one final time, igniting the ember to a white-hot flame. With no words spoken, love spilled between those sheets and healed us both, wrapping us in a cocoon that neither time nor space could weaken. For the first time in either of our lives, we were finally home.

Finally secure.

Finally loved for who we were.

I stared at my coffee mug, groggy from lack of sleep, but I didn't mind. Today, I'd woken with a new sense of belonging. The feeling was foreign to me, but I wrapped it around me like a shield. For the first time since I was a child, I felt like I could take on the world and win, thanks to Bo.

Years of reading romance novels still hadn't prepared me for a man like Bo. Fictional heroes seemed perfect, but with Bo, the perfection came with knowing that like me, he had a past that molded him to be the man he was. As Jolene had said, "*They're just words on a page. Real men come with baggage you gotta fix. Muscles that keep you safe. And hearts that beat only for you.*"

I smiled when I thought back to the early morning hours and

how much Bo's heart beat for me.

"She's lookin' dreamy," Poppy whispered to Cali.

Cali turned in her seat and studied Poppy, looking back to gauge my mood. "She looks like a woman who has found a man she can trust."

Poppy looked back at me and took my measure. "No doubts?" she asked.

I shook my head slowly. "No doubts. Bo was the best decision I've made in my life. He makes me feel safe. Wanted. Needed in a way I've never felt."

Poppy's face melted into a mask of warmth, and her eyes began to glitter with moisture. "I'm so happy for you."

I reached across the table and grabbed her hand. "You could have the same thing," I whispered. "You just need to let down your wall around the man who holds your interest."

Poppy pulled her hand back and grabbed her cup of coffee, acting as if she didn't have a clue what I was talking about. "Someday," she shrugged.

"Are you willin' to risk Nate findin' someone else?"

She'd wrapped her lips around her coffee cup and was taking a sip when I brought up Nate. She choked on the coffee, sputtering the brown liquid on the table.

"Nate?" she coughed, trying to clear her lungs. "Why on earth do you think I want Nate?"

"For goodness sake, Poppy. You don't think we're ninnies, do you?" Cali snapped.

"No one is callin' you a ninny. I just don't understand where you got the idea that I have a thing for Nate?"

"How about the fact that when he's around, you watch him out of the corner of your eye. Or the fact that when he showed up at the ranch, you hightailed it like a jackrabbit into the barn."

"I only had a T-shirt on. It wasn't proper."

"That didn't stop you from walkin' around in front of Bo and Devin," I pointed out.

"They're like brothers!" she exclaimed.

"And Nate's not?" Cali smiled.

Poppy opened her mouth, then closed it. "Look, he's . . . he's, well, hot. Gorgeous. And way the hell out of my league. I'd only be courtin' trouble if I set my sights on him. Maybe I watch him," she shrugged, "but what woman wouldn't? He's—"

"—hot, we get it, you've said that already," I interrupted.

"Well, surely you've noticed?"

I looked at Cali and shrugged. "I suppose he's hot. But nothing compares to Bo."

Cali nodded. "Nate has a certain appeal, I suppose, but Devin's way hotter."

Poppy snorted. "In the looks department, Nate wins hands down."

I had her, and she didn't even know it. "Yes, I've read when you love someone, you prefer them to all others. That even in the face of superior beauty, love blinds you to it."

"Exactly," Poppy agreed. "You don't see his hotness because you're blinded by love."

Lord, she was hardheaded. "*Ooor*," I drew out, "you don't see we're right because *you're* blinded by love."

Poppy blinked. "That's not it," she denied.

"Pitter-patter versus a stampeding mustang, Poppy. Which is it?" I asked, reminding her of what I'd said a few days before.

Her eyes widened in shock, and she began shaking her head rapidly. "No."

"Yes," Cali and I said in unison.

Bernice, Eunice, and Natasha walked into the diner, drawing our attention away from the matter at hand. It was just as well. Poppy looked like she needed a good half-day to chew on the information.

"We're grabbin' coffee to go, then headin' over to check on old man Craig before we visit Boris at the hospital."

"Old man Craig?" I questioned.

"The old man who lives on the property next door. The one the herd was on. We figured he might be unsettled by all the activity over at our place. He's in his seventies now and doesn't like surprises, seein' as he's got a bad ticker."

"Didn't the sheriff go over and talk to him?" Cali asked. "Seems like that would be a likely place to start, since the fence was taken down between the two properties."

"No idea," Natasha shrugged. "And it doesn't matter. We're his neighbors, and he's an old man. It's our duty to make sure he's okay."

And he might have information about Boris and Natasha that could help Bo.

"We could go for you," I blurted out. "There's no need for you to drive all that way when I know you'd rather be at the hospital. We could pick up a Bundt cake at the store and take it with us as a peace offerin'."

Natasha blinked, then smiled. "That would sure be a help," she said, digging in her purse. "He likes lemon poppy seed. I'll just give you some money and you can say it was from me and Boris."

I held up my hand to stop her. "I've got it covered. It's the least we can do. If you'd like us to run any more errands for you, just ask. The guys are gonna be tied up all day investigatin', so we've got a ton of time on our hands."

"All right," Natasha beamed. "You three sure are a godsend. I don't know where Boris and I would be if you hadn't been here when he got sick."

I shuddered thinking about it. Probably burned to a crisp in their beds.

"Be safe," Bernice said as they turned to leave.

I grinned. "Bo told you to keep remindin' me of that, didn't he?"

"If a man's any man at all, his first priority is always the safety of the ones he loves," Eunice threw out.

Bernice turned and looked at her. "Did Odis Lee teach you that?"

Eunice rolled her eyes, then turned and headed for the door.

"She's an 'Unapologetic Bitch' when it comes to that old coot."

Cali gasped, "Bernie, you gotta give him *One More Chance*," referring to Odis Lee's years of spying on their family for her grandfather. He'd finally manned up when he saw it would hurt Cali, who was like a daughter to him.

Bernice beamed at Cali for using a Madonna song title. "Gotta say, I love havin' you back like this, butterbean. Love has helped you *Open Your Heart* to the world around you."

Cali's smile softened. "I'm an Armstrong. We can rise above anything."

Bernice's eyes welled, and she cleared her throat, mumbling, "And don't you forget it."

"Never," Cali laughed, "You'd never let me."

"Bernie!" Eunice shouted from the door. "Get the lead out, sister. Boris is waitin'."

"Tell him we'll be by later to visit, and we'll sneak him in a piece of pie," I said.

We waved the aunts and Natasha off, then headed for the nearest grocery store to find a lemon poppy seed cake.

Cake in hand, we headed out of town. The drive to old man Craig's place took twenty minutes. When we pulled in, we were met by an old goat that was chewing on grass. His face reminded me of an old man, and I wondered if that was why the cranky old man had chosen him for a pet.

I looked toward the house and found the gentleman in question sitting on his front porch, rocking slowly as residual wind from the storm the night before whipped around us.

The difference between the two ranches was glaring. Boris and Natasha had state-of-the-art everything, right down to the spacious barn and outbuildings. Old man Craig's home was small, weathered, and broken down by life. It didn't look like anyone had run a coat of paint over the clapboard house in years. And the roof had seen better days. I was angry just looking at the place. If he had family, they were obviously ignoring him to the point of neglect.

I waved and called out, "Hello," but he just kept on rocking.

The girls shrugged at me, so we slammed the car doors and headed for the front porch.

Old man Craig eyed us suspiciously as we approached, so I put on my warmest smile. "Mr. Craig?"

"Who's askin'?"

"Well, I'm Sienna Miller, and these are my friends, Poppy Gentry, and Cali Armstrong. We're friends of Boris and Natasha."

He locked onto the lemon poppy seed cake Cali was holding and jerked his head toward it. "Is that for me?"

Cali looked down at the cake, then held it out to him. "Yes, sir. We came by to check on you. To make sure you're doin' okay after the storm, and to see if all the ruckus goin' on next door was botherin' you."

His eyes narrowed. "What ruckus?"

"Didn't the sheriff come by and speak to you?"

He leaned over and spit what looked like tobacco into the dirt yard, then wiped his mouth with the back of his hand. My stomach lurched a bit, but I held my smile. I needed to gain his trust so I could ask him questions.

"Maybe he did, maybe he didn't. I'm old. Sleep a lot, you know. He could have come by, and I didn't hear him. So why don't you tell me what's goin' on instead."

Cali looked at me for direction. I looked at Poppy. We weren't investigators, but I'd read enough romantic suspense to know that when talkin' to a witness, you have to hold your cards close to your vest. I mean, I doubted this old man had anything to do with what was happening to Boris and Natasha, and he couldn't possibly have killed Clint Black, but I'm pretty sure Sheriff Moore would be pissed if we said too much.

"Well?" he asked angrily, snatching the cake from Cali's hand.

I took a deep breath and went for it. "Mr. Craig, the Winkles' house burnt down under mysterious circumstances, and then a section of the fence between your two properties came down, allowing their herd to escape. We recovered them, but evidence suggests foul play. The police think someone is purposely tryin' to hurt the Winkles."

I left out the fact Clint had been murdered. He was old and didn't need to be unnecessarily frightened.

Craig didn't even blink when I told him what happened.

"Why does the sheriff want to talk to me? I can barely walk from the bathroom to my bed without usin' a walker."

I looked at the girls to see if they found his lack of surprise concerning. They looked at me and smiled.

Guess not.

"Well," I started, then looked around his property. Nothing had been done in years. There was no way he could be involved. He didn't have the strength. "Mr. Craig, has anyone ever come around here asking for access to survey the land? Maybe a man about medium height with tattoos on his arm?"

Recognition registered on his face, and he looked at the three of us, slowly taking each of us in. "I've never seen you three before. Are you from town?"

The sharp turn in the conversation surprised me.

"No, we're from Savannah. We came for the week as guests of the dude ranch."

"Women came all the way out here on their own just to ride horses?"

That seemed rather sexist to me, and Poppy appeared offended as well, because she bit out, "Why can't women go to a dude ranch on their own? We can do anything men can do."

"Settle down," he snapped. "You young folk are always goin' off half-cocked. It'll get you in trouble one day."

This was getting us nowhere. "Mr. Craig, did you see the gentleman who came around to do the survey?" I asked again.

He hesitated a moment, then nodded. "About a month ago. Asked if he could have access."

"Do you know where?"

"You mean specifically?"

I nodded with excitement. This might be the break we were looking for.

He rose slowly, shuffling his feet, and all three of us rushed to his aid until he was standing firmly in place.

He turned and pointed up the hill. "Over that ridge is a cave. He went in there several times. It sits on the property line, mind you, so most of the cave is on the Winkle side."

"Have you ever been in it?"

He shook his head. "Bad legs. Got shot in the spine during the war. It was before I bought the place. Black called it a veritable gold mine once. That he thinks Civil War soldiers must have camped out in there. Said he found some buttons. He gave me a couple hundred bucks for them and asked if he could come back.

But he never did. I was hopin' he was right about the Civil War stuff. I could have used the extra money."

I stretched my neck and rose to my tiptoes, trying to see the opening.

"You're welcome to go up and look inside. Black said it's not full of bugs. Smooth walls and dry. Cool, too. Said it felt like there was air conditionin' inside."

I looked at the girls. "Should we?"

"Does this fall under 'Be safe?'" Cali asked.

I smiled. "Probably not. But Mr. Craig here knows where we are, so what could happen?"

"I won't say *famous last words*," Poppy chuckled.

"We can call it into the guys if you'd rather wait?" I said.

"No, it's fine. It's not like we're gonna go inside, right?"

"Right," I said, shrugging. "No flashlights."

"I've got a bunch in the livin' room if you want to look inside. Could be more Civil War stuff in there, and I could sure use the money."

How could I say no to that?

"Um, sure. I can look if you want."

Poppy gave me a look, then headed inside and found a flashlight.

"Ready," she said as she came out.

I put my hand under Mr. Craig's arm and helped him back to his rocking chair. "Do you want a piece of the lemon cake before we go?"

"I'll save it for later," he smiled, patting his stomach. "Just had breakfast."

"Okay. We'll be back in a jiffy," I said.

"Take your time. Might miss somethin' valuable inside."

I nodded and stepped off his porch. Poppy and Cali followed me, and we didn't say a word until we were out of earshot.

"You're not really goin' inside, are you?" Cali asked.

"I'll shine the light inside. If I see anything, I'll get it. But not unless the crown jewels are involved."

"Then why did you say the only reason you couldn't go inside is 'cause you had no flashlight?"

"I don't know. I guess I didn't want to appear chicken."

"Chicken is good. Chicken keeps you alive and spider free. And snake free!" Poppy cringed, shuddering in disgust.

"Good point," I agreed, shuddering in solidarity.

We made it to the top of the rise, then scanned the outcropping of sharp, jagged rock for anything that looked like a cave.

"Do you see it?" I asked hopefully.

Cali shook her head at me, slightly annoyed. "Maybe it's further up? Let's give it a few more feet, then head back."

We hiked up the rocky rise, sliding on stones, holding on to each other to keep from falling, and we still didn't see the cave.

"Maybe he's confused about the location. Let's go back and call the guys. They can look for it," I finally said.

We started to turn when a sharp sound echoed across the muggy air.

"Did you hear that?"

We stood stock-still and listened. The sound of metal hitting something solid grew louder.

"Okay, I'm officially spooked. Can we go back?" Poppy asked in a strained voice.

I nodded empathically and turned to head down the hill. Whatever that noise was, it was definitely man-made. And considering Mr. Craig lived alone, that could only mean one thing. Someone was on his property without his knowledge.

We made it five feet before movement caught my eye. A woman I recognized immediately stepped out from behind a bush about ten feet away, startling us. She was holding a gun with a phone plastered to her ear. If I'd been the damsel in distress type of woman, this would have been the moment I swooned from fright.

"Got them. We'll take care of it."

Red, the woman I'd danced with the night before, hung up the phone and slipped it into her back pocket. Then she leered at me and winked. "You should have taken me up on my offer, gorgeous," she called out. "Now I have to kill you."

"Oh, shit!" Poppy gasped.

"Devin's sixth sense better kick in quickly," Cali whispered.

"Maybe I can flirt my way out of this," I offered.

They both looked at me in disbelief.

"What?"

Red strode the ten feet separating us and stopped in front of me. "How'd you figure it out?"

"Um," I mumbled. *Figure out what, exactly*? "We looked at the geological survey," I lied, stalling for time.

She narrowed her eyes. "Black said you couldn't see it on the map."

See what?

"He must have lied."

"Who else knows about the gold?"

Gold? I glanced at Cali. She had her best poker face on. Devin really was rubbing off on her.

"Answer me," Red bit out.

Here goes nothing. "The sheriff, Bo, Devin, Nate, Natasha, and Boris. We figured it out last night. We just didn't know who was involved. They're headed here now. We came ahead to check on Mr. Craig to make sure he was okay."

Red's mouth pulled into a sneer, and icy fingers of fear ran down my spine. Something told me I'd said the wrong thing.

"Then I have nothin' to lose," Red stated cryptically. She

grabbed my neck and pulled me to her mouth for a quick, hard kiss, then shoved me back.

"We're goin' for a little walk. Since they don't know who's involved, we'll keep it that way."

I closed my eyes. I was so stupid.

"I'm T.S.T.L."

"We all are," Cali replied, grabbing my hand. "From now on, I'm listenin' to Devin."

"Works for me. Books and more books," I said, trying to keep the fear out of my voice.

"To Live or Die," Poppy whispered.

I turned my head. "What?"

"Let's go," Red growled, shoving Cali first.

"Don't touch her!" I shouted.

"To Live or Die," Poppy ground out.

It hit me slowly what she was saying. She was referencing a romantic suspense book where two friends were held at gunpoint, and one of the friends rushed the bad guy so the other could escape. It didn't end well. The hero's friend died.

"NO!"

Red put her hand on my chest and shoved, ordering, "Get a move on."

Poppy lunged then. She went for the hand holding the gun and screamed, "Run!"

I leapt for Red's waist and tried to take her to the ground. "Wallflowers don't leave a woman behind," I grunted.

Cali joined in the fray, jumping on Red's back, and the weight of the three of us took her to the ground. The gun went off on impact, and I froze. I looked down with trepidation and saw bright crimson blooming freely across a chest.

"Poppy!"

"What?"

"You've been shot!"

"No, I haven't." Looking down at Red, I pushed her off the top of Poppy, rolling her to her back, and snatched the gun from her hand, throwing it behind us. Blood spread across her chest at an alarming rate, and an eerie gurgling noise bubbled up from her throat.

Pressing my hand on the gaping hole in her chest, I shouted, "Call 911!"

Cali started to pull her phone from her pocket, but an angry voice bit out, "Nobody move," stopping her.

We spun around to find the bodybuilder woman from last night holding the gun I'd just tossed away. My eyes closed while I berated myself. In the confusion and fear, I'd forgotten about the metallic hammering we'd heard. I should have known Red wasn't working alone. She'd popped out from behind a bush, away from the noise.

"We need to call for an ambulance," I snapped. "She'll die without help."

As if Red was following a script on how to die theatrically, she drew a rattled breath one last time, grabbed the front of my shirt, spasmed suddenly, and closed her eyes.

Her chest never rose again.

"That's unfortunate," Bodybuilder Lady said. "Jennifer was a good friend."

I looked down at Red. She didn't look like a Jennifer. Jennifers were perky and friendly, not villainous killers.

"Get up and grab her arms. We need to hide the body."

"This is ridiculous. Our men will be looking for us by now, and my aunts know we came here. You won't get away with this."

"Jennifer's granddad will convince them you never made it here."

"Mr. Craig?" I gasped.

She looked at me and grinned. "Convincin', isn't he?"

I'd say.

I looked at the girls. Poppy was covered in Red's blood, and the color had drained from Cali's face, her eyes widened in pure panic. Icy claws of fear shuddered down my spine.

We might not make it out of this.

I turned to the woman and tried to reason, "Look . . . What's your name by the way?"

She studied me for a moment, scanning me from head to toe, then shrugged and said, "Alice."

Alice. Appropriate, since I felt like we'd fallen down a rabbit hole.

"Look, Alice. Right now, you haven't done anything. Jennifer is the one who held us at gunpoint and threatened to kill us. So why don't you let us go, and we'll leave your name out of the whole thing." My voice shook as I spoke.

Alice shook her head slowly and raised the gun higher. "I killed Black. So you see, I'm in this up to my neck." What hope I might have had fled like a mouse chased by a cat. "So grab her arms and get movin'."

Poppy crossed her arms. "And if we refuse?"

Alice turned her gun on me and pointed it at my forehead, pulling back the hammer.

Poppy moved quickly, followed by Cali, while I tried unsuccessfully to keep calm. They both grabbed one of Jennifer's arms and then looked at Alice.

"Up the hill about ten feet, then turn toward the fence line."

If I was going to die, I wanted to know why.

"Jennifer said something about gold," I said in a long, shuddering breath.

Alice motioned up the hill to Poppy and Cali with her free

hand, but kept her gun trained on me. "Jennifer and Black found the entrance while he was doing a survey. He could see somethin' in the images he took, and they investigated. There's a cave with an opening on this side of the property, but the gold sits on the Winkles' side. Jennifer knew he would tell them, so she made a deal with him. Keep quiet, and she'd cut him in. Then the old man had a heart attack, and Black got the idea that in his condition, he wouldn't be able to keep the ranch runnin'. He decided to make sure the Winkles came to that same conclusion. He burned down the house and set the cattle free without consulting us. I wouldn't even have known he was over there workin' if I hadn't seen him leave. When I confronted him about what he was doin' over there, he admitted what he'd done."

"So you killed him?"

She shrugged. "He became a liability. We knew people would start diggin' into what had happened, like you ladies did at the weddin'. We had to get rid of him before he lost his nerve and talked."

Just like Poppy, Cali, and me.

I swallowed hard, praying Bo had figured out we were missing.

"Got him," Bo growled. "Clinton Theodore Black." Devin and Nate moved behind him and looked over his shoulder at the screen. It had taken them most of the night and into the morning before they'd hacked Shelton Geological.

"Pay dirt," Devin mumbled. "Now all we need are his accomplices."

"I'll call Moore and let him know," Bo said, grabbing his phone.

Devin reached into his back pocket and pulled out his phone, swiping 'Call Calla.'

When it went to voicemail, a trickle of caution tumbled through his brain. Scowling at the phone, he hit redial. He got the same response. Searching through his contact list until he found Bernice's number, he hit 'Dial.'

"Hey handsome," Bernice said.

"Is Calla with you?"

"Nope. She's runnin' an errand for Natasha."

"Where?"

"Old man Craig's house. She took him a lemon poppy seed cake."

That news settled in his gut, and it rolled around like a lead weight.

"Thanks," he bit out, then ended the call. "We need to get to Craig's house. Calla and the girls went over there for Natasha, and Calla's not answerin' her phone."

"I'll call Sienna," Bo responded, pulling out his phone. He found her number as all three men started heading for the door. It went to voicemail as well. "Nothin'. We should have locked them up in the jail," Bo growled.

"They're probably shoppin'," Nate supplied casually, but Bo heard a note of apprehension in his voice.

They moved with urgency and piled into Bo's truck. "Anyone got Poppy's number?" Bo asked, looking at Nate. Devin turned and looked at him as well.

Nate pulled his phone out and hit 'Call Poppy,' mumbling, "Calla gave it to me last night. I forgot I had it."

For the first time since he'd called Calla and got no answer, Devin grinned.

"She's not answerin'," Nate growled. "Floor it."

"Now you're worried," Devin muttered as Bo punched the

accelerator.

Nate glared at Devin. "I'm not as apt to overreact as you two are."

"You think we're overreactin'?"

Nate's jaw tightened. "No. They find trouble without tryin'."

The twenty-minute drive to Craig's home served to tighten the mood in the cab. By the time they pulled in front of the old man's house, you could cut the tension with a knife.

Bo scanned the yard looking for Poppy's car. It was filled with rusted equipment that had seen better days and an old goat tethered to a chain. Poppy's car was nowhere to be seen.

An old man was sitting in a chair, gently rocking the day away. Bo approached him.

"Mr. Craig?" Bo asked.

"Who's askin'?"

Bo stuck out his hand. "I'm Bo Strawn."

Craig stared at his outstretched offer, then rose his own shaking hand to grasp Bo's.

"What can I do for you?"

"We're lookin' for three women. They were supposed to come by here. Have you seen them?"

Craig's eyes darted to Devin and Nate. "I think I would remember three beautiful women stoppin' by."

"So you haven't seen them?" Devin asked.

"Nope. Just me and Bob."

"Bob?" Nate asked.

"My goat," Craig answered, pointing in the direction of the tethered goat.

Devin glanced around the porch, then through the window looking into the dining room. Something yellow caught his eye. On an old wooden table sat a yellow Bundt cake, and a piece was missing.

Turning to Bo, he said casually, "They're probably next door playin' with the pigs. I'm sure they're fine. They never get in trouble."

Bo's eyes shot to his, and he nodded. "Sorry to bother you," Bo said between clenched teeth, then turned swiftly and headed down the stairs. All three men folded into the truck before Devin spoke.

"Bernice said they were bringin' lemon cake over when they checked on the man. There was a new one sittin' on the table inside. I saw it through the window. He's lyin'."

"If he's lyin', then they're in trouble," Bo growled. "We need to come in from Bullwinkle Ranch and search his land. Whatever's goin' on, Craig's clearly involved, and they must have stumbled across it. I'd bet my life they never left here."

Fear coursed through Bo's body and squeezed, constricting his lungs.

Hold on, baby. I'm coming.

"I'll call Moore," Devin stated, pulling out his phone. The call went directly to voicemail. "You got your gun?" Devin ground out. "Moore's not pickin' up."

Bo nodded. "Since Moore's tied up, we'll go in hard on horseback," he stated flatly, controlled. "And when we find whoever's holdin' them, I'm not a cop. Do what you need to do."

Devin looked at him. "Extreme prejudice?"

"Yeah," Bo returned, then punched the accelerator.

Twelve

WHEN FATE DECIDED TO DUMP ON YOU, SHE DID IT WITH STYLE

A HUGE CHASM SPREAD OUT in front of us, deep in the bowels of a rocky cliff. It was located on the border of Craig's and Boris and Natasha's property. My mind couldn't wrap around the size of it. An oily stench of rotten dirt and rancid water permeated the air, choking me. The walls were smooth, eroded over time by water, yet they sparkled in the dim light of the torch Alice carried. Gold, silver, and other minerals winked back at me like stars in a night sky, peeking out between the solid rocks like veins in an arm.

We'd traveled deep into the ground, winding through narrow passages until I was turned around, but I was sure we had crossed the Winkles' property line. The gold had to belong to Boris and Natasha, like Alice had said. But even so, I was confused how Jennifer and Alice thought they would extract the precious metal from the walls without anyone noticing. It would take dynamite to bring the walls down, releasing the treasure from its eternal resting place.

Poppy and Cali let go of Jennifer's arms, then bent at the waist to catch their breath. I turned to Alice as my heart thundered in my chest. Now that we were hidden away, she could dispose of us easily.

"Grab those shovels and start diggin'," Alice barked out. "I don't want her stinkin' up the joint."

Her lack of anguish over her friend's death was disgusting. To Alice, Jennifer was only a partner in crime. One less person she had to share the bounty with.

I looked at the shovels. If we dug slowly, it would buy us time for the guys to find us. My stomach dropped at the thought. How *would* they find us? It took a geological survey to find the cave in the first place. I looked at the girls. It was up to us to save ourselves. When their eyes landed on mine, I mouthed, "Tybee," then my eyes darted to Alice, reminding them that Poppy and I had taken out Gayla Brown with a heavy piece of driftwood.

They both gave me a sharp nod. My friends were nuts, not stupid. They'd figured out, like I had, that help would have a hard time finding us in the belly of the earth, and that if we wanted to live, we had to take matters into our own hands.

They moved to the two shovels, leaning against the rock wall, and picked them up. I took one of them from Cali. She was exhausted from dragging Jennifer inside, so I'd take the first shift digging.

I searched the floor looking for a large area where we could dig. Water had found its way into the caves from underground springs, or flowed in during rainstorms. After last night's rain, water had puddled near a narrow fissure in the rock. The ground surrounding the opening was dark and muddy. It would make digging easy and quick. I turned my head and found a patch of dry earth that looked to be mixed with rocks. That area would take much longer to dig a hole deep enough to bury a body. Or four. I had no doubt when the hole was done; she would pull the trigger.

Pulling the shovel behind me, I walked over to the dry patch of dirt and drove in the edge of the shovel. It tore through the earth easier than expected.

Dammit.

I pretended to struggle so Alice would think the digging would take a while. We needed time. There would be no do-overs if we screwed up.

Poppy moved to my side and began digging next to me. I muttered, "Slowly," under my breath, and she nodded that she heard.

"Alice?" Cali said. I stopped digging to look at her. "You do know that the only way to get that gold out of the rock is to blast it, don't you?" Alice's face shifted slightly in confusion, and she looked at the wall. "I saw the pickax when we first came in. Have you dislodged any of it?"

Alice stood up and touched the wall, running her hand along the surface, and I cursed. This was the opportunity that we were waiting for, and Poppy and I were too far away to hit her over the head with a shovel before she turned.

"Do I set it against the wall and light it?" she asked.

Cali looked at us and rolled her eyes. "I think you drill holes in the rock and insert the dynamite inside."

Alice swung around. "How do you know this?"

"I read a romance novel once where the hero was a gold hunter."

"What else did you learn?"

"The gold is threaded through the rock. You have to crush it to extract the metals," I hollered.

The wheels turned behind her eyes, then she began to laugh. "Black was right. We do need to buy the Winkles' land. There's no way I can get the gold without them hearing."

It hit me out of the blue. Clint would have known that the only way to get the gold out was to blast it because of his job. No wonder he didn't tell her what he was doing. I had no doubt he planned to buy Boris and Natasha's land if he was successful and claim the gold for himself.

Alice began to pace, so I kept my eyes on her as I pretended to dig.

"What do you think she'll do now?" Poppy whispered, keeping her own eyes on Alice.

"I don't know. I think it's clear the jig is up. Two people are dead, and now she knows she can't get the gold out without Boris and Natasha knowin'."

Alice exploded in a hard, loud, "Son of a bitch!" causing me to jump. Poppy and I turned and froze, holding our breath.

Alice banged the gun against her head twice, and I flinched. I stared at her, speechless, as she took a long, shuddering breath and sobbed, understanding that she was finished. Panic grew across her features, and I held my breath. She was about to do something, and I was afraid to find out what.

Alice took a few deep breaths and then looked at us. Time stood still as we waited to learn our fate. We didn't have to wait long. She raised her gun and began to back out of the chasm.

"Sorry, ladies. I can't have witnesses."

I expected her to start firing at us; instead, she ran through the only opening in the cave and slammed a door made out a sheet metal shut. We moved at the same time, running at the door, slamming into it with our weight. It held with a groan. A loud sliding noise, like metal on metal, echoed on the other side. We pounded, shouting at Alice, but she didn't answer. The sound of pounding feet bounced off the walls until they disappeared, shrouding us in silence.

We turned and looked at the cavernous chamber. The light from Alice's torch, shoved into a holder on the wall, flickered and dimmed a bit. Once the fuel burned off, we'd be cloaked in darkness. And with the exception of the fissure where the water escaped, there was no exit. We were caged like a fox in a hole.

When fate decided to dump on you, she did it with style. Twenty-five years I'd waited to be happy. Cali had waited twenty-seven years after losing her parents as a child. And Poppy. If any of the Wallflowers deserved to be happy, it was her, and now we were trapped deep beneath the earth with no escape. We had air, a little water on the floor, and no food. We could last for a week or more while Bo, Devin, and Nate searched for us, but I felt like our luck was running out.

Well, at least the air was cool. We'd be comfortable while we starved to death.

"Try your phones," I said in a panic. "Maybe we can get a call out."

"Down here?" Poppy replied, pulling out her phone. "It would take a miracle and a cell tower the size of Georgia."

Cali already had her phone to her ear. She turned concerned eyes toward us and shook her head.

"We're done for," Poppy said a little hysterically. "There is no way they will find the openin'. Not if she puts that dead bush back in place. I couldn't see the openin' in all the undergrowth until she pointed it out."

Her lungs contracted and filled in great gasps, and she began to pace.

"Poppy? Are you claustrophobic?" I asked.

"No. I'm deathrophobic."

"We're not gonna die," Cali said patiently. "Devin won't allow it." To back up her assertion, she moved to a large boulder and sat down. "We might as well get comfortable while we wait."

"You're that sure he will find us?" Poppy questioned.

"They will," I stated with authority. Like Cali, I felt it deep in my bones. Bo wouldn't stop until he found us. Wouldn't sleep until he had me back in his arms.

Poppy looked between the two of us, then walked to her purse and picked it up. She sat next to Cali on the boulder, then opened her purse and pulled out a book. "We might as well read while we wait," she said, then flipped the book over so I could see it. Linda Howard's *To Die For* sat in her hands, the edges singed from the fire. She grinned. "I wanted to research. See if Bo followed Wyatt's train of thought. It must be a good sign that it made it through the fire."

I sat next to her and pulled the book from her hands, smiling. *"I have a rule,"* I began, quoting Blair Mallory from one of my favorite Linda Howard books. *"Walk out, crawl back. If a man does the first, then he has to do the second to get back on good terms with me."*

"Bo didn't crawl. He came ridin' in on a stallion," Poppy chuckled.

The image of Bo galloping toward me on Goliath flashed through my memory. He would come for me. I knew it. Bo didn't back down. He didn't stop until he'd gotten what he wanted, and he wanted me. Wanted us. No, he wouldn't stop until he found us, and my heart rate began to slow with the knowledge.

Opening the book, I started to read chapter one. I paused when the torch flickered. Its light began to dim rapidly, then it hissed and went out. Darkness veiled us, and I grabbed Poppy's hand. We moved closer together, then I turned my phone on to cast light in the chasm. "They'll come," I whispered.

Cali looked at us both and repeated my sentiment. "They'll come."

Bo waited as Nate rode up the rise. He'd gone down to check the old barn at the back of Craig's property. By the look on his face, he'd found something.

"Poppy's car's hidden inside under a tarp," he bit out. "No sign of the girls."

"Did you see Craig while you were lookin'?"

He shook his head. "I crept up on the house and looked inside. No sign of him. Goat's gone, too."

Devin swung into his saddle and scanned the property. "We need to find them. If he's spooked, then whoever has them is as well."

Fear crept in for a moment, then Bo shook it off like water. Fear clouded his judgment, made him weak. He needed to be sharp if he was gonna find the Wallflowers. Find his sun.

"Head across the property to the east side," he ordered Nate. "Devin, search the south side, and I'll search the west."

"They're still here," Devin growled. "I can feel it."

Bo nodded. He felt it, too. They were waiting to be found. "Keep in touch," Bo bit out, turning Goliath west, and took off.

Hours passed with no leads, and the fear Bo had been tamping down began to rise again with a vengeance. The sun was setting on the horizon, making it hard to see. Night was coming, and the thought of Sienna and the Wallflowers trapped someplace in the gloom of the darkness sat heavily in his gut. They needed flashlights to keep searching, or they'd never find them. Bo pulled out his phone and called Moore.

The sheriff answered on the third ring. "Did you get Hawthorne's message?" Bo growled.

"No, what's up?"

"The girls have disappeared. They came to Craig's property to check on the man, and now their car's parked in his garage covered by a tarp. He ran after we visited him. I need volunteers to search the property and plenty of light."

"The old man is at the heart of this?" Moore questioned.

"Yeah. Now send me what I need."

There was dead air on the line, then Moore sighed heavily. "I've got a six-car pileup, and people are trapped. I need the light to cut them out."

Bo's eyes closed, and he gritted his teeth to keep from roaring in frustration. "Send them when you can," he bit out, then hung up and swiped 'Call Bernice.' He didn't want to do it, but he had no choice. He needed light, and he needed people.

Bernice answered on the second ring. "We expected you back by now. What are you up to?"

"We've got trouble," Bo started. "The girls are missin'."

A long pause. "What do you mean, missin'?"

"Craig's involved in what's goin' on over at the Winkles' property. The girls must have figured it out. Now they're missin', and their car's hidden in his barn."

Bernice only hesitated a moment to take in all he'd said. "We'll be there in twenty minutes," she rushed out. "What do you need?"

"Lights. As many as you can find and the people to use them. My gut tells me they're still here somewhere. We need to find them quickly, and we can't do that without volunteers."

"I'll get right on it," she mumbled, then, in a soft whisper, said, "Find my girl. Find them all," before hanging up.

Sunset bled across the sky, beckoning in the night. Bo scanned the area looking for anything that would clue him in to where Craig was hiding the Wallflowers. He didn't know why he was certain they hadn't left the property, other than an ache in his gut any time he considered looking elsewhere. He could feel Sienna waiting for him. Could feel her presence on the property. And until he'd searched every inch, looked under every bush, he wouldn't leave.

Crickets began to sing as he kicked Goliath and headed up the hill. He'd searched from the road to the house. Once the lights arrived, he'd fan the volunteers out, and they'd search from the house up. Until they arrived, he'd keep searching.

He stared at the fence between the Winkles' property and Craig's.

How the hell does ruining the Winkles play into this?

Pulling out his phone, he dialed Devin.

He answered on the first ring. "You got them?" he asked anxiously, his deep timbre deafening in Bo's ear.

Bo's heart skipped a beat. A part of him had held out hope that Devin had the girls and hadn't called him yet.

"No. Not yet. Lights are comin', volunteers, too. Let's meet back at Craig's house. I want to run this through from the top. I want to know why Craig went after the Winkles."

"I've been thinkin' about that as well. Why now after all the years they've been neighbors?"

"That's what we're gonna find out. I'll call Moore back and find out if he found Black's hotel room yet. Maybe the contents of his room can shed some light."

"I'll call Nate and meet you in ten," Devin stated, then hung up.

Bo called Moore again. "Did you find them?" Moore asked after one ring.

He heard a loud screech from a siren and waited for it to fade. "Not yet. I'm comin' at this from another angle. Did you find out where Black was stayin'?"

"My men found it. He was stayin' out of town. They have his belongin's, but I haven't looked at them yet."

"Are they on the scene with you?"

"Yeah. I'll check and see if they have it bagged and tagged in their unit. Give me ten, and I'll call you back."

Bo hung up and then turned Goliath in the direction of the house. Ten minutes later, he pulled the stallion to a halt and slid off.

Devin and Nate rode up a few minutes later as Bo knelt in front of Craig's front door picking the lock. He stood when the bolt slid into the doorframe.

"Did you reach Moore?" Devin asked.

"Yeah, he's checkin' with his men. They found Black's hotel out of town. He hasn't looked through his things yet."

The three men scanned the living room. The furniture was old and worn, but clean. A newspaper was strewn on the arm of a recliner, and Bo stared at it. He lived in a technological world now. He couldn't remember the last time he'd read actual print news.

"Let's flip the place," Devin growled.

Bo moved to the dining room table and began going through his mail. "Bills. Junk mail. Nothin'."

He moved to the bedroom, while Devin tossed the living room. On the bedside table was a brochure for a timeshare in Aruba, and one for Chevy trucks. Bo picked up the timeshare and found a two-story condo circled on the inside flap. He glanced at the Chevy brochure and found a bright red dually cab marked with a star. Craig either expected to come into money or *had* come into money. Bo started to open the drawer to check the contents, when a picture frame caught his attention. He snatched up the frame and stared into the face of a woman with red hair. The same woman who'd danced with Sienna the night before.

Tossing the picture onto the bed, he pulled the drawer out and dumped the contents. Nothing of significance appeared, so he moved to the closet. He clicked on the light. The bars and shelves were practically empty. Exactly what he expected. He moved to the bathroom. Empty. No bottles of pills. No shampoo. He'd taken everything and wasn't coming back.

He was certain, then, that dead or alive, the Wallflowers were still on this property. There was no way those three would have been taken by a fragile old man. They'd have clawed his eyes out before they would have gotten in a car with him.

Bo moved back to the living room. "Find anything?"

"Nothin'," Devin growled.

Nate walked into the room from the kitchen holding a book and held it up. Bo read the title. "*How to Prospect for Gold*"

"Odd subject for an old man to study, don't you think?" Nate asked.

"Could be an old book, somethin' he's had for years," Devin replied.

"Was still in a box on his counter. Amazon order."

"So it's new."

Bo looked at Devin. "Is there gold in Georgia?"

Devin nodded. "All over. My cousin took her kids pannin' for gold."

Lights flooded the darkness outside, and Bo turned for the door. Twenty plus cars lined the yard. Men and women of every age and size peeled out of their cars holding flashlights.

The cavalry had arrived.

Bernice and Eunice moved toward them, followed by Natasha, Troy, and Brantley.

"Have you found them?" Bernice shouted.

"Not yet. I'm waitin' for Moore to call me back. He's got Black's personal possessions, so we might get lucky."

"Where do you want us to start?"

Bo descended the steps and walked the group to the edge of Craig's house.

"Fan out in a line until you reach the property line, then begin moving forward that way. If you find anything, call it in. We'll join you in a few minutes," Bo explained.

Bernice nodded and jumped into action, shouting at the volunteers to get their butts in gear.

Moving back to Devin, Bo pulled out his phone and dialed Moore again. He was tired of waiting.

Moore answered on the second ring. "I'm gettin' the bags now," he said without prelude. "We had a goat on the road causin' problems."

Bo paused. "Did you say goat?"

"Yeah."

"Do any of the vehicles involved in the accident have an old man in them? About seventy, with a balding head?"

"Yeah. DOA. We haven't pulled him out of the wreck, yet. The driver's on a helicopter headed to the hospital, but it doesn't look good for her."

Bo's heart raced. "Did you recognize her?"

He expected Moore to say she had red hair, but he described a woman who sounded like the one who'd danced with Calla.

"The old man is Craig. The driver, a friend of his granddaughter, if the pictures in his house are correct. I'll send Nate to the hospital. If she's coherent, he'll get her to talk."

Nate moved to Bo's side. "Head to the hospital. The woman who danced with Calla last night was with Craig. He's dead. She's been life-flighted there."

Nate peeled off their group and headed to Bernice. She gave him her keys, and then he was gone.

"I need you to look for anything that might pinpoint a location on Craig's property," Bo barked into the phone, returning his attention back to Moore.

"On it," Moore answered. "Breakin' the seal now."

Bo waited. The sound of plastic and paper being shuffled

sounded down the line. "I've got his clothes, toiletries, and a satellite image."

Bo narrowed his eyes. "Did he mark the image?"

"Yeah. There's a circle."

"Can you take a picture of it and text it to me?"

"Affirmative. Sendin' it now."

"When you can, send one of your men with the original to me."

"Will do. Good luck. I'll get there as soon as I can," Moore answered, then hung up.

Moments later, Bo's phone vibrated. He opened the image and turned the phone until it lined up with the hillside. "That way," Bo growled, pointing toward the direction Bernice and the volunteers were heading. Devin went into the house and came back out with two flashlights. He handed one to Bo.

"Let's go find our women."

"Cali?" Poppy whispered into the darkness. "Why are you so certain that Devin will find us?"

I could feel Cali smiling. "Because he said my only job was to love him, and that his job was to protect me. I'm holdin' up my end of the bargain, and I know he will his."

Poppy hesitated for a moment, then I heard her turn her head on the dirt floor and look at me. We had slid off the rock to lie on the floor. We didn't know how long we'd be down here before someone found us and had decided to conserve our energy.

"Why are *you* so sure that Bo will find us?"

I thought about that a moment. "I suppose it's because he never quits. Look at what he's overcome. His mother abandoned him, leavin' him to a father who drank himself to death, and he overcame all that to become a cop. He wears a badge every day, not carin' he may be puttin' his life at risk, just to keep people safe. He's a hero, and heroes don't quit."

Poppy sighed into the gloom. "Okay, I feel better now."

"When we get out, I'm gonna order a greasy hamburger and French fries from the nearest burger joint," Cali said, yawning. "I'm starvin'."

We'd missed lunch and dinner, and our stomachs were rumbling. Raising my phone, I pushed a button so it would illuminate the cave. It was one a.m., and my phone was at fifteen percent. Poppy and Cali's phones were in the same condition. Pretty soon we'd have no light at all.

Time for a distraction.

I sat up and emptied my purse in front of me. I'd stopped at the liquor store in town and picked up a small bottle of green magic fairy potion, since we'd lost my other bottle in the fire. I'd meant to leave it in my room, but I'd forgotten about it in my purse. Now seemed as good a time as any to pull it out.

"Got it!" I cried out. "Anyone up for some magic potion?"

The girls sat up and stared longingly at the bottle like it was a lobster covered in butter. I unscrewed the lid, took a drink, and then passed it to Poppy. They each took a good swig, then we all lay down on the cold ground and smiled. Thank God for green happiness in a bottle.

"I think we should be makin' noise," Poppy said. "We heard Alice usin' the pickax when we were outside."

"I think she was tryin' to draw us into the cave. I saw the pickax at the opening of the cave, not down here. I doubt they can hear us," Cali said in defeat.

I turned and looked in the direction of the fissure. *Could sound get out that way?*

"There's a fissure over there that may let out sound."

"Should we try?" Poppy asked.

"We should save our energy and try in the mornin'. They're probably restin' right now, waitin' for the sun to rise."

"Then let's get some sleep so we have enough energy to scream our lungs out," Cali yawned, so I doused my light.

We scooted together for warmth, chests to backs, and I grabbed Poppy's hand for comfort. Resting my head on my free arm, I closed my eyes and thought about Bo.

Was he sleeping?

Was he outside the cave right now trying to find a way inside?

Was he searching somewhere else?

Sleep claimed me quickly, thanks to the green magic fairy potion. The sound of water dripping into the puddle followed me under. Its plopping lulled me until nothing but the trickle permeated my awareness. Somewhere between consciousness and dreams, I felt warm arms wrap around me and breath, hot and sensual, hit my shoulder. Lips I'd recognize anywhere ran up my neck, nipping one spot then another, and then a warm, whispered voice rumbled in my ear, *"Wake up, baby."*

I turned and burrowed into Bo's body.

"Are you coming for us?" I asked, my voice thick with sleep.

"We're comin'. Just hold on."

"We're hidden," I said, kissing his chest.

"It won't matter. I won't stop until I've turned the farm inside out. I'll find you."

"Look for the gold."

"Where?"

"Behind the bush."

Bo jerked awake. It was five a.m., and he and the volunteers had headed back to Craig's house to regroup and get some coffee. He'd dozed off for a minute, a cup of coffee perched in his hand, after little sleep the past week and a half. He was waiting for the sun to rise so they could search again.

He scowled at the yard, trying to remember what he'd been dreaming. Closing his eyes, he heard Sienna's voice, and it curled around him like warm honey. His life had been gray until she walked into it. Her light had pulled him out of a half-life. Chased away the clouds. Now his past didn't matter, because she'd erased all the pain. She was *his* once in a lifetime reward, and he wouldn't stop looking until he was holding her in his arms again.

"Sun's startin' to rise," Devin mumbled in the chair next to him.

Bo raised his hand and rubbed at his face. "Has Nate called in?"

"Yeah. Woman's name was Alice. She died on the table. He's on his way back now, and Moore's headed to her house. With any luck, he'll find a map that says, 'X marks the spot.'"

Bo's head tipped back, and he closed his eyes. They couldn't catch a fucking break. "Are we huntin' in the wrong place?" Bo asked his friend, unsure. Panic was starting to cloud his judgment. "Did they get the girls off the farm, and we're just spinnin' our wheels here?"

Devin shook his head. "My gut says they're here. I can feel that Calla's close by."

Bo pulled out his phone, found the picture Moore had sent, and looked at the satellite image again. "What did Black find?" he asked, staring at a dark space in the image.

"We've searched that area. There's nothin' but hills and rocky cliffs. Whatever's on that image may have brought him here, but it doesn't mean that's where they've hidden the girls."

"It's the key to findin' them," Bo said. "I can feel it."

Nate pulled in front of the house and climbed out of Bernice's Jeep. His long strides ate up the ground in front of him. Stopping in front of Devin, he opened his hand and dropped a key on the table sitting between the two men. "That was in Alice's pocket. I Googled the serial number. It belongs to an old lock they stopped makin' in nineteen seventy-four. Whatever she was doin' before she fled, she locked it up."

"We've checked all the outbuildin's," Devin sighed.

"We're not lookin' for a buildin'," Bo stated, looking at the map. "We're lookin' for somethin' in the ground. Somethin' only a geologist would see." Bo's eyes snapped to Nate. "Gold."

Devin jumped up and went inside the house. A minute later, he exited carrying the book Craig had ordered from Amazon. Flipping through the book, he stopped and scanned the pages. Granite, quartz, iron ore, to name a few, were normally found with gold. He turned the book and showed Bo and Nate a picture of the rocks.

"If Black stumbled across gold while surveyin' the Winkles' property, that would explain burnin' down their house," Bo said. "If they were ruined, they'd have to sell to the highest bidder."

"So how does Craig play into it?" Nate asked.

Bo looked at the book, then back at the image. "The gray area Black circled, it's primarily on the Winkles' side. But the property line is here," he pointed, "putting a small amount on this side of the land. Craig must have known."

"So we're lookin' for what?" Nate asked. "A hole in the ground?"

"No," Devin said, looking at the book. "A cave."

Bo turned as Devin flipped the book around. On the page was a black and white photo of miners standing at the opening of a cave. The picture looked to be at least a hundred years old.

"Look for the gold," he mumbled, remembering his dream. "Find Natasha. She'll know what outcroppin's are on both sides."

"She's at the hospital," Bernice called out, standing in the doorway. "She didn't want Boris to be alone. I told her I'd call her when we found the girls."

"Call her. Ask her to come back," Devin barked out.

"Do you know where they are?" Bernice asked, her voice trembling.

Devin moved to Calla's aunt and wrapped her in a hug. "I'll find her," he vowed low. "I promise."

"I know you will," Bernice answered, returning his hug briefly, clearing her throat as if her moment of worry was an embarrassment. "You're an Armstrong now, and we always win."

A slow grin pulled across Devin's mouth, and he winked at her.

The sun rose high enough in the sky that it bounced off the window, blinding Bo with its reflection. He turned and watched as the horizon blazed bright orange, then melded into a golden hue the color of Sienna's hair.

"We need to move," Bo barked. "Send Natasha to find us when she gets here."

Nate took the steps two at a time, and Devin followed. They ate up the ground as they headed for the rise, then turned toward the fence line. "We fan out and keep movin' until we find them," Bo ordered.

"If we're right about the gold," Nate murmured, "that means the old man and his accomplices killed for it."

"Troy said Craig was as mean as they come. That ramshackle house, this barren land, he must have looked across the fence at what the Winkles had built and choked on it daily. If the gray spot on the map is what we think it is, that means the Winkles own the gold. That must have sat like bad beer in his gut," Bo grumbled.

"Considerin' my woman's missin', I don't give a fuck," Devin growled.

Bo nodded. He completely agreed.

They worked their way slowly, stomping on any surface that looked like it could hide a cave opening. After an hour of playing whack-a-mole, Natasha showed up and began pointing up the hill. They moved to her and helped her climb the rocky surface. It took them ten minutes to reach the outcropping. It was covered by grass, barely visible from Craig's side of the property.

Bo climbed the side of the grassy hill, looking for an opening. He made it halfway up when he stopped and listened.

"Do you hear that?" he shouted.

Devin and Nate followed him up the side, stopping next to him, neither talking as they listened to the wind whipping around them. Then they heard it.

"Are they singing?" Nate asked, looking at Devin.

A slow smile crept across his mouth. "The 99 Bottles of Beer song?" Devin asked Bo.

"Yeah. They're at thirty-three," Bo laughed, as the tension he'd been carrying for the past day melted away.

"They're alive?" Natasha asked.

"They are right now," Devin grumbled, jumping from the mound. "I can't guarantee it once we find them. I may wring her scrawny neck for puttin' me through this twice in one week."

Bo slapped Nate on the shoulder and followed Devin down. They began searching the mound for the entrance. It took them five minutes to find the fake bush, and another five to find the sheet metal covering the opening. The girls couldn't hear them over their singing. Bo smiled as he took the key from Nate.

When they slid the bolt free and swung the door open, the singing stopped abruptly. Devin rushed through the opening first, flashing his light in the huge cavern until he found the three Wallflowers. They caught Poppy with a green bottle halfway to her lips, frozen as she shielded her eyes from the light. Cali gasped, "Devin?" as she stumbled to her feet, then she shouted, with as much indignation as she could. "What the hell took you so long?" then covered her mouth with a grimace.

Tears began to well when Bo stepped through the opening. My muddled brain, thanks to the green magic fairy potion, wasn't firing on all cylinders, so I stood there and stared at him like he was an apparition.

He looked exhausted. His hair was sticking out in every direction, but he still looked sexy as hell.

He began moving toward me, and I unstuck from my position on the boulder. Then I began running. I launched myself into his arms a foot away. He caught me, buried his face in my neck, and squeezed the life out of me.

"You found us," I sighed into his ear.

Bo squeezed me tighter, then, in a low, growling voice, vowed, "If you ever put me through this again, I'm lockin' you up and throwin' away the—"

"I won't," I interrupted. "From now on, we're listenin' to you. We promise. No more takin' risks. Only books and more books."

His body relaxed against me, then he pulled back and cupped my face, kissing my forehead, mumbling, "Thank Christ," against my skin.

I clutched at him, drinking in his warmth to ward off the cold that had settled deep into my bones.

A low rumble from Nate, its tone accusatory, broke the air, and I pulled back from Bo. "We're up all night, worried you're lyin' in a ditch somewhere, and you're gettin' drunk?"

Poppy was reaching for the bottle of Absinthe when I looked in their direction. She snatched it from his hand and put the cap back on. "No reason we can't die happy," she bit out, then turned and picked up her purse, shoving the bottle inside.

"Let's get you out of here," Bo said, wrapping his arm tightly around my shoulders.

"Shine your flashlight over there so I can find my purse."

Bo raised his light, and the minerals buried deep within the rock sparkled brightly like diamonds. "Jesus," Bo whispered, moving the light slowly across the wall. "Boris and Natasha are sittin',"—he smiled—"on a gold mine."

Red hair caught my attention in the low light, and I closed my eyes. In the darkness, we'd forgotten about Jennifer.

"You need to call the sheriff," I called out, nodding toward Jennifer's body.

Bo swung the light until it illuminated her body. "Is that the granddaughter?"

I nodded.

"How'd she die?"

I looked back at the girls. "We were strugglin' for her gun, and it went off. Are we in trouble?"

"No," Devin barked out. "You were defendin' yourselves. Justifiable if the gun proves to have any of your fingerprints on it."

"It won't," Poppy called out. "Sienna tossed the gun by the barrel but never touched the trigger. Alice took it with her when she left."

Nate shone his light on her as she spoke, and he froze. In the low light, it was hard to see, so he'd missed the rust-colored bloodstain on the front of her shirt. "Jesus, you're injured," he growled low, a hint of panic in his tone, as he reached for her.

Poppy pulled back and shook her head. "It's hers," she answered, nodding toward Red.

"Alice and Craig are dead," Bo announced, his voice rough and angry. "They fled together and caused a pileup in their hurry. Craig died at the scene. Alice died at the hospital."

I blinked, and sat on the boulder to steady myself. If Bo hadn't figured out where we were, nobody would have found us.

"We might have died if you hadn't found us," I mumbled, near hysterics. "They were the only ones who could have told you where we were."

Bo heard the panic in my voice and moved to me, pulling me back into his arms. "We didn't find you. You saved yourselves, once again. You and your horrendous singin'."

That broke through my panic and I glared back at him. "We are not horrendous singers."

"You suck," Nate called out.

"We *so* don't," Cali snapped.

"Babe . . . it was caterwaulin'," Devin chuckled.

Bo grinned. "Feelin' better?"

I shrugged. "I was until you said my singin' sucks."

"Let's get the fuck out of here," Devin said.

Bo smiled and wrapped his arm around me. "Come on, Pavarotti, let's get you home."

Hours later, after a shower that involved lots of soap *and* lots of hands and tongues, we were back at Bullwinkle Ranch at Natasha's insistence. She wanted to thank us for discovering the gold mine with an old-fashioned Bullwinkle Ranch campfire and cookout.

It felt like half the town wandered the property as music blared from speakers. I wasn't sure how she managed it, but she had a full bluegrass band and a pig rotating on a spit. Ice-cold beer flowed freely, lightening the mood of all partygoers.

We may have lost out on our chance for a real cowboy adventure due to all that had happened, but we hadn't missed out on the 'End of the Trail' bonfire and cookout.

We laughed and raised our glasses, reveling in the atmosphere. Boris was recovering, the ranch was safe, Bo and I were together, and once again, the girls and I had come out of a deadly situation unscathed because the power of friendship and love could not be defeated.

What more could a Wallflower ask for?

"I'm keepin' the gold from Boris until he gets stronger," Natasha said above the music. "He might have another heart attack if he knows we've been sittin' on a fortune all these years."

"I'd keep it from the son, too," Poppy mumbled under her breath.

I nodded in response. How such loving people had ended up with a son like that boggled my mind.

Bo curled his arm around my shoulder and began to draw me away from the crowd. "Where are we goin'?"

"You'll see," he said, pulling me into the horse barn.

Inside, Goliath was saddled, and a large pack was laid out across his back.

Troy held his reins, grinning.

"What are you up to?" I asked.

Bo flashed me a quick smile, then stuck his left foot into the stirrup and climbed on the horse's back. I crossed my arms and looked up at him, raising a brow. Bo crooked his finger. I stepped closer. In a single fluid movement, he reached down and picked me up, sitting me across his lap just like one of the heroines in my romance novels.

My white knight in Wranglers.

A strong arm wrapped around my waist as the other reached out to take the reins, then, with a, "Let's go," and nudge of his boot, he urged Goliath to take off into the pasture.

I turned and wrapped my arms around his waist, laying my head on his shoulder. "I thought I wasn't allowed on anything with four legs."

A slow grin pulled against his mouth. "As long as I'm with you, you can do whatever you want."

Such a Neanderthal.

The sun began to set as we made it to the top of the rise. Bo pulled Goliath to a halt, and we looked back at the ranch below us.

"It's beautiful here, isn't it?"

I turned to look at Bo. His eyes were a sparkling silver, and they were staring at me instead of the view below. "Yeah. Beautiful," he said, then brushed a kiss across my mouth.

We kept riding up the rocky hill until we came to a wide meadow full of endless pink and purple wildflowers. The sky above it bled from orange to red, kissing the field. As we rode across the meadow, the wind blew the flowers softly, stirring them until their fragrance filled the air.

Bo reined in Goliath near a babbling brook. The cool water washed over the smooth rocks, sparkling like crystal in the fading sun. I took in the scenery and filled my lungs. The air up here was as clean as the water trickling down the stream.

"You didn't get your overnight underneath the stars," Bo whispered in my ear. "So I'm improvisin'."

I turned in my seat and smiled like a loon. "We're campin' out?"

"You're cute when you're excited," Bo chuckled.

I felt carefree now that the mystery had been solved, so I batted my eyes like a Southern belle and asked, full-on Georgia peach, "When else am I cute?"

His smile widened. "When you're flushed with passion after takin' my cock."

I gasped. Then I sputtered. "You are…are…"

"Yeah?"

"Naughty. Very, very naughty."

Bo pulled me sharply into his chest. "You haven't seen naughty yet."

My breath froze in my lungs at the promise in his words. "I'm gonna climb off now," I sputtered.

Smirking, Bo slid me slowly to the ground, then followed gracefully like he'd been born to be in a saddle.

"Do you miss bein' on a ranch?" I asked as he pulled the pack from the horse's back.

"Sometimes," he answered. "Times like these," he said distantly, looking around the meadow. "You can't think in the city, not like out here."

"Savannah's not exactly a huge, sprawlin' metropolis."

"No," he grinned. "It's just the right size for a country boy like me."

Bo started to lead Goliath to the water, but I stopped him with my hand.

"Teach me to ride?"

I expected Bo to say no. Instead, he grabbed my waist and lifted me onto Goliath's back. Before handing me the reins, he looped a long rope, used to tie off the pack, into the horse's bridle, and then walked him to the center of the meadow.

"Loosen your grip," he called out.

I did as he said, then sat myself deeper into the seat like Boris had taught me.

"Now ride," he said, smiling.

I gave Goliath a nudge with my boots, and he began trotting. Bo kept a tight hold on the rope, walking in circles as he watched me bounce on the horse's back. My hair flew behind me as we picked up speed, and soon I was cantering. I felt free riding on the beast's back, while Bo kept me safe, like I could spread my wings and fly. Laughing with the freedom that comes with being at peace with your world, I grinned at Bo as we circled wide. I was one with the arrogant beast. I had not a care in the world. No mother criticizing me. No father ignoring me. It was just me, Bo, and a beautiful sunset putting the world to bed.

"Sun's settin', rein him in," Bo called out, so I pulled back until he stopped.

"I could do that all day!" I cried out. "How do you not miss this?"

Grinning at my enthusiasm, Bo led the horse near the stream and helped me down. "Growin' up on the back of a horse, I never saw it as entertainment."

"Tell me about your father," I said softly.

He'd mentioned he was dead, while we lay together in the early morning light the day before. But I didn't push him. We were happy, content in our cocoon, so I'd let it go.

"He was a proud man," Bo began. "Too proud. He took my mother's abandonment as a personal affront. He should have brooded over her for a month or two and moved on."

He'd been taking off Goliath's saddle as he spoke. Surprisingly, there was no anger in his voice, only resignation.

"Did you blame him when she left?"

He shook his head, then led Goliath to the stream to drink. He was making sure the horse was taken care of first like I'd read about in historical romance novels. Knights and cowboys alike knew their mount was the most valuable thing they owned. They took good care of them because their mounts were the difference between life and death most days.

I smiled at the thought. Bo was old school.

"Do you blame your mother for your father leavin'?" Bo asked, catching me off guard.

"Yes," I answered immediately. I hadn't thought about it. No searching my subconscious for the answer. I blamed her for taking him away from me, and I also blamed her for keeping my biological father away.

"Have you ever looked for your biological father?"

I shook my head. "All I know is that he was a gym manager. I don't even know the name of the gym or if she was tellin' the truth about the affair. She won't talk about it."

He searched my face, gauging my answer. "Do you want to know?"

"Of course. I have another family out there. I could have brothers and sisters who look just like me. Who act just like me."

"I take it you don't look like your siblin's, and that bothers you?" Bo approached on silent feet, watching me.

I rolled my lips on my teeth, searching for the right words. "My whole life I wanted to fit in. My brother and sister made sense with my parents. I didn't. Once I found out why I didn't, all I could think about was finding those who were like me. I wanted to belong. To make sense."

Bo's eyes glittered, and he reached up and grabbed my neck, pulling me closer to his body. "You belong to *me*," he ground out. "You make sense to *me*. My past haunted me for years, and in the stretch of a week, you made it all disappear. I keep thinkin' it will end. That somethin' this special isn't meant for me. Hell, I keep lookin' over my shoulder waitin' for someone to walk up and take you away." I opened my mouth, and then I shut it.

I didn't even know how to respond to that. "I'll find your father if he's out there," he continued, "but even if I don't, you belong. Don't ever think you don't."

How could a man be this wonderful? I loved him. No ifs, ands, or buts. I loved him and his stormy gray eyes that brightened when he laughed at me. Loved the way his eye twitched when I'd pushed him too far. The way he came for me and never gave up. I. Loved. Him.

"I won't disappear," I whispered, running my hand down his face. That scared little boy who had lost so much stared back at me from inside Bo's gaze. "I'm caught, and I'm stayin' caught."

"Damn straight you are."

"And you're caught, and you're stayin' caught," I let him know.

He grinned. "A man would have to be nuts to walk away from you."

"I thought you said you were nuts?"

"Nuts for you," he whispered.

A falling star flashed across the sky, drawing my attention up. It reminded me of how I'd stared at those same stars a few nights ago, wondering if fate had finally smiled down on me. She had.

"So," I said, snuggling in closer, "are you goin' to feed me, or what?"

Bo looked at my mouth. "Or what," he replied softly.

I mentally pumped my arm.

"Does it involve bein' naked?"

He nodded.

"Does it involve ropes?"

He raised a brow.

"What? A girl can dream, can't she?" I drawled, batting my eyes again.

"Naughty." Bo grinned. "Very, very naughty."

Thirteen

LARRY DWAYNE DANIELS

Three days later . . .

BO STROLLED INTO JACOBS' LADDER and looked up. The Wallflowers were sitting at what they'd deemed 'their table,' toasting each other with shots. The green liquid glistened in the light above them. It looked like cough syrup to Bo, but his woman's eyes always glazed over when she drank it, her mouth pulling into a sexy grin, and the effects of the liquor on her mood were spectacular. One shot, and they were on their backs within five minutes.

Sienna looked down at him, and she stuck out her tongue.

Bo raised a brow.

She raised one back, and he saw the challenge in her eyes. He looked back at Jacobs' office and considered taking her up on it, but it would have to wait; he had a man to interview. Larry Dwayne Daniels had woken up the night before, and he wanted a word with the man.

Bo mouthed, "Later," to Sienna, and her eyes hooded with

anticipation.

Fucking spectacular.

Turning to the bar, Bo took a seat on a stool next to Devin. "Daniels is finally awake," Bo said.

The beer Devin had lifted to his lips paused. "You headed there now?"

Bo nodded. "I came by to see if you wanted to join me."

Devin put his tongue to his teeth and whistled. Nate looked up from across the restaurant and jerked his head, raised a finger to stop a tirade his aunt was having, and headed in their direction.

Bo watched Nate as he approached, grinning when he caught the big man's eyes darting to the Wallflowers.

"What's holdin' him back from Poppy?" Bo mumbled to Devin.

Devin looked over his shoulder at the Wallflowers. "Abusive father. He used to beat him *and* his mother. He's got it in his head he's predisposed to follow in his old man's footsteps due to his genetic lottery. He keeps a tight rein on his temper because of it."

"So he doesn't date?"

"Not more than a couple of weeks, and that's not often. He's married to his bar rather than a woman."

"He ever lose control?" Bo asked as Nate walked across the restaurant toward them.

"Only once since I've known him," Devin smiled.

Bo's forehead creased. "What's so funny?"

"What's funny is, the only time I've seen him lose his cool was at Craig's place."

Bo lifted a brow.

Devin looked over his shoulder, then back. "After you called, tellin' us to meet you back at the house, I found Nate checkin' an old rickety outbuildin'. When he saw me ride up, he asked if they'd been found. When I said no, he put a fist through one of the walls, then proceeded to dismantle the entire buildin'."

Bo whistled low. "He's in deep."

"He's in deep," Devin agreed.

They both turned to watch Nate walk up.

"What's up?" Nate asked, stopping in front of both men from behind the bar.

"Daniels woke up," Bo stated, trying to hide a smile. "I'm headin' there now to interview him."

"Good," Nate ground out, "it's about time we knew what's goin' on."

"Can you keep an eye on the girls while we're gone? We don't want them out of our sight until we know what we're up against," Devin said.

Nate looked up at the girls and nodded. "None of them will get past me this time."

"Easiest way to keep an eye on them is to introduce them to Gertrude. The way they sing, they'll love her," Devin chuckled.

Nate grinned. "They might actually get Gert to shut up with their caterwaulin'."

Devin cringed. "Never heard women that bad at singin'."

The girls burst out laughing, and all three men turned to look at them.

"Did you hear that Poppy tried to sacrifice herself so Calla and Sienna could get away?" Bo mumbled, keeping his eyes on Sienna.

There was silence for a moment, then Nate growled, "You wanna repeat that?"

Bo turned and leaned on the bar. He held Nate's eyes for a moment. They were glittering with anger. "Craig's granddaughter was gonna shoot all three of them, so Poppy decided she would sacrifice herself. She lunged for the gun and told Calla and

Sienna to run."

Nate's eyes shot to Poppy, and his nostrils flared. "She's got no sense."

"No. She's got no man to fight for her," Devin said, tapping the bar twice with his knuckles before stepping away and heading for the door.

Bo followed, looking up at Sienna. When he caught her eyes, he held up his phone. She nodded and dug her phone out of her purse. Bo answered on the first ring. "We're headed to the hospital to interview Daniels. We don't want you ladies leavin' until we know what's goin' on. Nate's got your back."

"Roger that. We'll stay here and wait for your return," she answered, saluting him as he opened the door to exit.

Bo's lip twitched. They were taking the whole 'we'll listen to you from now on' to heart.

"Sienna?"

"Yeah?"

"Dinner at your place tonight. I'll teach you how to cook pasta, then I'll worship you while you practice."

She gasped, then, and in a breathy voice said, "Lookin' forward to it."

Beautiful. Fucking spectacular. "Later, baby . . . Love you."

Her eyes warmed as she looked back at him. "Later, Bo. I love you, too."

Devin grinned at him. "She can't cook worth a shit, either?"

"As bad as her singin'."

"Good thing they're worth lyin', stealin', or killin' for," Devin laughed.

"Amen."

Twenty minutes later, they walked into Daniels' hospital room. He looked like he'd been pounded with a sledgehammer. Both eyes were swollen, and his nose had been broken. Bo figured he'd eat through a straw for a few weeks, and he didn't give a shit. Daniels had gone after his woman with a gun; he'd shake the hand of the man who nearly beat him to death.

"Wake up," Bo barked.

Daniels jerked, swallowing. He opened his eyes to slits and scanned the room.

"Who are you?" he rasped out, his voice dry.

"I'm Detective Bo Strawn, and this is Devin Hawthorne. We need to ask you a few questions about the truck you crashed last Saturday."

Daniels expression turned cautious. "What truck?"

"The truck," Devin hissed, leaning down so the man could see him better, "you used to chase three women through the streets of Savannah."

Daniels color turned ashen, and he swallowed hard. "I don't know what you're talkin' about."

"Yeah, you do. You pulled a gun on them as they left the Tap Room, thinkin' you'd score easy money," Bo taunted. "What I really want to know is why you chased them."

Daniels raised a shaking hand to a cup resting on his bedside table and brought it to his mouth. He struggled with the straw, then winced as he swallowed.

"You gonna answer the man?" Devin bit out.

"I want a lawyer," was his response.

"You'll get a lawyer once you're discharged. And a comfortable bed in county lockup. What I need to know is why. Are these women still in danger?"

Daniels looked between Bo and Devin, weighing his options, then shook his head slowly.

"So no one else is lookin' for them?" Devin growled.

Daniels closed his eyes and shook his head again. "I'd been drinkin' and heard one say she was Calla Armstrong. I figured I'd make a quick buck seein' as she's loaded. I hadn't been tweaked in days, and I was desperate."

Bo looked at Devin to gauge his reaction. His hands were balled into tight fists, the knuckles white. "If you weren't already broken, I would beat you myself," Devin rumbled low. "That's my woman you went after."

Daniels moved further up the bed, looking at Bo for help. "I'm done," he whispered. "Her father already put me in the hospital. I'm not goin' anywhere near her."

Bo's eyes shot to Devin. "Isn't her father dead?"

Devin nodded slowly. "Describe this man."

Daniels looked at Bo. "He'll kill me."

"Hawthorne's not gonna kill you," Bo sighed.

"Not him." Daniels jerked his head at Devin. "Her father."

"Her father is dead," Devin growled, "so start talkin'."

"I'm tellin' you I can't," Daniels shot back. "He's associated with the Serpents. A nomad with no club affiliation."

Bo narrowed his eyes. "And he told you he was Calla's father?"

Daniels nodded.

"He said her name?" Bo ground out.

Daniels shook his head. "He said, 'Nobody fucks with my kids.' I assumed he meant Armstrong, since I was goin' after her."

Jesus, this guy is an idiot.

Bo pulled out his phone and flipped through the pictures Sienna had taken during their stay at the ranch. He found one of the three Wallflowers together and held up his phone. "Which one?"

Daniels squinted at the photo, then raised his hand and pointed to Sienna.

Bo gritted his teeth. If this man beat a punk half to death over his kid, and Daniels was goin' after Sienna . . . *Christ.*

"You're an idiot," Devin growled. "You went after the wrong woman."

Daniels narrowed his eyes at Devin. "Fuck you, man."

Devin shook his head. "Tweaker with no brains who goes after the wrong woman *and* gets manhandled by a middle-aged man isn't exactly Einstein."

"I need a name," Bo bit out.

"I'm not givin' it to you, man."

"You're givin' it to me," Bo growled.

"He'll kill me," Daniels bit back.

Bo's smile turned sinister. "I'll kill you if you don't."

Ten minutes later, they exited Daniels' room with a name. Knox. One name. No last name, just Knox.

"You're gettin' good at lyin'," Devin chuckled.

"Bite me," Bo said. "What are the chances this Knox is Sienna's biological father?"

"I'd say slim, but it makes you wonder why the hell he went after Daniels. Mistaken identity?"

"A nomad biker? They survive by knowin' everyone and everything."

Devin rubbed a hand across his face. He had no answers.

"How the fuck do I tell Sienna her father may be a biker? And how the hell do I find a biker with one name?"

"You could lie. Say you can't find him."

Bo shook his head. "If he's who he says he is, this guy knows Sienna's his daughter. It's only a matter of time before he comes sniffin'. She needs to be prepared."

"You wanna head to the Tap Room and knock some heads?" Devin asked.

"Thought you'd never ask," Bo grinned.

"I don't think we sounded that bad," Poppy grumbled low in my ear as Nate led us away from his apartment. We'd been playing with his adorable bulldog Gertrude, singing along with her to an Italian opera.

He turned at her whispered complaint, rose both brows, and shook his head. "Never heard three more *tone-deaf* Georgia peaches in my life."

"Four," I chuckled. "Gertrude is one of us now."

"Oh, wouldn't she look darlin' in a studded UG shirt," Cali said. "There are a few at Frock You I could cut down to size and take a Bedazzler to."

Poppy and I nodded, smiling wide at how cute Gertrude would be in a custom shirt. Nate stopped in his tracks, turned, and pointed right in Cali's face. "No fuckin' bedazzlin'."

"But—"

He glared her into silence.

She looked and me and bit her lips to keep from smiling.

I grabbed her hand so the big man didn't explode and pulled her around Nate, heading for our table.

"He's testy," Poppy muttered as we climbed the steps. "He's been on edge all afternoon."

"That's true," I answered. "He's been glarin' most of the day."

"Devin gets grumpy when we haven't . . . *you know what.*"

"Cali, you've been together a little over a week. You're still in the honeymoon period. You haven't had time *not* to have time for *you know what*."

Now she had me saying 'you know what.' Pretty soon, I wouldn't be able to say 'ass,' without slapping my hand over my mouth.

She settled in her seat before answering. "We went twenty-four hours once. He was a bear by the time he got home. When I asked him why, he said it's because he needed to work off his frustration."

"How is that the same?" I questioned.

"He was frustrated at me."

"What had you done?"

"Pulled an all-nighter at the office when we got back from the ranch."

Poppy and I snorted.

"Do you think when men find someone they want, their bodies need *you know what* all the time?" Poppy asked.

I looked at Cali and smiled. "Yeah. Most definitely."

She bit her lip. "Do you, um, think it's the same for women?"

Cali and I both nodded . . . rapidly.

Poppy chuckled. "You both look like bobbleheads."

A loud, husky female voice rang out from below, and we looked over the railing into the restaurant. Nate's aunt Martine was leaning on a table with a bunch of college boys, smiling seductively.

Nate's aunt was a sassy redhead who was born and raised in Glasgow, Scotland. She had a quick wit and a smile that turned heads, and a body that stopped traffic. She was in her mid-forties, unmarried, and flirted with every man between eighteen and seventy. I'd watched her interact with men most of the afternoon and decided she liked flirting with the college crowd best because she could rattle them easily.

"Did you hear Nate say she's puttin' down roots in Savannah and will be managin' the bar for him?"

"Yeah. I wonder where she's stayin'?"

"With his mother, Devin said."

Poppy's phone began to ring, so she pulled it from her purse. I started to ask Cali if she was hungry, but my attention snapped to Poppy. She'd gasped at whatever she heard on the phone.

"I'll be right home, Momma," she rushed out and stood,

swiping her phone off.

"What's wrong?" Cali asked.

"Nothin'. I need to go."

I looked at Cali. "We promised Bo we'd listen from now on. You can't leave until he calls."

Poppy grabbed her purse from the chair, mumbling, "*You* promised. It has nothin' to do with me. I need to go," then fled the table.

"Poppy!" I called out, but she ignored me and hit the stairs two at a time.

I searched the restaurant for Nate. He was behind the bar, and his focus was on Poppy as she rushed through the crowd. Before I could call out to him, he threw a bar towel down, muttered something to a waitress, and then headed swiftly toward the door Poppy had just exited.

I fumbled for my phone and started to dial Bo's number, but it rang in my hand.

"Bo?" I rushed out.

"You're in the clear, baby. Daniels won't be comin' after you. Tell the girls."

I looked at the door Poppy had fled through, and relaxed. Whatever her problem was, we'd find out soon enough. At least she was safe.

"You there?" Bo asked.

"Yeah," I answered. "So, we're safe?"

"Yeah, you're safe, baby. I'll meet you at your place in a few hours. There's somethin' I need to look into first, then we'll talk."

"Talk?" I questioned.

"About your biological father."

I blinked. Bo said he would look for him, but it didn't occur to me he'd do it so quickly.

"Are you sayin' you found him?" My heart pounded in my

chest.

"We'll talk when I get to your place."

"Bo—"

"When I get there, baby."

"Please," I whispered into the phone, my tone begging.

There was a pregnant pause, then Bo whispered, "Fuck."

"Please tell me what you know."

"He goes by the name Knox, but his given name is David. David Tyler. I just got the confirmation, but that's all I've got."

"How did you find him?"

"I'll tell you when I get to your place."

"Bo, please."

"I've told you all I'm gonna tell you without bein' there."

"Is it bad?" I asked, my stomach dropping like a lead ball. *What if he's a serial killer?*

"I don't know yet. I gotta go to the station and run his info."

"Okay," I answered breathlessly. I'd just have to be patient. "I'll tell Nate when he gets back that we're in the clear."

"He left you alone?"

"Poppy got a call that upset her, and she ran out. Nate took off after her."

Bo sighed. "That lasted all of three days."

"What did?"

"You promisin' to listen."

I narrowed my eyes. "Uh, we did listen. Poppy is the one who ran out."

"Right. So, she's the weak link now."

"Weak link?"

"Yeah, weak link. She doesn't have a man who'll lose his shit if somethin' happens to her, so she does what she wants. The weak link in your Wallflower chain. It's only as strong as its weakest member. Meanin' she'll break, and you'll follow suit."

"You're an ass," I snapped. "What does havin' a man got to do with anything? I promised to listen 'cause you're a lawman, and you have more experience with bad guys than me, not because you'd lose your shit if I disobeyed. You're not my father."

Bo grew quiet. I could hear him breathing on the other end, so I waited.

"Point made," he growled. "But *I'll* point out that listenin' to me has nothin' to do with bein' disobedient and *everything* to do with lovin' someone enough not to worry them."

My heart fluttered. He loved me. "You're right," I breathed out. "And I love you, too."

"Christ, you drive me nuts."

"Ditto," I smiled. "So, do you want me to call Nate?"

"No, I'll call him and bring him up to date."

"Okay, then," I said.

"Sienna?"

"What?"

"You're worth the heartburn."

I smiled. He was referring to his comment when he'd rescued me from the tree.

"You, too," I whispered.

"See you in a few hours," Bo said, then hung up.

"I take it we're in the clear and can roam the streets of Savannah without a bodyguard?"

I nodded. "Bo may have a lead on my father," I said excitedly.

Cali blinked. "How? Who? Where?"

I chuckled. "All I know is his name may be David Tyler. But he called him Knox for some reason."

"Like a nickname?"

I shrugged. "Cali, do you think he'll like me?"

The thought he might not accept me started rolling around my head like a gerbil in a wheel.

Her smile softened, and she grabbed my hand. "He'll love you. Just like I did the moment I met you. Just like Bo does. You're impossible to hate."

My bottom lip trembled. "Sorry, residual angst from my family. I'll worry about it when it happens. Right now, I'm worried about Poppy. What do you think is goin' on with her mother?"

"No clue," Cali answered. "Since we're free to go, do you wanna follow her and find out?"

I stood instantly. "I've been to her mother's house a few times. We can check there first."

We both grabbed our purses and headed downstairs, waving at Nate's aunt as we left.

"Did you notice how Nate chased after her?" Cali said as we hurried through the crowded sidewalk. "I wonder if he's feelin' the same thing, too?"

"We can only hope," I sighed. "Watchin' her is frustratin'."

We made the long walk to Cali's building and climbed into my beat-up car. As much as I hated to part with my silver Honda, it was time. New life. New man. New wheels for the new Sienna.

Poppy's mother lived on the outskirts of the city, in a less than desirable neighborhood. I'd met her several times in the past two years. She'd been stunning once, but life had beaten her down. Yet, every once in a while, I saw a spark in her eyes, and I knew she'd been a spitfire in her youth. A trait her daughter had inherited. Poppy looked just like her, too. No one would doubt that she was her mother's daughter.

As we rounded the corner to her mother's house, I caught sight of Nate sitting on his motorcycle. He was parked two doors down, like a sentry guarding a castle. He turned his head as we approached and climbed off his bike.

I came to a stop next to him and rolled down the window. "I

take it since you're here, Bo didn't call you."

Nate shook his head. "Just got off the phone with him. Poppy ran inside as I pulled up. What's goin' on with her? She looked like she saw a ghost."

"No idea. We're gonna find out, though. You wanna come inside with us?" I asked.

Nate looked at the house, then back at us. "Yeah."

I smiled. He definitely looked like a man on the hunt. "I'll just pull over," I said, then rolled up the window and gave Cali big eyes.

"This should be interestin'," she mumbled.

Shirley Gentry's home was neutral. Mushroom-colored siding wrapped around the house, a throwback from the early nineties when vinyl siding was king, with gray planters on either side of the black door housing dying flowers. There was no color to distinguish it from the other lifeless houses on the street. In fact, the neighborhood as a whole gave off the air of having given up.

As we approached the door, I could hear voices inside. Poppy seemed to be yelling at someone. Nate heard it, too, and moved in front of us. He didn't bother knocking; he just grabbed hold of the worn-out screen door, ripped it open, and pushed through the front door like he owned the house.

We all came to a screeching halt inside a tiny living room, made smaller by the three people presently filling the space to capacity.

"What the fuck is goin' on?" Nate growled.

Poppy turned at his question and blinked. "What are you doin' here?" she gasped, her face ashen.

"Better question is, who the fuck is he?"

Cali and I looked at the middle-aged man. His face was hard, scary even, and he was dressed like a biker. There was something familiar about the man. He was big and broad, had hair the color of wheat, but it was streaked with gray announcing his age. His eyes were dark brown, hiding intelligence. And even though he was in his mid-fifties, he was a good-looking man.

He stared back at us, his eyes wandering from Poppy to me, and he smiled. Wow. His smile was like looking into the face of the sun. It warmed his features, softening the rough edges.

Poppy turned and looked at the man, then, in a voice filled with ice, bit out, "This is my father. Wallflowers, meet David Tyler, the bastard who knocked up my mother and then disappeared from my life."

Cali gasped beside me, and I froze in place. A loud roaring in my ears began to drown out the noise around me, and the room tilted slightly before righting itself. I heard Nate growl, "Fuck me," as he whipped out his phone. And I just concentrated on breathing.

The room spun as I looked at the man. Recognition slowly crept in, but when it did, it hit me like a freight train. I looked just like him. Same hair, same eyes, same smile. And he was watching me with a smile on his face, as if he was proud of what he was seeing.

How can this be?

Cali grabbed my hand and held on tight. I squeezed it back to ground myself to reality. "It has to be him," she whispered. "You look just like him."

I didn't know whether to laugh or cry. It felt like I was on an episode of *Punk'd.* "Knox?" I questioned. "Is…is that your name?" I continued on a shuddering breath.

The man with golden hair the color of mine nodded his head, mumbling, "Yeah, baby girl."

Nate grabbed Poppy's hand and pulled her behind his back, then bit out in a strained voice, "Strawn, you need to get your ass over to Ms. Gentry's house. STAT. Knox is *here*, and we've got a clusterfuck on our hands."

Poppy stared at Nate, confused. Her brow pulled into a sharp line, and she looked at me. "*What's* goin' on?"

I looked at her, really looked at her for some sort of similarities.

There were none. She was the spitting image of her mother. I looked back at Knox. Same hair. Same stubborn jaw. There was no way this could be true. "Are you Poppy's father?" I asked anxiously.

He nodded slowly.

Poppy looked at me, her brows pulling into a line of confusion. "Why are you askin' if he's my father? Did you drink too much green magic at lunch?"

I swallowed hard. Now, for the moment of truth. "Are you… are you *my* father?"

Poppy gasped, "What?" looking for all the world like she thought I was nuts.

He looked at Poppy, back at me, then smiled with eyes I looked back at daily in the mirror. "Yeah, baby girl."

Oh. My. God.

I blinked. Ms. Gentry shouted, "You bastard!" and my eyes shot to Poppy. She'd turned white as a ghost as she stared at her father. *Our father.*

Reaching out my hand, I whispered, "Poppy."

She whipped around and looked at me as if she'd never seen me before, and stepped back out of my reach, shaking her head rapidly in denial. I watched her wiwth trepidation as the truth sank in. She seemed off balance, her eyes wide as if in shock, her face pale with bitterness and rejection as she panted. Nate had been watching her closely, so when she didn't rail against her father for yet another deceit, he stepped up next to her and whispered something into her ear. She shook her head, her breath coming in great gasping gulps, then she tittered on her feet and reached out for Nate's arm before her eyes rolled back in her head.

To be continued . . .

Stay tuned for Wallflowers: One Heart Remains
Coming Soon!

About the Author

CP Smith lives in Oklahoma with her husband and five children. She loves football, reading, and card games. Writing for her is about escape. She writes what she loves to read, and leaves the rest to those with better imaginations.

Made in the USA
Monee, IL
20 February 2023